TIME PASSAGE

A Time Travel Romance Novel

Elyse Douglas

Broadback Books

For Vito and Mary and those train adventures.

"Time does not change us. It just unfolds us."

~MAX FRISCH

TIME PASSAGE

CHAPTER 1

O n the full moon night of Wednesday, November 9, 2022, I killed him. There was no doubt he was dead. No breath. No movement. His face the color of white paper. Eyes open, staring at nothing. I didn't check his pulse. Stayed away from him. I hit him with the heavy, ornate gold clock. It's an antique, I think, and it cost a fortune, not that it would have mattered to him. He was bleeding from his right temple, where I hit him.

My mind whirled, my pulse jumped, my throat tightened. We'd argued, and it had turned violent. We had argued before, but never like this. He grabbed my hair and jerked me around, slapping me. His ugly words were still fresh in my ears.

"I should have ditched you months ago," he shouted. "I gave you everything. I made you! If it wasn't for me, you'd never have made it in real estate! You'd be nothing but a loser waitress, waiting on tables at some pathetic excuse for a restaurant."

"Let me go, Cliff! Stop it!"

"I'll kill you!" he roared, slapping me again.

I'd broken free, gasping for air, stumbling

backwards.

He staggered about, whiskey glass in hand, his face twisted in anger. "How many times, Cindy? How many times have you been with him? How many times have you been with Kevin? Stop lying and tell me!"

"I wasn't with him! I've never been with him. Never! I've told you that a hundred times! You're drunk, and when you're drunk, you get crazy and think everybody's out to get you," I said, my voice shaky.

"I'll kill you!" he shouted again, hurling his whiskey glass at me. I screamed and ducked as the glass sailed over my head and shattered against the wall. And then he came at me—lunged at me like an animal—before I could run. Drunk or not, he had rage, adrenaline and a strong body, and he shoved me down on the sofa. He fell on top of me, slapping my face and cursing me.

I kicked and screamed, sure he was going to kill me, when his strong hands squeezed my throat, angry breath puffing from his clenched teeth. I strained for breath, a hot white light of panic exploding in my head. In a desperate reflex, I kneed him in the balls, and he jerked up, writhing in agony, his hands releasing my neck. As he howled in pain, I twisted and kicked and shoved him off, and he tumbled onto the white carpet with a thump.

With a pounding heart, I sprang up and stumbled, white dots swimming across my eyes. I swayed, staggered ahead, swayed again and braced myself against the black marble mantel, feeling a raw, burning throat and the metallic taste of blood.

From the corner of my eye, I saw him spring up, wobble, then come for me, his face flamed, his eyes wild. My blood ran cold. I knew he was going to kill me.

I don't remember seeing that antique clock or reaching for it. I do remember swinging it at him as his big hands reached for me. I remember the dull thud of the clock as it thumped against his head. I remember I'd never felt so scared or so strong as the adrenaline pumped through me.

And then, there was a ringing silence, and there he was, bleeding on the white carpet, his body still, his flat eyes empty, staring at nothing.

I was sick. I felt darkness encircling me, like an evil presence, like death itself. The clock slid from my hand and bounced on the carpet near Cliff's head. My breath came out in shallow puffs, and I was frozen to the spot. I didn't know what to do. My mind locked up, and I was in a motionless trance. Should I call the police? Should I call my friend Alina? Should I call 911?

I lowered my spooked eyes on him, feeling the urge to vomit. I fought it. Was he dead? Yeah... He was dead, and I had killed him.

And then I didn't do anything I should have done. I'd been in trouble with the cops before, when I was a teenager. I'd hung out with a bad crowd. I'd stolen things. I'd done jail time. I'd been called everything from a cheap whore, to a hoodie thief, to a gold-digging bitch.

I hated jail and swore I'd never go back, no matter what. The cops scared me. The lawyers didn't care. So, I had a record. Would anybody believe me if I told them I'd killed the famous billionaire Clifton Prince in self-defense? No, of course not.

I felt my stomach pitch as I made a dash for the door, grabbing my long, sealskin coat, my gloves, and my purse. Hurrying down the burgundy and silver carpeted hallway, I finger combed my hair, which must have looked a mess. I was sure my face looked a mess.

Downstairs in the spacious, gleaming lobby, my smile was forced, my steps measured, not rushed, as the pleasant doormen, Pedro, held the glass doors for me and asked if I'd be back soon.

Just before exiting, I lowered my gaze, in case my face was bruised, or my eyes swollen. I didn't know how I looked.

"Oh, yes, I'll be back in a half hour or so," I said, as casually and as brightly as my trembling voice could utter.

I fled the place, wearing my coat, black slacks, a fuchsia turtleneck sweater, and pumps. It was a chilly November night, with scattered, moving clouds, about forty-five degrees. What was the date? November 9, 2022.

I was scared and nauseous, and my head felt like it was on fire. That's what fear and horror do to you when you've done the unthinkable; when you've done the thing you never thought possible; the one terrible thing you thought you'd never do: kill another human being.

CHAPTER 2

I walked aimlessly downtown from East 63rd Street, with no direction in mind, because I didn't have a mind. It was a muddled mess of chaos.

Cliff Prince was dead. He was thirty-five years old, and rich, with a fine, handsome face, and roguish black eyes that I'd immediately found attractive when we met, two years ago, at a gallery opening cocktail party in the Chelsea district of New York City. I was one of the servers passing around hors d'oeuvres.

Was Cliff a millionaire? Billionaire? He'd inherited much of his money from his family, and then he'd made more in technology, buying and selling companies. I didn't really know what all that meant. That's what he told me. I didn't care.

And, yes, just after I'd killed him, my whole life flashed before me in seconds. I saw myself as a thirteen-year old girl, my drunken, low-life father slapping me around, my frail mother trying to fight for me but ending up on the floor, and my younger sister, Casey, fighting for me and then slapped to the floor and curled into a ball as he kicked her. And then he left us. And then he was killed in some back alley knife fight in Tulsa. Good riddance.

When I was twenty, Mom died from a swollen liver and pneumonia.

But I'm not looking for pity. Pity means nothing. Pity is for losers, and despite all that has happened, I have never felt like a loser, and I never intend to.

I did well in school—straight A's mostly—mostly to prove to the world that I wasn't a low-life dumbshit, who lived in a banged-up trailer, in a not-so-prosperous trailer park in Florida.

I'd excelled in English and math, and since I was eight, I'd kept a journal, writing about people and family events—or to be more accurate, family disasters. I was interested in people and their reactions and their words and feelings, but as I got older, I wasn't so interested in keeping a record of my day-to-day emotions and the insanity of my life. I avoided anything that was painful.

Once, after doing jailtime, I was forced to see a head-shrink instead of the usual social worker. She had a lavish, well-designed office, with lots of family pictures in silver frames on her desk and many diplomas conspicuously displayed on the walls. She even had a nifty, shiny Italian espresso machine.

She said that, as a kid, I'd coped by escaping into myself and hiding my feelings. She said I'd witnessed the feelings and emotions of others instead. "Avoidance and lashing out irrationally," she'd said, in a wise, calm voice.

But I couldn't stop staring at her gray fitted suit and her diamond ring, the diamond the size of an ice cube. Okay. Whatever. Maybe I was jealous of her normal life, her education and good job, and her fat diamond. Maybe I wanted to meet a rich guy and get a fat, sparkling diamond ring, too. I was pretty enough. I knew that.

My younger sister, Casey, was my best friend. She'd always tried to protect me from Dad and from the world, but she'd failed. Dad was strong. Casey wasn't. Dad laughed whenever Casey took swings at him. Dad just gave her a shove, and she went tumbling.

Casey had been a frail child, but she had the heart of a lioness. And then she was killed in a car crash when she was sixteen and I was eighteen. I'm not sure I've ever recovered from that. Casey deserved so much better. She deserved kindness and a chance at life, and I deserved to have my little sister, whom I loved more than my own life.

As I said already, I was pretty, and as I write this, I still am. Like most things in life, it has been a blessing and a curse. The boys flirted, my male teachers flirted, and older men gave me a lusty smile and a wink. I fought off most men, kissed a few in high school, and dated one of my high school teachers on the sly. He was twenty-six and unmarried. He was actually a nice guy, and I learned a lot from him. I learned good manners, listened to good music, and read good books; and I learned that not all men are jerks.

He broke my heart when he married someone else. I thought he was going to marry me. That one set me back. I was prettier than his wife, but she must have had something I didn't, but I didn't know what that was.

Snow flurries drifted down, and the world seemed peaceful, and as they dusted the tops of cars and my shoulders, the anxiety of my mind cooled. I kept walking downtown, unable to connect any dots or fit together the scattered pieces of my life. I was just broken, inside and out, my mind burning with misery. I didn't know what to do or where to go.

I had a beautiful, two-bedroom condo on West Broadway and Chambers Street, and I had plenty of my own money. I was a successful real estate agent, thanks to Cliff's influence and contacts, as he always liked to throw in my face. But I had worked hard, learned the business from the ground up, and I had proven myself. Clients liked me and they recommended me to their friends and family. I was proud of that. It was the only real thing in my life I was proud of.

But all that was flushed down the toilet now. Everything I'd worked for and built up would come crashing down as soon as the cops found Cliff's body.

It wouldn't be long before Cliff's unanswered cellphone and texts would raise suspicion, and building security would call, knock on the suite door, and then enter and find him dead.

They'd find him lying on that luxurious carpet

with the antique clock next to his head, next to that sleek, silver-gray Italian sofa that cost a fortune. But everything in that extravagant, elegant room cost a fortune, in that high-rise, three-bedroom suite on the sixty-second floor, overlooking lower Manhattan, the Hudson River and the distant New Jersey hills.

It's pathetic, really. It's an old story. Poor Girl meets Billionaire. Billionaire thinks Poor Girl is a hot-looking waitress who, like every other young, attractive woman in New York, wants to be a model or an actress. I said to myself, "He's handsome. He's eyeing me. He's rich because everyone in that room is rich. If I play my flirtation just right, he might even buy me a big, fat diamond ring. Awesome, girl. Go for it!"

Cliff Prince offered me a new and exciting life, and I didn't hesitate, did I? I took it.

The wail of a police siren snapped me from my thoughts. Two police cars raced by, their dome lights swirling. And just like that, I was back in the present, recalling the horror of what I'd done. Fear burned like fire.

I had to form a plan, and fast, or I'd be in jail for a very long time.

CHAPTER 3

O kay, so it was a simple plan. Hail a cab and get to The Moynihan Train Hall, across the street from Penn Station, and take an Amtrak to somewhere. Anywhere. If Cliff's body was found soon, the airports were too dangerous, and I was too shaky to rent a car and drive. Besides, they would be able to trace the car. If I took the train, I could change trains en route as many times as I needed, and then I could vanish, or at least have the chance to.

Then I had a hopeful thought. I knew a guy, a shady guy in Chicago. I had always known shady guys. Anyway, if I could get to him, I knew he'd hide me and give me a new identity. As I said, he was shady, with good, shady connections. I'd met his sister at sixteen when I was in juvenile detention for shoplifting. We'd hit it off and stayed in touch. I'd call her and ask for her brother's number.

Three cabs streamed by. One was free, so I flagged it down, climbed in and told the driver where I was going.

"They say we're going to get a few inches of this snow," he said, in some accent.

I stayed quiet, my heart still racing, and I was perspiring, even though I was also shivering. I was in shock, no doubt about it.

"And it's before Thanksgiving," the driver continued. "Early... Way too early for snow. What about that, huh? And they say the globe is warming up. What the hell does anybody know about anything anymore? You know what I'm saying? Everybody's shootin' off their big mouths, and they don't know nothin' about nothin'."

I breathed in impatience. I did not want to talk to the man. "Yeah, right."

Easing back in my seat, I buckled my seatbelt. The driver kept blabbering on. I didn't answer, and he didn't seem to notice, obviously enjoying the sound of his own voice. My mind kept turning back to Cliff.

Cliff Prince was rich, handsome, and arrogant, but not what you'd call nice. I'm not the only one who thought so. He had few real friends, a lot of enemies, a brother who despised him, and a sister who wouldn't speak to him. But despite all that, he didn't deserve to die.

He wasn't the worst man I'd dated or lived with, but he did get aggressive when he drank too much. That's when the monster burst out, and then no one wanted to be around him, not his friends or business partners. I'd usually managed to avoid him when he got drunk because he didn't do it often. But this time, a business deal had gone bad, and Cliff had hit the whiskey hard.

I should have locked myself in my room or just left

and returned to my condo until the storm passed. Shoulda, woulda, coulda. I didn't because Cliff didn't want me to. He'd wanted to talk, and then I knew why. He thought I was sleeping with one of his buddies, Kevin Tyler. I wasn't. I didn't do that. For all my faults, I was faithful when I committed myself to a relationship.

Smart girl I was. I should have left him the last time he slapped me, shoved me down on the bed, and ripped off my top. Yeah, I guess you could say he did get violent before, but I'd let it go. I'd managed to fight him off and lock myself in the bathroom until he left. Yes, that's when I should have got the hell out of there. I should have left him.

But I didn't leave him because he had money, and he spent money on me, and he gave me money, and he kept sending real estate clients my way. I know, I know. I was a mercenary girl, and now I was paying for it.

So, yeah, he gave me money when we started dating. I won't say how much, but for a poor girl who came from a shabby trailer park, let me just say it made me feel good, and powerful, and free. What a laugh. Free. What a way to learn that money is good to have, but it isn't everything, and it can get you in big trouble. And it can be an addiction. I didn't love Cliff, and I should have left him, but I liked what money could buy. I was a fool.

I left the cab on Eighth Avenue and hurried toward the train station. Inside the huge, lofty train hall, with its soaring skylights and steel cathedral ceiling, I glanced about, already feeling watched. It was quiet, with stores and malls on the sides, an escalator in the center leading down to the tracks, and ticket windows on the left.

The bored ticket agent said the Lakeshore Limited traveled to Chicago, via Albany, and it was scheduled to leave in forty-five minutes—a lifetime, but I'd been lucky. I didn't have the cash, which wasn't good, so I used a credit card to pay for a one-way trip to Chicago, feeling tension in my shoulders and in my gut, feeling a headache coming on. Now, all I had to do was stay calm and not to let the terror take me over. I was already growing paranoid that everyone was looking at me, accusing me of murder.

My attention was drawn to a homeless woman who sat on a side bench near a closed deli. There were five or six shopping bags stuffed with items gathered around her, like a protective shield. She saw me and smiled. It was a kind smile, not a pleading, suffering one. The long coat she was wrapped in was too large for her frame, her gray hair was plastered to her head, and her thin face and sagging eyelids gave off a kind of weary contentment. But there was something else about the woman that startled me: she reminded me of my mother. Her sad eyes. Her stooped shoulders. The slight tilt of her head.

I didn't move for a minute or so, and we just stared at each other. Glancing about, on edge, I ambled over to her, and she lifted her old, watery eyes on me.

"Hello, young woman. You're awfully pretty, you know."

I swallowed. Those were exactly the same words my mother used to say to me. Exactly. The same. *You're awfully pretty, you know.*

"Who are you?" I asked, feeling my skin crawl. The entire night was just too weird.

"Nobody."

"Everybody's somebody," I said, searching her face.

"How old are you, young lady?"

"I'm twenty-five."

The lady cocked a questioning eye. "I bet you went to college and you're real smart, aren't you?"

I couldn't stop a burst of dark laughter. "No, I didn't go to college and I'm not smart at all. If I was smart, I wouldn't be here."

"And what's your name?"

"I'll tell you my name if you tell me yours."

"My name don't matter anymore. I'm nobody now. That's my name. Nobody. Now, tell me yours."

Yeah, she reminded me of my mother, but she wasn't my mother. But I felt sorry for her, even though I knew she wouldn't want that. "My name is Cindy Downing."

The woman's face warmed. "That's a fine name. A good and fine name for a pretty girl with reddish blonde hair and shining blue eyes. Yes, a fine name, Cindy."

I shrugged a shoulder. "Yeah, I guess so."

The woman leaned her head back and looked me

over anew. "Why are you so scared?"

I swallowed again. "I've had a bad day."

The woman studied me. "Yeah, I see that. Do you know what else I see?"

I didn't say anything. She was freaking me out, and I wanted to go.

"The night will swallow you up. Hear me?"

"What?"

She nodded. "I know all about the night, Cindy. I live in it, and I move in it, and it speaks to me. The night has kept me alive when others are long dead. You have to be quiet, of course, to hear it speak, because it doesn't use words, you know. It has its own words. But if I'm quiet, it speaks to me. Yes, the night will swallow you right up, and your life will never be the same again."

The whole scene seemed a nightmare, and I wanted to get the hell away from that woman. It was time to go. I reached into my purse for my wallet, removed a twenty-dollar bill, and extended my hand toward her.

She stared at it. "That's a lot of money for an old woman."

I didn't know what else to say. "It's not much. Not the way prices are today, it isn't. Please take it."

With a shaky, blue-veined hand, the woman reached and took the twenty, quickly stuffing it into her right coat pocket. "Thanks, young lady. Something good will happen to you for this. I just know it."

I sighed a little, my spooked eyes moving,

searching, blinking. "I hope so. I can use it. Do you have anywhere else to go?" I asked, glancing around again, spotting a cop near the front entrance, staring out the windows. Perspiration formed between my breasts and on my back.

"I'm just where I need to be, young lady," the woman responded. "Don't you worry none about me. You just go now and catch your train. Somewhere out there, the big night will hide you. You'll be okay."

I gave her a half-smile that probably looked more like a twisted grin. "Take care of yourself," I said, and I meant it, even though I knew the woman probably wouldn't live much longer.

I checked the departure board, and saw the blinking letters: ALL ABOARD. Finally, I could board the Amtrak train to Chicago.

I joined a line forming near the escalator, keeping my head down, taking the opportunity to glance at my cellphone to see if there was any news. Thank God, there wasn't. But it was too soon. With any luck, Cliff hadn't been found.

It seemed an eternity before the line inched ahead, and I stepped onto the escalator and glided down, being one of the few passengers who didn't have luggage.

Leaving the escalator, I walked briskly down the concrete platform toward the rear of the train, ducking inside the third coach from the rear, finding it wasn't crowded. The seat I chose was three from the exit doors, just in case I needed to escape quickly.

I sank down in the seat, leaned my head back, and closed my eyes. I took several deep breaths and tamped down the mounting hysteria. While my heart thudded in my ears, I willed the train to move, pressed my forehead with the heel of my hand and blurted out, "Move, train! Move, dammit!"

A man across the aisle shot me a glance.

When the train finally lurched ahead, I let out a breath. I had made it. At least for now, I was on my way. Would I make it to Chicago before the police boarded the train searching for me?

CHAPTER 4

There are good dreams, and there are bad ones. A bad dream startled me awake, and I blinked, wiped my eyes, and realized the bad dream I'd just awakened from wasn't as bad as the waking dream I was living in. And, of course, it wasn't a dream, and I couldn't pinch myself and wake up.

I was on a train heading for Chicago to change my name and hide somewhere—who knew where?—probably for the rest of my life. But who was I kidding? The cops would find me, eventually. Cliff's family would make sure I was found, no matter where I hid. They had the money.

Thankfully, no one had sat on the seat next to me. I'd been asleep for over an hour, and as much as I dreaded it, I pulled my cellphone and checked the news. Terror rippled up my spine. There it was, already a shouting headline on CNN!

BILLIONAIRE TYCOON CLIFTON PRINCE FOUND DEAD IN NEW YORK LUXURY SUITE! GIRLFRIEND SOUGHT!

There was a photo of the two of us in happier days,

his arm around my waist, Cliff wearing a tuxedo, and me in a killer cocktail dress, showing plenty of cleavage. My smile was gushing and forced, and he had the high-wattage smile of a movie star. Even as the panic rose, I had to admit that we'd been a lovely couple.

The weight of the moment was suffocating. I dropped my cellphone into my purse and couldn't stop my scared eyes from moving. That's when I became aware that my lip was sore, and my left eye was throbbing in pain where Cliff had struck me. I turned my face toward the window and saw my vague reflection in the glass. Why hadn't I felt the pain before now? Shock? It didn't matter. Now that my photo was all over the internet, I wouldn't have a chance. Somebody would recognize me, or maybe they'd already recognized me, and I'd be in jail before morning.

My mind felt bruised, and I couldn't think. I was a stupid girl in headlights, and a big and fast police car was going to flatten me like roadkill on a back Florida road. I tried to swallow away a lump, but I couldn't. I needed a drink, wine, beer, water, whatever, but I was too scared to move. I'd be recognized.

So, I sat with my head turned aside, staring out into the night, as lights blurred by, as the train thundered ahead, the moan of its whistle reminding me of that trailer park back in Florida. The freight trains would come rumbling across the tracks at all hours of the day and night, shaking the trailer. I got used to them, and they seldom awakened me, even when their hollow whistle blasted and echoed.

I squirmed when I recalled that the train conductor had taken and punched my ticket and then placed the stub into the metal tab above my seat. He'd seen my face. He'd said, "Good evening." He'd smiled at me and stared at me a little too long. Did he notice my eye? My sore lip? Why didn't the homeless woman say anything? Maybe she didn't see so well? I should have brought a hat to help disguise my face. I should have stopped at an ATM and taken out more cash, so I wouldn't have to use credit cards, which are so easily tracked. I should have done a hundred other things, but I hadn't been thinking so good, had I?

I had to get off at the next stop, whatever that next stop was, and make a run for it. It was my only chance. Was the next stop Poughkeepsie, New York? Albany?

I slid out of my coat and placed it on the seat next to me. I grabbed my purse, left my seat and, with my head bowed low, worked my way down the aisle until I came to the bathroom. Stepping in, I closed and locked the door, and faced the mirror.

Surprise. My lip wasn't so swollen. Lipstick would cover it, and my eye, although a bit puffy, wasn't as bad as I'd imagined. I applied lipstick, and then concealer and blush, especially around my sore eye. I leaned in, taking a closer look. Not bad. Not bad at all, except that I still looked like the girl on the CNN website. Not bad at all meant that I'd be easily recognized.

Returning to my seat, I saw the conductor working his way down the aisle. I sat and turned toward the window, pretending to be lost in thought, and it wasn't hard to pretend.

I heard the conductor say, "Next stop, Poughkeepsie, New York. Poughkeepsie, next stop, in about ten minutes."

And then he leaned in toward me and lowered his voice. "Everything all right?"

I didn't turn to face him. "Yes, everything is just fine, thank you."

"Well, you let me know if we can make your trip more comfortable."

I looked at him through the window's reflection and he was just a smudge. "Thank you."

He lingered. I sweated.

What he said next paralyzed me. "You look familiar."

"Everybody looks like somebody else," I said, wishing he'd leave.

"Yeah, okay. That's cool."

I was certain he was suspicious. Why didn't I look at him? He was in his early thirties and not bad looking. I was certain he had returned to get a better look at me. I had to get off at Poughkeepsie.

I sat forward, getting ready to shoot up as soon as the train pulled to a stop. If the conductor was standing nearby, I'd blow by him, exit the train and disappear into the night.

I heard the whistle and the ding of bells as the

train approached the platform and squealed to a stop. That's when I saw them: two policemen on the platform, hands stuffed into their jacket pockets, chatting, their breath smoking. I jerked my glance away and plotted an alternate escape.

What escape? There was no escape. It was over. I was caught. I pushed up and headed to the bathroom, a useless idea. Inside, I closed and locked the door, leaned back against it and waited, feeling like a trapped animal. My heart kicked, my saliva was thick. I chewed on my lower lip and waited. And waited. And waited.

When the train jolted, moved and gathered speed, I was breathing through my teeth, sweat on my face, my neck, my back.

Minutes later, as the train was clicking along the tracks, I made my move. I unlocked the bathroom door, slid it open and, after a deep breath, I stepped out. I was surprised to see that the coach was nearly empty, only three other people remained, a 40s something business-type woman at work on her laptop, an elderly man reading a newspaper, and a 20s looking guy staring into his phone across the aisle from my seat. I thought that was strange. Weren't most passengers traveling to Albany or Chicago?

When I saw that no one was waiting for me, not the conductor or the cops, I ducked my head and returned to my seat, sitting on the edge of misery. Staring out into the night, I flirted with the idea of getting off at Albany and turning myself in. Wouldn't that be the right thing to do? After all, I had killed a man, even though it was in self-defense. Should I, for once, do the right thing and tell the truth? Wasn't it time I grew up and accepted responsibility for my actions? Isn't that what my mother had tried to hammer into me when I was a teenager, running wild and stealing clothes, makeup, and food?

As the minutes ticked by, as the train pushed on, I stared at my reflection in the window, and realized I didn't like that image of myself, as vague and blurry as it was. I had lived callously and selfishly, indifferent to others, and apathetic about the consequences of my actions. So, yes, maybe it was time I turned myself in, pleaded my case and accepted the outcome. If I had to go to jail, then fine, I'd do my time and then I'd be free to start again. Start a brand-new life.

But the thought of going to prison completely paralyzed my body, mind, and soul. What if I was found guilty of murder and sentenced to twenty or thirty years? If I survived in that hell of a place, I'd be too old and too broken to start again. I'd seen women who'd spent only ten or fifteen years in prison. One woman who lived in our trailer park had spent ten years in a Florida prison for killing her boyfriend in self-defense. She was an old, shattered hag at fifty-two. And I'd met other former cons along the way, and they were mean, broken, and darkly depressed.

The train shuddered. I got the shakes. My hands shook, my throat tightened, and my right eye twitched. What the hell was I going to do?

That's when it happened, something I'll never be able to explain. So why am I writing this? Because I have to. Because it happened, and it was crazy and terrifying, and it completely changed my life. Because I have to write it down and try to make sense of it. Because no one will ever believe it.

I heard a whooshing sound. The train rocked, and when I glanced toward the window, I saw we'd entered a tunnel. And that's when it happened. I felt floaty and detached, the first signs something wasn't right. I thought it was my nerves, or my mind was tuning out from all the stress. A chill rippled up to the top of my head. I felt flushed, and my eyes got blurry.

On impulse, I shot a glance toward the guy across the aisle, who'd been surfing his cellphone. It was completely weird. He was fading in and out, solid one moment, ghost-like the next. And then he was gone. Vanished! What the hell!?

Sure I was having a breakdown or a heart attack, I gulped in air and tried to stand, but the train shook so violently I couldn't get to my feet. A puff of cold wind blew across my face; it had a scary scream to it, just like in the movies. And then a smoky, yellow fog engulfed the coach. I was certain it was poison gas, and I was going to die.

In my crazy head, I thought the cops had found me and someone had hired them to kill me and toss my body off the train. My chest tightened, my throat burned, and I was sure I was close to death.

I peered into that churning fog and saw crackling light: red, green and blue, like little firework explosions, dazzling. In frightened wonder, I watched as bright blue threads of light crawled along the sides and ceiling of the train, like an electric current.

The train bucked hard. I braced for the thing to jump the tracks, go barreling off a cliff, and crash.

When the electric, blue current reached me, I felt the shock of it, the sting of it, the pain of it. I screamed. It jolted me from my seat, and I bounced down hard, only to be jolted again. The last time, I thought I would shatter into pieces, and I fainted.

CHAPTER 5

I returned to consciousness slowly, reluctantly, my breathing staggered. My head was leaned back and someone above was trying to get me to drink water from a glass. I choked the first two times.

"There, there, there, now, young woman," a reassuring male voice said. "You just relax, and we'll try again. Open your mouth a little wider. Come on, you can do it... just a little wider."

My eyes were glued shut and my head pounded. I'd lost all track of time and place, and the last thing I remembered was standing in Cliff's suite, sipping champagne from a crystal flute while he took a drink of his whiskey.

I finally managed to drink some water, and it felt cool on my burning throat.

"Very good, very good. That will make you feel better," the soothing male voice said.

With effort, I forced my eyes open, squinting into the dim, flickering light that came from a glass globe ceiling attachment.

"Feeling better now?" the male voice asked.

Slowly turning my head, I gazed up into the face of a gray-bearded man with a bushy mustache, calm eyes, and a smiling mouth. I figured he was in his middle-to-late fifties, from his wrinkled forehead, his crow's feet, and the bags under his eyes.

I licked my lips and found my voice. "What happened? Where am I?"

"I'm Dr. Harlan Broadbent. You fainted, and I was summoned by the conductor to assist and examine you."

My foggy brain struggled to make connections. I slowly lifted my head and sat up, turning my attention out the window. The train was rocking through wide open country in early evening, passing trees, rickety shacks, and endless, waving fields of long grass, all sliding smoothly backward.

My sleepy eyes opened fully. I saw black smoke billowing past the window and heard the moan of a train whistle as the train wheels went clicking along the tracks.

Was I in a private car? My seat, and the surrounding seats, were velvet, spacious and plush. The décor was lavish, with beautiful, detailed woodwork and brass fixtures. Everything looked retro, as if the train had come from a museum and was the set for a historical Hollywood movie. On the ceiling, ornate, mother-of-pearl globes gave off muted light, not so bright, but relaxing, casting everything in a romantic glow.

"Where am I?" I asked, my eyes returning to Dr. Broadbent. He wore a curious, black, cutaway coat with silk lapels and a high starched collar, a black bow tie, and black and gray striped pants. His wire spectacles enlarged his dark eyes. He looked more like a butler from the TV series *Downton Abbey* than a doctor. I sensed something was wrong, but my head hadn't cleared enough for me to work it out.

"First, young lady, may I ask your name?"

I hesitated, my mind a tangle of memories, thoughts and faces. I simply couldn't remember, and it scared the hell out of me. I was sure I'd had some kind of seizure or a stroke.

"I... I can't remember. How crazy is that? I just can't remember."

He studied me. "I must say, with some small surprise, that you favor a woman I have treated in the past. You have similar features."

"I don't know my name. I just don't know it. Why is that? What the hell has happened to me?"

"Just calm yourself now, young woman. You must have had a shock. In good time, your memory will return to you, and all will be well."

The conductor drifted over and whispered into the doctor's ear. Dr. Broadbent nodded confidently, and the conductor gave me one final, wary glance before leaving the coach.

I kept my voice low, but my temples were pounding. I felt for my purse, but it wasn't there. "Where's my purse? My cellphone?"

Dr. Broadbent questioned me with his eyes. "We did not find a purse either on you or beside you."

I looked left and right, but it wasn't there. "Where

is this? What is this?"

At that moment, a woman came into view, and she stood next to Dr. Broadbent. Her pretty face and intelligent eyes held concern as she leaned, looking me over.

"And how are you feeling, Rosamond?" she asked, with sweet concern.

I blinked, confused. "Rosamond?"

"Yes... are you feeling better, dear friend?"

"Dear friend?" I stammered out. "I... I don't know."

Dr. Broadbent looked at the woman. "Do you know this ailing young woman?"

To my shock, the woman said, "Yes, of course I know her. Her name is Rosamond Adams."

"And who are you?" the doctor asked, straightening his spine.

"I am Nellie Cummins," she answered, standing erect, meeting his gaze.

"And where have you been while this poor creature took ill and fainted? And why is she dressed in such immodest attire? I have never seen this mode of dress and it is the reason I had her brought back to this private car, away from prying eyes."

"That is none of your affair, sir. It is Rosamond's and my affair, is it not?"

Dr. Broadbent adjusted his spectacles, wiggled his nose and narrowed his eyes into slits. "Just so, young woman."

Nellie was about my age, also a blonde, with a slim figure and refined features. She wore a royal blue bustle dress, heavily trimmed, pleated and ornamented with lace, and it fit her figure to perfection. But it was her hat that drew my eyes. It was made of violet crepe and blonde lace, trimmed with two short, violet ostrich feathers and a spray of tea roses.

Even in my numb state, I thought it looked fabulous, and I thought I must be having one helluva dream—or I fell and hit my head and knocked myself silly. Why were these people dressed in such extravagant clothes from another time?

My stalled mind tried to punch through the walls of mental chaos and remember who I was and what had happened, but my blurry headache only grew worse.

"So, I will repeat, where were you when this young woman suddenly took ill and fainted?"

In defiance, Nellie raised her chin. "I can assure you, sir, I stepped away from my friend for necessary minutes to visit the lavatory. Upon my return, I saw Rosamond hunched over in her seat. That is when I summoned the conductor, who summoned you."

Dr. Broadbent said, "I do not recall seeing you when I was summoned."

"Well, I can assure you it was I who sought help for my dear friend. I stepped aside for only a moment to consult my gentleman friend. In any event, henceforth, I will see to it that Rosamond is cared for. I thank you for your kind attention and professional expertise, but we will not require your services any further."

Dr. Broadbent looked Nellie up and down with disapproval, sniffed, turned, and left the compartment.

I didn't know what to think or what to say. They spoke so formally, so stiffly, so weirdly.

Nellie eased down beside me, slowly and gently, her cool eyes appraising me. I noticed she sat forward because the back of the bustle bunched up behind her. I thought, why would any woman wear a thing like that?

"What particular confidence trick are you undertaking?" Nellie asked.

I had no idea what she was talking about, so I didn't say anything.

"Are you working alone or in partnership?"

Again, I didn't speak.

"Where did you purchase your garments? I've never seen any like them. They are manly and odd. They are, well, I don't know quite how to say it. They are quite immodest and unsuitable for a woman of your favorable physical attributes."

I looked down at my expensive slacks and turtleneck sweater and wondered what had happened to my coat, purse and cellphone. I stayed silent, trembling inside and out. I knew I was over my head and that something unthinkable had happened. I began to get flashes of things: I saw Cliff's suite. I saw his dead body. I remembered hailing a cab and entering the train station. I remembered speaking to the homeless woman and giving her twenty bucks.

As I stared into Nellie's frosty eyes, I sensed darkness tunneling in around me and I nearly fainted again. Was it fear or hunger?

"I can help you, if you take me into your confidence," Nellie said crisply.

I said, "Do you know me?"

Nellie's mouth tightened and then she said, "No..."

"Then why did you tell that doctor you did? Why did you call me your friend?"

Nellie narrowed her eyes at me. "Did you want him hovering over you, asking all sorts of personal questions?"

"No..."

"Well, then, I dispatched of him, didn't I?"

I looked at her carefully. "Who are you?"

"I told you, Nellie Cummins. Where are you from? I don't know that accent."

"From Florida... but I live in New York."

One of her eyebrows shot up. "New York?"

"Yes."

Nellie kept her suspicious eyes on me. "Where are you going?"

"Chicago."

Nellie arched an eyebrow. "Chicago? Dearie, if you're going to Chicago, then you are on the wrong train."

"What are you talking about? I bought a ticket to Chicago. I'm going to Chicago."

Nellie shook her head. "This is the train to Denver. We arrive in about five hours."

That floaty feeling returned. "No way. It can't be. What is this? What is all this?"

Nellie sighed. "Did you hit your head or something? What is the matter with you?"

Frustration and fear brought angry words. "I don't know what the hell's the matter with me, okay?! I don't know what happened, why I'm here, or how I got here. I don't know shit, okay!?"

Nellie drew back, startled by my outburst. She blinked several times before she spoke, in a measured voice. "You speak coarsely, and it is unladylike. You must come from the Lower East Side."

"Just tell me what's going on."

Nellie adjusted her hat. "Have you eaten recently? I always get out of sorts when I'm hungry."

I shook my head, then massaged my forehead with a hand. "I don't know. No."

"Then perhaps we should order you some refreshments."

I ignored her, desperate to clear my head. "Why are you here, and why are you dressed like that?"

"Like what?" Nellie asked, taking mild offense.

"Like you're in an old movie. Like you've just stepped out of *Gone with the Wind* or something."

"An old what? Gone with what?"

I heaved out a frustrated sigh. "This is friggin' crazy!"

Nellie rose, impatience rising in her face and voice. "And I think you are not right in your mind, whoever you are."

"And I think you're the one who's crazy! Just tell me where I am."

Nellie gave me an icy glare. "You are on the Central Pacific Railroad, traveling to Denver, Colorado. This is a private car, not occupied on this leg of the journey, but it will be occupied once the train arrives in Denver. That's what that lascivious-eyed conductor told me, anyway. The occupants will be the wealthy industrialist, Mr. Horace T. Bakersfield, and his wife. They will travel from Denver to San Francisco. You are here because you fainted. I happened to see you as a I passed, coming from the lavatory. Concerned, I called the conductor, who summoned the doctor. They gently lifted you and carried you in here. I followed them, and I heard you say, you didn't know your name. That's as much as I know."

I let my brain process that. "Okay... why did you lie and tell the doctor you knew me? Why did you say my name was... what was it, Rosamond Adams?"

"I told you. So he would leave us. Leave the coach."

"Okay, whatever. Fine. Just tell me what day this is," I said, trying to get anchored in time and place. "I'm completely lost."

"It's Wednesday."

I tried to remember the date I'd left New York. "Wednesday, November 9?"

Nellie faced me. "Perhaps I should call the doctor back."

"No! Just please tell me. Is it still Wednesday, November 9?"

Nellie answered with a shake of her head. "No. It is November, but it's the sixth of November. Wednesday, November 6, 1880."

My blood surged, my heart kicked, and my voice rose in disbelief. "What!? Did you just say it's 1880?"

Nellie turned and started to leave. "I will call for Dr. Broadbent."

"No! Don't leave. Don't call him."

Nellie stopped, but she didn't turn. "Who are you, truly?"

I fumbled for my name, and when it popped into my head, I blurted it out. "I'm Cindy Downing. *That's* my name. Cindy!"

Nellie did a slow turn, her eyes round with new interest. "And are you ill, Miss Downing? And, if so, what is your particular illness?"

"No... I'm not ill. I'm freaking out. I'm lost in the middle of some kind of shitshow, but I'm not ill. I'm not sick."

Nellie's face tightened in displeasure. "Your speech is blunt and common."

What could I say? I guess I *was* blunt and common.

"And are you alone, Miss Downing? Are you not travelling with anyone? A man, perhaps? Your mother or sister? A chaperone? Forgive me, but I noticed you were seated alone when you fainted, and no one, except the conductor and the doctor, came to your assistance."

I considered that, lowering my voice, trying to put all the scattered pieces together. "I'm alone. I was on a train that didn't look like this, and we were on our way to Albany, New York, when something happened, and I passed out."

Nellie took steps toward me, her expression changing, but I couldn't read her. There was just the hint of a smile, although her eyes remained cool, as if there were calculations going on in her devious little head. "All right, Miss Downing. I am going to order you some food, and while you eat, I would like us to converse and get to know each other."

"I can't find my purse. I don't have any money."

"Do not worry about funds just now, Miss Downing. If I'm going to help you, I'll have to know you better, won't I?"

Nellie's tight little smile unnerved me. If I was dreaming, and I didn't believe for a minute that I was, then I needed to find out what had happened. Why did these people believe they were living in 1880?

Had I completely lost my mind? I had watched stupid *YouTube* videos about time travel, and time slips, and time portals and time whatever, but I didn't believe them. Not really.

But now? My mind whirled, my pulse rose. Had I somehow blinked out of the twenty-first century into the world of 1880? Had I time traveled? Just because you don't understand something doesn't mean you stay stupid when it's in your face. That's not how I'd always survived. Whatever had happened, I'd faced it and dealt with it.

And then Nellie said, "Does madness run in your family?"

CHAPTER 6

I ate at a linen-topped table in the private coach compartment. A white-haired steward, wearing a white coat and black tie, brought the food on a silver tray, covered by what he called a "cloche"—a silver, dome-shaped covering. He eased the tray down and removed the cloche, and I was intoxicated by the delicious smell of the food. The conductor arrived as the steward withdrew, and he told us we'd have to leave as soon as I'd eaten.

Nellie flashed him a killer smile and told him, tartly, that we'd leave when we were good and ready, and not a minute before. He scowled, pivoted, and retreated.

The sirloin steak was excellent; the baked potato with butter, fluffy; the peas, overcooked; the bread roll warm and tasty. I ate like a wolf while Nellie kept her eyes on me, also like a wolf.

"Will there be anyone in Denver to meet you?" Nellie asked.

I swallowed a piece of steak, chewed, then reached for a glass of water. After I'd swallowed, I said, "No."

"What will you do?"

Not wanting to think about it, I kept eating. Food never tasted so good. "I have no idea."

"You may be in luck," Nellie said, in a cheerful tone.

I stopped eating and looked directly at her. "What does that mean?"

Nellie's smile held secrets. "I can help."

"Do you live in Denver?"

"No. I've never been."

"So, why are you going?"

Nellie made a vague gesture with a hand. "I know a family you can stay with."

"If you've never been, how do you know this family?"

"Through friends."

I continued eating, and we didn't speak again until I'd cleaned my plate and drained the water.

"I could use a drink," I said.

"A drink?" Nellie asked, with confusion. "You have water."

"No, I mean, something with booze in it, like a vodka martini."

Nellie's face was blank. "What is that? A vodka martini?"

I lowered my eyes on her, wondering what planet she was living on. "You know, like a vodka martini. Lots of vodka, a touch of vermouth, and a big, fat, green olive. Don't tell me you've never had one?"

Nellie shifted her eyes. "I have no idea what you're talking about."

I sat up. "Okay, I'm talking about booze. Alcohol.

Vodka."

Nellie turned defensive. "I know about whiskey and beer and, of course, peach and apple cider. I do not know about martini."

I stared hard at her for a long, disappointed moment, and I thought, *How sad. No vodka martinis in 1880.*

The food relaxed me and satisfied my gnawing hunger, but the gentle motion of the train and all the stress and confusion made me sleepy.

"You look fatigued," Nellie said. "Perhaps you should lie down and rest. You have not sufficiently recovered from your illness, and you must have your strength when we arrive in Denver. We'll be there in only a few hours."

"Maybe we should talk about those friends of yours in Denver," I said. "Until I can figure things out, I'll need someplace to stay."

In a smooth, level voice she said, "I think it best if you rest for a time. Meanwhile, I'll make some plans for us. So, relax, Miss Downing. All will be well."

I was heavy and felt drugged by anxiety. I stood and stepped over to a red velvet loveseat settee, and lay down, feeling exhausted and lost. I closed my eyes, wanting to escape, willing myself to sleep, praying that when I awakened, I'd be back on that Amtrak train, in 2022.

Sometime later, I heard voices—a male voice and then Nellie's—but I could only hear fragments of their conversation.

"Can you do it?" the male voice asked.

"Yes..."

"But... We could... if... Let's hope..."

"Don't worry," Nellie said.

"It's just that..."

"Don't worry, Percy."

I strained my ears to hear more but I couldn't, and then I fell back to sleep.

A touch on my shoulder awakened me. I'd been dreaming I was making a *TikTok* video about living in 1880, and I was laughing hysterically.

"Miss Downing," Nellie said, "we must get you in proper attire before we arrive in Denver."

I sat up, putting a hand to a yawn. "What time is it?"

"It's nearly eight o'clock in the evening. I have let you sleep too long, and the conductor is making threats."

"Did you say attire?"

"Yes, you can't meet my friends in your present attire, and with that hairstyle."

"Why?"

Nellie sighed. "Because they simply won't do. My gentleman friend has a private stateroom, and he has agreed to let us dress there."

"I don't have any other clothes. What you see is what you get."

"Not to worry," Nellie said, casually. "We are about the same size, and I have just the dress for you. You will look quite lovely in it."

I stared at her and then I pointed at her dress. "Am I supposed to wear one of those?"

"Yes, Miss Downing, of course. Now, we don't have a lot of time, and we must not tarry."

I could have said "No." I could have refused to go with her because the street-smart girl in me said I couldn't trust her, and she was up to something. But I had no other options, did I? I didn't know anyone, I had no money, and I had nowhere to go. I knew I wasn't hallucinating, and I knew I wasn't dreaming, so all I had was the reality I was living in and, frankly, for now, I was screwed. I'd have to go with it and hope I'd survive whatever I was about to face until I could find a way out.

I followed Nellie out of the private parlor car, through the empty dining car, with its linen tablecloths, silverware, and crystal glasses, to the passenger coaches. As we moved through the coaches, along the narrow aisles, I felt every passenger was staring at me as if I were some convicted felon or freak. Everyone was dressed as if they had just stumbled in from one of those Jane Austen movies the Brits produce, like *Pride and Prejudice,* a book I'd actually read a few years ago.

We came to a polished mahogany door, and Nellie knocked twice. The door opened. A man in his early thirties, dressed in a black suit, white ruffled shirt and silk black bow tie, stood stiffly, looking me over. His black hair was center-parted, with a pomaded, retro look; his dark eyes wary; his face craggy, not quite handsome, but not ugly either. I sized the guy up as being clever, charming, and cunning. I'd seen a lot of faces like his in my twenty-five years: stock brokers, politicians, lawyers, and Cliff Prince.

He stepped back, his voice low, his eyes nervous. "Come in."

Once inside the stateroom, he closed the door and gave me a curt nod. "I'm Percy Blackstone."

He didn't offer to shake hands, and that was fine with me. "Cindy Downing."

The room contained an upper and lower berth, a half sofa, a narrow desk, a snug bathroom and a clothes closet.

I saw an open trunk placed on the floor near the lower berth, with clothes packed inside. The trunk looked heavy, a square-shaped box with wooden straps and a gold latch that could be locked.

Percy and Nellie exchanged a nod, the kind of nod that I interpreted as, "So far, so good."

Percy pointed at the door. "I'll just be going and let you two go about your business."

The sleep had helped my state of mind. The food had also helped. I felt better, although I still had a slight headache, and my body was stiff and sore as if I'd worked out in a gym, too long and too hard.

When Nellie removed the bustle dress from the narrow closet, I didn't say anything. I watched in curious wonder as she laid the beautiful burgundy dress across the lower bed.

She told me it was a silk taffeta dress, and it was awesome, to say the least, with the trimming, the opulence, the expensive laces, and the multitude of fabrics, all on the same gown. It must have taken a seamstress days to make the thing, and it couldn't have been cheap.

Nellie reached into the trunk and removed undergarments, trimmed with lace. They were long, loose-fitting underpants that split and overlapped in the middle, which, I guessed, allowed for easy bathroom access. There was a chemise, a corset, a stiff-looking petticoat, and a bustle made of wire and fabric.

I knew what was coming, and I wanted no part of it. The dress was beautiful, but I couldn't imagine stuffing myself into those undergarments, never mind the petticoat and the corset. I'd be unable to move around in that paraphernalia. It was absurd.

I put my hands on my hips and said, bluntly, "I'm not going to wear that. Any of that."

Nellie straightened and gave me a cool glance. "Miss Downing…"

"Just call me Cindy, okay? Nobody calls me Miss Downing. You don't need to be so formal."

Impatience flashed in her face and voice. "We have little time to discuss this. You cannot make your appearance before my friends wearing those immodest and bizarre-looking clothes. Did you not see the cold stares you received as we strolled through the passenger coaches? They believe you to be a loose woman, or one who has escaped from a sanitarium. That should tell you the truth of it, and why you must put on that dress."

I lifted my chin in a challenge. "Okay, fine. And who are these friends of yours, Nellie Cummins, and why are you and Percy, or whatever his name is, being so friendly to me when you don't even know who I am? I can see it in your face that you think I'm crazy or I've just dropped in from some other planet, which, believe it or not, I have. So, who are these friends, and why are you helping me?"

Nellie's icy stare was a little scary, and her voice dropped an octave into a threat.

"You are trying my patience, Cindy. As I see it, you have little choice in the matter. You either do as I say or you will be tossed off this train into the frigid winter night, where you will freeze to death, or starve to death, or end up with some very unsavory types who will have their way with you. I have heard that this is a very harsh and vulgar part of the country, filled with ruffians and scoundrels."

Nellie set her chin and our eyes clashed.

"Now, do you understand me, Cindy? You have no money, no friends and nowhere to go. I am giving you the rare opportunity to meet wealthy and decent people, who will protect you and look after your every need."

My grappling, restless mind sought an escape, but there was no escape. I kept circling the same question: what was this girl up to? It couldn't be good.

I kept my hands on my hips. I kept my poker face, and I struggled to keep my cool.

"Who are you, Nellie, if that is your right name? And what do you really want from me? Like you just said, I have to go along with whatever it is you've got planned for me, so you might as well tell me everything. Right?"

I could almost see and hear her brain working. The room filled with silent tension.

CHAPTER 7

"SO YOU WANT the truth, then you shall have it," Nellie said, with ugly superiority. "My true name is Rosamond Adams."

That certainly got my attention.

"I was raised in a tenement on the Lower East Side of New York by a shoemaker and a seamstress. I was always pretty, and I was always intelligent, and I spent much of my time desperately searching for schemes and methods to escape that crowded, miserable neighborhood and better myself. My parents constantly fought and constantly struggled to get enough money to pay the rent and put food on the table."

I nodded, thinking that Nellie and I had some things in common.

Nellie continued. "I married an older man when I was sixteen. He was a drunkard, and he beat me. A year later, I stole money from him, and fled. Weeks later, I learned he'd been kicked in the head by a horse and killed. When I was eighteen, I took up with a man who traded stocks, and he was successful, and we had fun for a time, until he lost everything on bad investments, and then he shot himself. I met other men, but they were louts, cheats, or brutes. As you can see, I kept falling into dirty coal piles where men are concerned. I turned twenty-four two months ago, and I was desperate, living with two other girls in one room, and working at Lord & Taylor on the Ladies' Mile. When a shopgirl friend told me about The Rose Daisy Agency, that they were looking for attractive, smart young women with refined interests, I seized the opportunity."

Rosamond made a sour face, and her smile was crooked. "What a lovely name, isn't it? The Rose Daisy Agency," Nellie said, her words alive with sarcasm.

"What kind of agency is it?" I asked.

Nellie glanced away in disgust, wetting her lips, stalling, as if telling me would make her sick.

"Okay, well, it sounds totally suspicious," I said. "Was it a high-end call girl agency?"

"I don't know what a call girl is. The Rose Daisy Agency is a highbrow mail-order business, owned and operated by Mrs. Rose Daisy herself, along with her bloated ogre of a husband, who looks like a rodent and tries to paw every young woman who enters the place."

Her dark expression suddenly transformed into pride. "A wealthy man paid ten thousand dollars for me, and I was to marry him."

I didn't see that coming. "Okay... Was?"

Nellie folded her hands, holding them at her

waist. "The agency mailed him an artistic drawing of me—a sketch—and he liked it. But then he demanded a photograph, which he agreed to pay for. So, I was sent to Horace Abbot's studio on Dey Street, and I had my photograph taken, which I found quite fascinating, but troubling."

"Why troubling?"

"Have you ever had your photograph captured by a camera?" Nellie asked.

"Yeah, many times."

Nellie's folded hands tightened. "Well, I've seen photographs, of course, and I've seen daguerreotypes, but I will just say that it was a good likeness of me… Maybe it was too fine a likeness for my nerves. I felt as though I were looking at my twin. I found the eyes looking back at me to be probing and eager, and it revealed more than I was… Well, let me say, more than I was comfortable with."

I thought about that photo of Cliff and me, the one where my smile was too wide and too forced, my eyes glazed from too much champagne and glittering with too much greed, and I understood what Nellie was trying to say.

Nellie flicked a hand in the air. "I'm talking too much. None of that matters now. Rose loved the photograph, and she promptly posted it to the wealthy man."

Nellie dropped her hands to her sides and squared her shoulders. "Well, anyway, he chose *me* to be his wife."

Mail-order bride? It seemed a fantasy and a

twisted joke. I had no idea how much ten thousand dollars was worth in 1880, but I assumed it was a lot. "So, you're on your way to meet and marry this man?"

Nellie avoided the question, and her voice became girlish. "As luck would have it, I met Percy only days before I was to board this train and travel to Denver. We have become, how should I say it? We are quite attached to each other, and he has asked me to travel with him to San Francisco. I told him about my particular situation, and he was very understanding. He said nobody will find us in San Francisco. He is a gambler—a very good gambler, and I am certain we will make a success of things there. He wants to open his own saloon, and I have a head for business."

That shocked my clogged brain into full working capacity. Now I knew exactly what Nellie and Percy were up to, and I turned cold. I took a little step backwards and shook my head. "No way, Nellie. No friggin' way."

Nellie crossed her arms and fastened her hard eyes on me, her mouth a tight line. "I'm afraid you have no choice."

"Oh, yes, I do have a choice and there's no way in hell I'm doing this. You're out of your mind. I'll get off the train and find someone to help me. I'm very resourceful, I can think fast on my feet, and I'm telling you, there's no way I'm taking your place. There's no way I'm going to marry some guy I don't even know. And anyway, he's seen your photo, and he'll know right off something's messed up. We don't look that much alike."

Nellie's voice was steady, and taking on strength. "On the contrary, we look remarkably alike. We have the same shaped face. The same slender neck, and if our features are not quite a perfect match, they are close enough. No, when I saw you being carried off into that private car, I couldn't believe my very good and timely luck."

"And I can't believe you're serious about this! It won't work, Nellie. Never. No way!"

"It will work, and I'm going to San Francisco!"

My stomach squirmed. "Okay, fine, go to San Francisco. So what? What will they do if you don't show up and marry this guy? The agency isn't going to send anyone from New York to search for you. And whoever this guy is, he's not going to take the time and money to run off looking for you, either. So, keep me out of it and go to San Francisco."

Nellie's face darkened. "You don't understand. He's wealthy. He will come after me. There is no doubt about it. I told Percy that despite what he says about us hiding in San Francisco, John Gannon will come for me. I was warned by Rose when I signed that piece of paper in New York. I was told that John Gannon is a ruthless man who owns considerable land and employs many people, including private law officers. They will come looking for me, even in San Francisco. Rose told me that the day I signed the contract."

I shook my head and shrugged. "Okay. Fine. Well,

that's your problem, Nellie, not mine. I've got other, bigger problems, and I didn't sign anything, and I'm not about to marry that guy. It just ain't gonna happen."

Nellie's posture tensed. "I was afraid you would respond like this."

"Yeah, well, duh!"

"I do not know what that word means, and it sounds offensive."

"Offensive? Good. I'm glad it sounds offensive, because I'm very offended. Well, girl, or Nellie, or Rosamond, or whoever you are, I've got to hand it to you, you're clever and quick."

"Yes, well, I've had to be, haven't I?"

"And you weren't going to tell me, were you? If I hadn't like, woken up and got my brains back, you were just going to toss me off the train and chug-a-lug off to San Francisco with your gambler friend, weren't you? Well, baby doll, it ain't gonna happen, because I am not getting off this train in Denver unless somebody tosses me off."

Nellie stared down, and when her eyes lifted on me, she'd slid her hand into a hidden dress pocket and retrieved a two-shot derringer with a beautiful pearl handle. She pointed it at me, staring with cold, even finality.

CHAPTER 8

I gave her and the derringer a long look. In all my wild, running days, I'd never had anyone point a gun at me. Like everything else I'd experienced in the last few hours, this, too, had a kind of fantasy, dreamlike quality to it. What nightmare of a reality was I in?

Nellie's expression was grim and determined. There was no mercy in her eyes. "Step back, Cindy."

There wasn't a lot of room, but I took two steps back.

Nellie kept her hostile gaze on me. "Dr. Broadbent is from Denver. I learned that from the conductor. And I also learned that he has treated John Gannon and his family numerous times. Now you know that John Gannon is the man I'm supposed to marry. I spoke your name to Dr. Broadbent. I spoke your name clearly. I said you were my friend, Rosamond Adams, distinctly, so the doctor will know you by that name."

I glanced around, considering an escape, so I decided to stall, so I could think of a way out. "Your name, Rosamond, is an elegant name. I'm sure your guy, Mr. Gannon, liked it as well. It sounds so romantic."

Nellie's smile was faint. "My father told me that if he couldn't give me wealth, then at the very least, he could give me a name that sounded like wealth. Now, there isn't much time, and I am weary of explanations."

I didn't say anything. I stared at that shiny derringer, thinking, if she shoots me and I die, where will I go? To some other world in the past... to the future?

A knock on the door startled me and shook me out of my thoughts.

"Who is it?" Nellie asked, tension tightening her lips and the skin around her eyes.

"Percy."

Keeping the derringer pointed at me, she backed up, released the lock, and stepped away from the door. Percy slipped in, closed the door, and locked it.

His worried gaze looked at me and then at Nellie.

"It was the only way," Nellie said. "She says she won't do it."

I could have said something brave like, "You won't shoot me," but I didn't feel brave. I felt a flood of fear, and I'd been living with that damned fear ever since I hit Cliff with that heavy clock. I felt weak from it and sick from it.

Nellie handed the derringer to Percy. Even under the dim light of the wall gas lamp, his hair gleamed as he estimated the situation.

"Are you sure?" Percy said to Nellie, in a near

whisper.

Nellie nodded. "I told you, it's the only way. I told you it would be the only way."

Nellie's breathing was deep. She was stressed. With a tight face of impatience, she said, "We're running out of time. Now get dressed, Cindy."

I felt a big lump in my throat, and I couldn't swallow it away. "I don't know how. If you want me to put that thing on, you're going to have to help me."

Percy exhaled a mounting anxiety. "Let's get on with it. We'll be in Denver soon!"

I don't know how to describe my transformation into a shiny new mirage of an 1880 woman. I removed my clothes and Nellie helped me put on the various undergarments, the petticoat, the corset, and the bustle. It was a feeling of gradually being tied up, shoehorned into the corset, fitted with the bustle and finally stepping into that voluminous dress that was nearly too big for the room. All the stuff beneath the dress gave it form. The corset molded the waist, and the bustle projected the dress out from behind.

And, of course, there was a hat. Every woman and man wore a hat. Mine was burgundy velvet, with silver gray brocade, black netting and off-white lace. The mirror provided was small, so I didn't get a full-length view of myself and, anyway, I was scared to death, trying to keep my heart from kicking its way out of my chest.

As the train was slowing down, arriving at the

Denver station, everyone was tense. I didn't see a way out, so I'd have to go with it. I would meet Mr. John Gannon and then I'd tell him the truth. I'd tell him what Nellie or Rosamond had done and hope he'd help me find my way in this world of 1880.

Nellie seemed to read my mind. "One last thing, Cindy. Just in case you're thinking about telling Mr. Gannon the truth about me. I warn you, from all I have heard about the man, he will not take kindly to it, and he will suspect you are involved in this little plot. If you value your life, I'd recommend you keep your mouth shut."

That little witch had thought of everything, and I wanted to slap her silly.

We were moving down the aisle to exit the train, me in front, Percy behind me, with the derringer hidden in his suit coat pocket, and Nellie bringing up the rear.

I was about to step from one unknown world into another, and it felt as if I were going to my death, like I was walking the plank on one of those pirate ships of old. The long, heavy winter coat that covered the bulky dress was hot and suffocating, and my breathing was coming fast. I was trapped, and I hated being trapped. It was the same sick feeling as being in jail, but it was even worse, and I never thought that would be possible.

We stood by the exit door, waiting for the train to come to a complete stop, its bell clanging, steam hissing.

Nellie said, "There will be a carriage waiting for

you. The coachman should be inside the passenger terminal searching for you. He'll have your description, the dress, hat and possibly the sketch or photograph. He'll drive you to the Gannon Mansion. Your trunk will be delivered on the platform. Be sure you have the driver load it in the carriage for you."

"What trunk?"

"You'll have a trunk, Cindy, so you don't raise any suspicions. I have thought of everything," she said, with a little lift of her haughty chin.

No, I didn't want to slap her. I wanted to punch her in the face. "Okay, whatever."

Nellie added, "You don't seem quite in your senses."

"Yeah, so maybe I'm not so in my senses," I said. "When is this marriage supposed to happen?"

"It was never specified. It depended on whether Mr. Gannon approved of me."

I thought about that. That could be good or bad. "Awesome!" I said, with a shake of my head. "And what happens if he doesn't approve?"

Nellie sighed. "You talk too much."

As the train platform came into view, the conductor came through and we stepped aside as he slid open the heavy steel door. A burst of cold, night wind washed over my face.

The train squealed to a stop and Percy barked, "All right. Go. Get off the train!"

I inhaled a shaky breath, gathered up my skirts, not gracefully, and descended the two steel stairs down to the wooden platform.

Behind me, a wiry, thin-faced porter appeared, tugging the trunk to the door. As he grunted with effort, he half-carried, half-dragged the thing down the stairs.

On the platform, a stocky man appeared, pushing a high wheeled hand car. He touched the brim of his cap and loaded the trunk.

"Where would you like this, Miss?" he asked in a deep, scraping voice, his face aged and lined, reminding me of a high school boyfriend's catcher's mitt.

What was inside that trunk, I had no idea.

I glanced around to see other passengers leaving the train and strolling into the train terminal. I pointed to the door. "Inside the terminal."

"Very good, Miss," the porter said.

I walked across the broad wooden platform to the terminal, as another gust of frigid wind chilled me to the bone, and I tucked my chin, while the porter clamped a hand onto his hat to keep it from flying away. My hat was secured by three pins, so it stayed firmly on my head, a new sensation.

I didn't look back at the train to see if Nellie and Percy were watching. I assumed they were hanging around, making sure I didn't slip back onto the train through another door.

Was this my punishment? Was the universe punishing me for all the shitty things I'd done in my life, hurling me off into some other time and place? Was this my punishment for killing Cliff Prince and running away?

CHAPTER 9

I pushed through the heavy oak doors, feeling the rustling of my skirts, another new sensation. Entering the warm passenger terminal, I glanced up to see an impressive rotunda interior with a golden dome, which gave the room an extravagant elegance. The large white clock with black Roman numerals hanging from the ceiling said it was 10:25. That seemed farcical. A joke. Could time really be measured? What time? Whose time?

Amazed by the luxurious decor, I paused, taking in the white and brown marble floor, polished and gleaming. There were stained-glass windows and glowing amber gas lamps, gold leaf features and long, mahogany benches, where passengers sat, waiting for travel notices. They glanced up often to view a dark green, overhanging schedule board above the ticket windows, which announced departures and arrivals from Chicago, St. Louis and Kansas City.

Letting my mind ramble to escape the angst for what was to come, I wished I had my cellphone to snap photos of this vintage place, surely long gone in the twenty-first century. I stared at the vivid, unreal world that was truly surreal, as I gawked at women in dark dresses, stylish, long wrapping coats, and elaborate hats, some with their hands tucked inside fur muffs.

I observed men in richly styled overcoats and top hats or bowler hats, sporting mustaches and beards. Some lounged on a bench, their legs crossed, engrossed in a newspaper, while puffing a cigar.

Others perused magazines or newspapers at one of the two golden domed, central newsstands. The fragrance of vanilla polish, cigar smoke, and wax wafted through the area, creating a strange yet intriguing scent that I had never encountered before. It was both alluring and unappealing at the same time.

The porter cleared his throat, and I turned to him. "Oh, I'm sorry. I've never been here before." And then, to my embarrassment, I realized I didn't have any money for a tip.

"Would you like me to park your trunk over by them benches, Miss?"

"Yes, thank you. That would be cool... I mean, nice."

Next to a long bench, mostly unoccupied, he slid the trunk from his hand truck, stood and tipped two fingers to the bill of his cap.

I made a face of apology. "I'm sorry, sir, I don't have any change."

His smile was thin. "Not to worry none, Miss. A gentleman took care of it. Now, a good evening to you."

I remained standing, because I didn't know how to sit in that bustle dress, with the back sticking out like I had two asses. Nonchalantly, I observed women seated nearby. They were perched forward, the bustle providing a kind of padding between them and the back of the bench. Again, I thought, *What an utterly stupid way to dress.*

Now that I was here, who was I supposed to meet? Nellie hadn't been clear. She'd said a coachman should be inside the passenger terminal looking for me. I didn't see anyone looking for me.

I cast my anxious gaze over the open spaces, to the two circular newsstands and the tobacco shop. I glanced at The Mirror High Grade Candy Shop that had a big, black-and-white CLOSED sign on the front door. The quaint-looking tea shop was also closed.

I wondered how I looked, with no fresh makeup and my hair piled on top of my head, where Nellie had placed it before pinning on the hat. Did I look authentic to this time, or was it obvious that I was from the twenty-first century? Well, no one stared at me, and I guessed that was a good sign.

Easing down onto the bench, I inclined forward, feeling the corset tighten, feeling like a bear in all that clothes. I especially hated the corset. But when I unbuttoned my coat, the lovely dress was visible, and I had to admit it was a stunning work of art. Where had Nellie found it? It must have cost her a fortune. Maybe John Gannon paid for it?

A man passed and then paused, the gleam of

seduction in his eyes. He touched the brim of his top hat, and then he winked at me. I sat up straighter. Was he the coachman? He didn't look like a coachman, not that I knew what a coachman looked like, except for what I'd seen in movies.

I slid my eyes down and away from him. If it was the coachman, I'd let him speak first, but the man moved on.

In the open space, I heard the echo of footsteps and the whisper of conversation nearby. I saw porters pushing wooden carts, loaded with trunks like mine, and canvas bags, and leather suitcases.

No coachman approached. I grew edgy. My hands grew clammy. Had Nellie bullshited me? Had the whole thing been a lie? But why? It didn't make sense, but then nothing made sense. Absolutely nothing.

What was I going to do? I saw a policeman, one of those policemen from an old black-and-white movie, wearing a helmet, a dark blue uniform with a stiff collar, polished brass buttons, and shiny black boots. He was swinging a police baton billy club. I couldn't help but think, *What a costumed drama!* I also thought, I'm desperate, and I might have to ask him for help. He wandered the space with a stern expression, his handlebar mustache impressive, twirled up at the ends.

I'd need a good lie, or he might suspect something and toss me in jail. Then what? I had no identification and no money, and I didn't know a single person in this town, or in the entire world.

Yeah, he'd definitely toss me in jail.

Just then, I heard a deep voice say, "Miss Adams?"

I glanced up, to my right, and saw a 30s something hulking man, who had to be well over six feet. He had the blunt face of a fighter, a thick, reddish, blonde mustache and dull blue/gray eyes. Those eyes expanded on me in surprise as if he recognized me, and as if that recognition startled him.

He wore a below-the-waist sheepskin coat, dark pants and high, chocolate brown boots. With a hunter's fur cap in his hand, he bowed awkwardly, his curly, chestnut hair long over the ears and carelessly combed to the side.

A bit scared of the man, I pushed to my feet, feeling Nellie's shoes pinching my right big toe. "Yes... I'm... I'm..." and then my voice just fell off into the echo of the footsteps and muffled voices.

He finished it. "Miss Rosamond Adams?"

I cleared my throat. "Yes."

He kept staring at me as if he were trying to understand something.

"Are you the coachman?" I asked thickly.

His lips were compressed with concern.

I repeated. "You are the coachman, aren't you? I mean from... that mansion? I'm sorry, my head's a little... I'm not thinking so good. It's all the travel, I guess."

He snapped out of his daydream or whatever. "Yes, Miss Adams, I am the coachman from the Gannon Mansion, come to fetch you."

He didn't offer his name, but I wanted to know it. "And what's your name?"

He hesitated, then bowed stiffly again. "I'm Thomas. Thomas Dayton, ma'am."

We stood still, him staring and not moving.

Finally, I said, "Should we go?"

Thomas jerked a nod. "Yes, Miss Adams. We've quite a distance to travel, and snow is in the wind, I think. Mrs. Grieve, the housekeeper, will be waiting for us to show you to your room, and she doesn't take kindly to people arriving in the late hours."

He had an odd accent I'd never heard before. Part Southern, part British... or an old Western accent?

"Is that your only trunk?" he asked.

"Yes."

Thomas pulled on his fur cap, and I watched, impressed, as he hoisted the trunk with an easy effort, settled it on his right shoulder and led the way out of the train station. Outside, I stared in wonder at the carriages of all types waiting at the curb, some drawn by white horses, some black, some chestnut.

Thomas led me left through the dark night, away from the terminal traffic, along a packed dirt path. He stopped near a black enameled, enclosed carriage, with glass windows, two glowing side lanterns, and two magnificent looking black horses.

Snow flurries drifted down, creating a magical moment of sight and sound. The elegant carriage, the raven black horses with white vapor puffing from their nostrils, and the sound of wind whispering through the surrounding trees calmed me like a sedative. It was the first time I'd pulled an easy breath since I'd killed Cliff Prince.

In that soothing moment, I remembered something an old boyfriend used to say to me. He'd been a struggling writer, who seldom wrote and mostly drank. Anyway, he was full of quotes and, unfortunately, most of the time, also full of whiskey and full of dreams that would never come true.

But the quote by Kurt Vonnegut came clanging into my head like a ringing bell: "Be careful what you pretend to be, because you *are* what you pretend to be."

Thomas tied the trunk securely to the rear of the carriage, then came around and helped me into the coach. I sat clumsily on a soft leather seat, squirmed and adjusted the dress, my butt, and my legs, until I was somewhat comfortable.

"Is everything to your liking, Miss Adams?" Thomas asked, watching me curiously.

"Yes, yes," I said with forced confidence, unable to stop the modern slang from popping out of my mouth. "Yes, cool. No problem... I mean, good. It's all good."

"There's a wool horsehair blanket to your right, and a muff for your hands, Miss Adams. Will you be needing anything else before we start off?"

"No, I'm good, thank you."

A moment later, the coach lurched forward, and we started off into one of the darkest nights I'd ever seen. The ride was a bit bouncy, but the sway of the carriage was pleasant, with only the occasional jolt when the wheels hit a rough patch of road.

I draped the woolen blanket over my legs, slipped my hands into the very warm fur muff, and then eased back as much as I could, watching the feathery snowflakes drift by the windows.

The motion made me sleepy, and I nodded off several times, awaking with a start, my mind alive, speculating as to what I was about to face. How could I marry a man I didn't know and live in this backward time? What would be expected of me? Wouldn't they notice I wasn't like them, didn't have their manners and didn't talk like them? If John Gannon realized I wasn't the real Rosamond Adams, would he kick me out? Beat me? Kill me?

There was a time some years back when I'd wanted to write novels. Now I felt as though I were living one, and I had no idea how it would unfold or how it would all end.

One valuable lesson I'd learned in jail was, for as much as possible, keep your mouth shut and don't let on how stupid and how scared you are. The more silent and mysterious you seem, the better. Inmates and female correction officers thought I was smarter than I was, or more dangerous than I was.

I figured that women in 1880 weren't aggressive or outspoken, so I'd say little, observe much, and try not to offend anybody. With any luck, Mr. John Gannon wouldn't approve of me, and he'd send me off with a few bucks in my purse.

If he did approve of me? I shuddered to think. I'd have to escape somehow and go where? I had no idea. Was there a possibility I could climb aboard another train, go east and enter that same tunnel and pass through the same time portal, or whatever it was, and return to the twenty-first century?

It was possible, wasn't it? A slim possibility, but possible?

CHAPTER 10

We moved slowly along winding roads, through dark walls of tall trees that moved and wheezed in a sturdy wind. Once, the carriage stopped, and I thought we'd arrived, but I couldn't see much of anything from the windows except black night and blurring snow. I heard the high, piercing cry of some wild animal close by, and it totally creeped me out. I slid down in the seat, cursing Nellie and Percy.

A moment later, the carriage advanced in fits and starts, taking a sharp bend with skillful care, then it went struggling up a hill, the back wheels fighting for traction.

Arriving at the Gannon Mansion shortly after 1 a.m., I finally saw the impressive estate. It emerged from the falling snow, resembling a solemn and shadowy fortress, adorned with large wrought-iron gas lanterns at the front entrance, and an enchanting wraparound porch that was a feast for the eyes.

As we drew closer, I was able to examine the red sandstone, Queen Anne-style mansion in detail.

It boasted turrets, a steep roof with cross gables, and tall stone column entrance pillars, but the most striking feature was an ominous onion-domed tower.

The carriage stopped. I grabbed a quick breath, and Thomas opened the door and peered inside. "We have arrived, Miss Adams. I trust your ride was comfortable, despite the snow and the rough patches of road."

"Yes, thank you."

I took his broad, rough hand and stepped down into four inches of newly fallen snow. I glanced about at the surrounding snowy trees, whose names I didn't know then but found out later: bristlecone pine, Colorado blue spruce, Douglas-fir, and narrowleaf cottonwood.

"If you follow me, Miss Adams, I'll escort you to the house and carry your trunk in presently. Mr. Hopkins, the butler, has retired for the evening, but Mrs. Grieve will be waiting."

I followed Thomas along a snowy stone walkway to the endless, wraparound porch, mounted the stairs, and stopped at a tall, heavy oak door with an impressive, golden, lion-face knocker.

The amber door lanterns cast Thomas in a soft glow, as he lifted the knocker and rapped twice.

A moment later, the tall door slowly opened, and a slim and staring woman gazed out, wearing a black dress, long to her ankles, high to her throat and covering her arms. She had a starched face, a tight mouth, and a tight bun on the top of her graying head. Her squinting, cool eyes said something like, "Don't waste my time," and her prominent, granite-hard jaw suggested a woman who didn't mind a good argument or even a fistfight.

I tried to smile, but I couldn't get my lips to do it.

Thomas removed his cap and said, "This is Miss Adams, Mrs. Grieve. Pardon me for the late hour, but the snow held us up some and the roads showed some ice."

Mrs. Grieve flicked him an impatient glance. "A little too late is much too late. Bring up the trunk, Thomas, and then off with you to the carriage house. There'll be some warm cider for you, so says young Dalton."

Thomas nodded, turned, and left for the carriage.

Mrs. Grieve's attention turned to me, and she gave me a curt once-over before her eyes revealed a moment's surprise, and she glanced away. It was obvious she didn't approve of what she saw. "Come on in then, girl," she said, backing away.

My stomach twisted. The last thing I wanted was to enter that house. But I did, and Mrs. Grieve closed the tall, heavy door behind me. Was it an iron prison door clanging shut and locking me in?

Even in the soft lamplight, the spacious marble lobby was an impressive, echoing space, with stained-glass windows, a gaslight chandelier, and golden oak paneling. To my right was the parlor, with an elegant, black and gray marble fireplace, the fire gleaming, the room richly styled in burgundy and gold. Before me was a wide staircase with a broad, ornately carved wooden banister and thick, red carpeting that led to upper rooms.

Mrs. Grieve glanced at me. "Will you be wanting any refreshment? Mr. Gannon instructed me to ask."

I shook my head. I was hungry, but it was too late to eat, and my stomach was a knot of nerves. "No, thank you. Could I just have some water, please?"

"There will be a pitcher and a glass in your room. Now follow me."

We started up the staircase, the carpet soft like moss under my feet. On the second floor, we moved along a dimly lit, long hallway that seemed to go on for shadowy infinity.

I felt apprehension and loneliness, but I accepted them as we passed elaborately hand painted vases on pedestals, featuring artistic flower arrangements that scented the air.

And there were portraits hanging on the walls, stern men in black, staring back at me with accusing eyes, as if I were an intruder.

At the end of the hallway, Mrs. Grieve stopped, pulled a set of jangling keys from her dress pocket, found the key, inserted it, and opened the door, entering.

I hesitated, and she turned back to me, impatient. "Well, come in, girl."

I bristled a little, and I wanted to say my name was Miss Adams, but I didn't. Mrs. Grieve was my jailor and, at least for now, I needed to keep my mouth shut.

I stepped into a large, beautiful room, with a fire

going in the white marble fireplace, and Victorian lamps with lace fabric lampshades, giving off a warm glow.

Feeling as though I'd fallen down yet another rabbit hole, I gazed at the spacious room, richly adorned in a lush, cream floral carpet, hardwood furniture with a bone-white finish and silver brushed accents. There was a loveseat and matching chair, round gilded mirrors, two landscaped oil paintings of the Rocky Mountains, and a four-poster bed with a silk canopy.

Mrs. Grieve turned to face me. "This is your room, at least for the time being. Mr. Gannon may have you moved, depending on whether it suits him."

I thought, *Suits him? What about me?* But I didn't speak.

"Your personal lady's maid, Alice Wells, will come presently and also, as per Mr. Gannon's wishes, you will have breakfast in your room in the morning. He will want to meet you tomorrow afternoon at one o'clock sharp."

Just then, Thomas appeared in the doorway, with my trunk resting easily on his broad shoulder. With Mrs. Grieve's nod of permission, he brought it in, stooped and lowered it near the closet doors, tipped his hat and left.

Mrs. Grieve folded her tight hands at her lap, lifted her imperious chin, and marched for the door. "I will say good night."

And then she was gone, closing the door behind her. I didn't move for a while, waiting for Alice.

I was utterly exhausted, and I needed to use the bathroom. Did they even have bathrooms? I removed my coat and hat and dropped them on the bed. I glanced around, spotting an open door and a softly lighted room.

I stepped inside and froze. I couldn't believe it. It was a golden bathtub. A big golden bathtub. There were also two oval porcelain sinks with gold fixtures, and a toilet with a pull chain. I stood there, staring. Placed on a golden rack were plenty of soft, white, fluffy towels. Scented potpourris sat on the sinks, and there was a lovely rose basin with a matching pitcher on a marble top cabinet.

"Well, it's a whole lot better than any other jail I've been locked up in," I said aloud.

I poured some of the water into the basin and, not finding a toothbrush, I used a washcloth to clean my teeth. I couldn't remember the last time I'd brushed them.

I managed to use the toilet, fumbling with that big dress and those crazy undergarments, but it wasn't easy, and I wasn't graceful, and I cursed, shifted about, and cursed again.

Back in the bedroom, I heard a light knock on the door, and I stilled. "Yes...? Come in."

My lady's maid entered, her eyes cast down. She bobbed a bow and closed the door behind her.

"Good evening, Miss," she said, in a formal tone.

"Hello..."

"I'm your lady's maid, Miss Adams, Alice Wells. I'm sure you are quite weary after your long journey.

I'll help you undress and prepare for bed."

I stared at her, a clear-eyed woman in her late twenties. Her posture was erect, and her chestnut hair combed back into a modified bun. There was an air of confidence about her, suggesting she was efficient and comfortable in her own skin. She wore a plain, loose, gray dress, simple black shoes, and a wedding ring. Although Alice wasn't a beauty, she was attractive, with thin lips, a sharp nose and alert eyes that swiftly evaluated me, then lowered.

"This must be late for you," I said.

"Not to worry, Miss Adams. Shall I help you undress?"

I was a bit self-conscious. No one had ever helped me undress, except my mother, a couple of female correction officers, and maybe a boyfriend or three.

I cleared my throat. "Yeah… cool…"

Alice gave me a look, and I realized my modern slang confused her. I made a mental note to drop all that. I didn't want to stand out. Standing out was never good when you were incarcerated.

I quickly said, "I mean, I'm a little cool… and… yes, I guess I'm tired and ready for bed."

Alice went to work, removing my dress, the petticoat, the corset, and the undergarments. I'd never felt so free and relieved, and at least fifty pounds lighter.

From the closet, Alice brought a cotton nightgown with embroidered primroses and trimmed with lace, and a pair of black velvet and floral silk embroidered slippers that actually fit, and they were incredibly soft, warm and comfortable.

Alice worked silently, with concentration, and I didn't speak, not knowing what I should say, and feeling it was better not to say anything until I got a sense of the place and the people.

Wearing the gown and the slippers, I sat before a massive, Victorian vanity while Alice left for the bathroom, and soon returned with a hot cloth. After gently blotting my face and neck, she wiped my hands. Finally, Alice brushed my hair in long, easy strokes, and I became so relaxed, I nearly dropped off to sleep.

I longed to take a hot bath, but by the time Alice had finished brushing my hair, I was completely wiped out.

At the door, she said my breakfast would arrive at eight o'clock and she'd come by at nine. I thanked her, she offered a little bow, wished me a "good night" and she was gone.

I switched off the lamps, climbed into bed and slid under the heavy quilt, feeling a crushing fatigue, too tired to think and too tired to cry.

My last thoughts hung in the air above me. In the morning, would I be back home in 2022? Would this nightmare be over? Would I wake up to find Cliff lying next to me? I'd tell him all about my silly, crazy dream and we'd laugh, and he'd reach for me, and the entire nightmare would just fade away like all bad dreams do.

But then, Cliff Prince was a bad dream, too, wasn't he?

CHAPTER 11

I awakened with a start, making a choked sound of fear. My eyes snapped open, and I lifted on elbows, feeling as if I were looking up from out of a well. The truth of time and place struck like a hammer, and I collapsed my elbows and dropped back, my head sinking deep into the pillow. I inhaled a few breaths and tried again, sitting up carefully, leaning back against the richly padded headboard.

It wasn't a dream. The nightmare hadn't faded into the night. I was in the Gannon Mansion, outside Denver, Colorado, living in 1880.

A moment later came a knock on the door. Then two.

After a swallow, I glanced over. "Yes? Who is it?"

The door opened and a young woman entered softly, stepping into the room, just beyond the threshold. She wore a blue uniform, a white apron and a cap bonnet, and she appeared to be in her early teens.

"May I enter, please, Miss Adams?"

"Yes... Yes, come in."

She gave a little bob of her head, took a tray from

a pushcart and entered, carrying a silver tray, topped with two silver dome covers.

"I have your breakfast, Miss Adams, as ordered by Mr. Gannon. May I place it on the side table by the bed, or will you be wanting it on the far table next to the loveseat?"

The smell of the ham and coffee awoke me fully. I was ravenous. The meal I had eaten on the train seemed like days ago.

I sat up. "Please put it near the loveseat. I'll come over."

"Yes, Miss."

"What's your name?" I asked.

The girl lowered her eyes. "I'm Tara, Miss."

"It's nice to meet you. What's your last name?"

"O'Hanlon, Miss Adams," she said, crossing to the loveseat and setting the tray down on a table with elaborately carved scrolled legs. I swung my legs to the floor and yawned. "What's on the menu? It smells good."

"It's eggs, ham, beans, buttered bread and coffee, Miss Adams."

"I'm so hungry. Who cooked it?"

"As I said, Miss Adams, Mr. Gannon ordered it for you and Mrs. Dockery herself prepared it."

"Mrs. Dockery?"

"The head cook... Mrs. Dockery is in charge of the kitchen."

Tara was a thin girl, with delicate features and slightly stooped shoulders. She had a pretty face, but her skin was pale, and her eyes nervous and watchful. She didn't look at me when she spoke.

"You can call me Cin..." Cindy said, then stopped, catching herself. "I mean, you can call me Rosamond, Tara."

Tara's gaze fell to her shoes, and she stiffened. "Oh, no, Miss Adams. I would not do that. It would be improper."

My feet found the slippers, and I stood, walked to the loveseat and sat, while Tara removed the domes. Steam rose from the eggs, ham, and beans. Under the second dome was sliced toasted bread, warm applesauce and a small silver coffee pot and a ceramic cup.

"This looks awesome!" I said.

Tara kept her gaze focused on the carpet. "Will there be anything else, Miss?"

I reached for the bread, spread some of the applesauce on it, and took a bite. I closed my eyes, falling into bliss. It was absolutely delicious.

"Oh my God, this is totally awesome!"

Tara stood stark still, eyes focused on the carpet.

I swallowed down the bread, and then reach for the coffee pot, poured the coffee steaming into the cup, blew off the steam and took an eager, careful sip.

I glanced up. "Where are you from, Tara?"

"I'm from New York, Miss Adams."

"New York? Really? How did you end up way out here?"

Tara still held the silver dome covers, her eyes shifting. "I came on the orphan train, Miss Adams."

I'd heard of orphan trains, but I knew little about them. "How old are you?"

"I'm thirteen, Miss."

"How old were you when you came here?"

"Nine years old."

"And how did that work? I mean, how did you get here?"

Tara shifted her feet. "A chaperone brought me. Both my parents died, and I was living on the streets."

I stopped cutting the eggs and looked up. "Both your parents died?"

"Yes, Miss Adams. Mother from the fever. My father from a fall while working."

"So a chaperone brought you here to the Gannon Mansion?"

"No, Miss. I was led off the train in Denver and taken to a public gathering in a church. There, I was selected by Mrs. Grieve to work here at the Gannon Mansion."

I tried not to show my alarm. "Mrs. Grieve? The head housekeeper?"

"Yes, Miss Adams."

Tara looked toward the door like a frightened rabbit ready to bolt. "I should be going, Miss. Mrs. Dockery will be asking after me. Will you require anything further?"

"No, Tara, thank you."

"I will come by later and clean out your fireplace, if that meets with your approval?"

"Yes, of course. Come anytime."

Tara curtsied and hurried from the room, closing the door softly behind her.

As I finished my breakfast, my mind was active, imagining the afternoon meeting with John Gannon. I dreaded it. I also thought about Tara. She had a sweet face and a shy manner that touched me. I wondered how many hours a day she worked, and under what conditions. I hoped Mrs. Dockery was a more pleasant woman than Mrs. Grieve.

After I'd inhaled the breakfast, and finished the coffee, completely buzzed, I left the loveseat, went to the closet and slid back the doors. To my surprise, I saw lavish gowns, day dresses and petticoats. Inside a wall of broad drawers I found corsets, corset covers, a dozen pairs of silk stockings, fans, gloves and hats. Obviously, they had prepared for the arrival of the real Rosamond Adams. Didn't this mean that John Gannon had already made up his mind to marry her? I gulped.

It was time to explore the trunk and its contents, so I sank down on the floor beside it, released the front brass latch, and lifted the heavy lid.

What I found, to use 2022 slang, nearly knocked me on my ass. I knelt over the trunk and rummaged through the clothes. There were undergarments, two day dresses, one gray and white, one a deep magenta, and one carefully packed stunning bustle dress of purple silk and crushed velvet, with a lavish matching hat with feathers. There were also two bonnets, a mirror, a hair-brush, two pairs of shoes, two books, and a brown bag of mostly broken gingerbread cookies.

But it was what I found at the bottom of the trunk that stunned me. There was a small change purse, a black purse with gold silk embroidery, and a black leather diary with an unlocked latch. Intrigued, I first removed the diary, then the change purse, and finally, the black purse, spreading them out before me on the carpet.

Sitting cross-legged, I reached for the change purse. It had a lovely flowers motif, crocheted with beadwork glass beads. With a twist of fingers, I released the ball clasp and opened it. I gasped. It was cash!

Excited, I shook the contents onto the carpet, spread them out, and took in a sharp breath. I couldn't believe it! There were twenty-two one-dollar bills, with George Washington's image. There were four smaller fifty-cent bills, which I had never seen before; I had no idea they'd ever existed. Finally, there were five ten-dollar bills with the image of some grumpy looking guy I didn't recognize. Lying beside the bills were seven shiny, thick-looking silver dollars. I said, "Wow!" much too loudly.

How much was that? Eighty-one dollars? In 1880, was that a lot of money? I had no idea, but what was it doing in that trunk?

I grabbed the black purse, opened it and stared bug-eyed. With anxious hands, I reached in and removed everything: a pair of rose gold earrings; a gorgeous, turquoise and pearl yellow gold necklace; a rose gold diamond ring that flashed with fire;

two brooch pins; a small gold watch; and a silver bracelet.

Stunned, I sat staring—breathing and staring at the money and jewelry, struggling to understand what they were doing there. Then I reached for the diary, turning it over and running a hand along the worn leather. My breath was coming fast as I released the latch, opened the diary and thumbed through the pages, finally coming to one of the last entries. My eyes widened on the words.

I met a gentleman, and he has captured my heart in a manner which has left me nearly breathless to describe and impossible to translate onto the page. He has been most candid with me and conveyed in fine speech and with impeccable manners that he is a gambler. Yes! But not a ne'er-do-well, rakish gambler of low station, but a successful one, a gentleman who comes from a good Boston family! And his fine name bears this out. Percy Blackstone. And what a lovely name it is, dear diary!

I quote here what he corresponded to me after our first meeting in New York, Thursday last.

"My dear Miss Adams, since our first encounter, I have no longer been master of my own heart. Your beauty, charm and good qualities have enslaved it, and thus I offer it to your acceptance. Please grant me the pleasure of another such meeting. Your lovely society was, to me, a source of the purest delight. When we meet again, then you may be the judge, therefore, from your own sentiments, how miserable a man I am when I am not in your company. Dare I say it, you have driven me

almost to despair."

I raised my eyes from the page and nearly gagged. Did people really write like that in the 1880s?

Turning the page, I found an entry about me, and I stiffened, nosing in closer.

There is an ailing young woman on the train about my own age; perhaps she is truly sick of mind. She doesn't know who she is or where she came from, and her dress and manner are quite foreign to me, and strange, and more than a little vulgar. Passengers had been talking, believing her to be a foreigner from some distant country, and some said she should be removed from the train, and others demanded action by the conductor. She was moved to a private car, and that's when I was seized by an idea.

But she is most attractive and, dare I say it, similar in body and facial makeup to me, so that she could pass as my sister. Fate has come to my aid when I needed it the most, and I have swiftly conjured a plan. With Mr. Percy Blackstone's help, I am nearly certain I can convince this poor, daft creature to take my place with Mr. John Gannon.

I will then be free to travel without any fear that Mr. Gannon will come after me and commit bodily harm. And then, San Francisco will be my new home, with my beloved Mr. Blackstone, and I know we will be blissfully happy together. My entire happiness depends on persuading this woman to take my place, and I will do whatever I must do to accomplish my goal. I must go now to work on my plan.

I lifted my eyes, smiling, delighted by the revelation, feeling a delicious satisfaction surge through every vein. Clever Nellie had screwed up big time, and made a bad mistake. No way would she have purposely given me a trunk containing her jewels, her money, and her private diary. No way! And I was sure that Percy Blackstone, from that good Boston family—yeah, right—knew about those jewels and the money. What would he do when he discovered what had happened, and, if Nellie was so clever, why hadn't she seen through Percy Blackstone's bullshit?

My grin started small and then grew into a triumphant laugh. In her impatience to toss me off that train, she'd given the porter the wrong trunk, or he had mistakenly taken it. Either way, it was Nellie's trunk! I was still laughing when I heard a knock on the door.

I slammed the diary shut, gathered up the money and jewels, stuffed them back into the purses, tossed the diary and the purses back into the trunk, and closed the lid.

More knocks.

CHAPTER 12

"IT'S ALICE WELLS, MISS ADAMS. May I enter?"

I unfolded my legs and stood up. "One moment, please."

I cast my gaze about the room. Where could I hide that trunk? No idea. It would have to wait.

"Yes… Come in," I said, running a hand through my hair and stretching my face, hoping to look awake.

Alice entered with a formal smile, her shoulders back, her head up, the perfect image of energy and efficiency.

"How did you sleep, Miss Adams?"

"Good… Just fine."

Alice went directly to the bed and began thumping the pillows.

"So, I guess I'm meeting Mr. Gannon at one o'clock?"

"Yes."

"What do you think of Mr. Gannon, Alice?"

Alice reached for the top sheet, tugged it up, smoothed it out and arranged the pillows. "He is a fine man."

I waited for more, but there wasn't more.

"Has Mr. Gannon ever been married?" I asked, keeping the formal style, since everybody was so formal.

"Yes, Miss Adams."

"You can call me Rosamond, Alice, if you want to."

Alice didn't look at me. "I beg your pardon, but that would not be proper, Miss Adams."

I tried again. "What happened to Mr. Gannon's first wife?"

"I'm not at liberty to say," Alice said, moving to the other side of the bed and drawing up the quilt.

"Not at liberty?"

Alice changed the subject, and not so subtly. "Will you be wanting a sponge bath or a soak in the tub, Miss Adams?"

"The tub, if that's all right."

"I will draw the water for you. The Gannon Mansion is the only house for many miles that has running water," she concluded proudly.

"Have you been here long?" I asked, hoping to develop a friendship.

"Four years."

"And where are you from?"

"Lowell, Massachusetts."

"I've heard of it, but never been."

"It's a mill town. My father and brothers work in the mills."

"And why did you come here?"

Alice hesitated, while she smoothed the quilt and carefully positioned the shams and throw pillows.

"My husband came for the gold, like many other men, even though I told him I thought it was all played out back in the 1860s. But he had the fever and so we came and for a time he panned for gold at the South Platte River."

Alice straightened up, examining her work, giving it a satisfied nod.

"Did he find any gold?"

Alice glanced over. "Yes, he did, Miss Adams, and two men killed him for it. A short time later, I found work here."

I'm sure my face registered shock. "I'm so sorry."

Alice shrugged, and her eyes stared ahead, her face falling into sorrow. "He was a good man, Callen was, but he wouldn't hear, and he wouldn't listen. I told him, 'When everybody is out looking for gold, it's time to get into the pick and shovel business.' He just laughed at me."

Alice blinked, clearing her sad eyes. "All right, Miss Adams, I will run your bath and prepare your clothes."

I followed her into the bathroom and watched as she adjusted the bathtub's porcelain levers. A weak stream of water poured into the tub, and the pipes above knocked and thumped.

I took a lukewarm bath in shallow water, while Alice cleaned the bedroom and prepared my clothes. I heard Tara enter and remove my breakfast tray.

When it was time to dress, I groaned at the plum-colored bustle dress displayed extravagantly across the bed, along with all its undergarment companions. But before I was stuffed into them, Alice brushed and styled my hair, artistically piling it high on my head, curling it, placing it, and pinning it. I decided to ask Alice another question.

"Are you surprised that Mr. Gannon wants to marry again?"

Alice continued working, checking the mirror often. "I have no opinion about that, Miss Adams."

I'd been picking at a thought, and being the curious, often annoying type who liked to ask questions, I risked being a nuisance. "In a house like this, there must be lots of rumors about me. I mean, it must be, well, a little weird to have a stranger suddenly appear."

"I couldn't say," Alice said, steady at her work, not looking at me through the mirror.

I gave up. Obviously, Alice wasn't going to volunteer any information about Gannon or the house.

Alice applied light makeup, lip salve, powder, and a subtle touch of rouge. We didn't talk until after I was corseted, petticoated and squeezed into that bustle dress. Once again, I had to admit that it was a beauty. It had a double-layered skirt, the top bunched to reveal an intricately patterned underskirt.

"Where did this thing come from?" I asked.

Alice took a step back and examined her work with great attention, scrutinizing me from head to toe. It was obvious that she was anxious and eager, wanting to ensure I looked my best for Gannon, a reflection of her own lady's maid skills.

Alice said distractedly, "Mr. Gannon had it made in France, according to the specifications the New York agency sent him with regard to your measurements. The dress arrived only a week ago. It was the dress he wants to see you in today."

Between the tightness of the dress and her last comment, I felt slightly nauseated. Gannon was obviously a controlling man.

The final touch was jewelry, which Alice brought from an ornate, gold jewelry box kept in a top vanity drawer. She held up a pair of stunning gold and black earrings for me to see. "These are 16-karat gold, also French," Alice said, proud of her knowledge.

After she'd fastened the earrings, she presented me with a simple flower brooch with black crystals and diamonds, and then she pinned it at the neckline of the dress.

Alice stepped back for a final appraisal of her work and invited me to take a look in the mirror. "Please have a look at yourself, Miss Adams, and be so kind as to tell me if you approve."

I stepped before the oval vanity mirror.

"Do you like what you see?" Alice asked, hope lighting up her eyes.

My eyes were round with surprise. I looked absolutely fabulous in that elegant, tucked-in-at-the-waist, bustle-in-the-back, totally awesome dress. I stared with a detached, emotionless gaze, finding it hard to believe that the woman in the mirror, with all that lusciously styled hair, was me. I looked like a royal princess from some British period drama. I blinked slowly, like a tortoise.

"Do you approve, Miss Adams?"

"Oh, yeah. I totally approve. You are amazing, Alice."

She accepted the comment with a small, pleased smile.

"Wow... and I love the earrings," I said, turning my head slowly from side to side. "I've never seen anything like them."

"You are quite lovely, Miss Adams. I believe Mr. Gannon will be pleased."

And then I had a dark thought. *I look like a princess, and based on that, I doubt that John Gannon will send me away. I mean, look at me! That's not good, is it? How could that be good if he doesn't send me away?*

I felt tension tightening my shoulders. "Well, I have about two hours until I meet him. What should I do?"

"Mr. Hopkins, the butler, is to take you on a tour of the house."

I looked at Alice in the mirror. "A tour? Okay..."

"You will be served some refreshments at noon, and then afterwards, you will be escorted to Mr. Gannon's private office."

I nodded again. "Okay... So, my day is all planned out."

"Yes, Miss Adams. I hope it will be a pleasant one for you."

"Yeah... sure. Cool... I mean, thank you."

After Alice had left, I continued staring into the mirror. With exaggerated enunciation, I whispered, "What the hell am I going to do?"

CHAPTER 13

The stately butler, Sidney Hopkins, arrived ten minutes later, along with Tara, who slipped in behind him, head bowed, clutching a broom and dustpan. Without a word, she went straight to work, bending over the fireplace, sweeping the hearth clear of soot and debris.

I learned later that one of Tara's many jobs included cleaning all the fireplaces and replenishing them with the firewood that she toted about in a large canvas bag. She rarely got to bed before eleven in the evening and she was up before dawn.

I wanted to say hello to her, but she was hard at work, and she kept her eyes down, avoiding me. It was obvious that she wasn't supposed to speak to me, or to any of the upper rank servants.

Mr. Hopkins regarded me with cool indifference, offering a little nod of his head. My smile was vaguely awkward and excessively bright.

"It's nice to meet you, Sidney."

He cleared his throat and lifted an eyebrow. "I'd prefer that you address me as Mr. Hopkins, Miss Adams."

"Okay... Well, then, it's nice to meet you, Mr. Hopkins," I repeated.

He stared over my head at the far windows, as if he were addressing a snowy fir tree. "Nice, is it? How interesting," he concluded, dryly.

Mr. Hopkins was in his forties, a tall, attractive, and refined man with autocratic features. His gleaming, pomaded hair was combed sideways with a perfect part, and he was gray at the temples, a feature that added distinction and class.

I later learned that Mr. Hopkins was the first employee hired by John Gannon when the house opened five years before, in 1875, and, when anyone questioned his abilities or authority, he reminded them of that fact, with an arrogant lift of his nose.

I heard him once say to a complaining underbutler, "Don't question me, just do as I say, sir. I was the first servant to be hired in this fine edifice, and I know the requirements of the place utterly, intuitively, and intimately."

Mr. Hopkins cast his worshipful eyes about, his voice as deep and rich as that of a fine Shakespearean actor. "The Gannon Mansion is one of the finest houses inside or outside Denver," Mr. Hopkins expounded, with superb articulation and pride. "And the society of the city of Denver, as well as the regions beyond, accord it great respect, as well they should."

Another bit of information I later learned was that Mr. Hopkins had never been married and was not inclined to do so. Rumors circulated that he'd once been smitten by a Chicago showgirl who had broken his heart, making him bitter about marriage, and about most women.

We left the room and began the tour.

"This house is made of Colorado," Mr. Hopkins said grandly, pointing here and there. "The stones used to build this four-level mansion consist of rhyolite from Castle Rock and red sandstone from the Garden of the Gods."

I nodded, not knowing what rhyolite was, or where Castle Rock or the Garden of the Gods were, but I tried to look intelligent.

While we toured the impressive mansion, Mr. Hopkins' tall stature and commanding gaze seemed to see everything—the slightest infraction, the minutest detail: a small smudge on a crystal glass in the dining room; the linen tablecloth hanging a fraction of an inch longer on the right side than on the left.

With a keen eye, he'd noticed that a flower arrangement "lacked balance and grace," and he'd demanded that the anxious servant girl reconstruct it, "Ensuring there is a dignity of color and presentation."

There were ten bedrooms, nine bathrooms and remarkable woodwork, with crafted fireplace mantels and three sweeping, ornate, multi-level oak staircases. The library had multitiered bookshelves, leather furniture, oversized windows, a lofty ceiling, and a massive stone fireplace.

I saw polished hardwood floors in the hallways, a

cozy sitting room, and a third-floor parlor, rich with burgundy color and heavy, Victorian furniture.

The jaw-dropping second-floor ballroom had white birch floors, one entire wall of mirrors, and a stage for an orchestra that featured a black grand piano and a harpsichord. There were stained-glass windows and interior oak woodwork that smelled of wealth, and I couldn't imagine how many servants were needed to keep the house tidy and clean.

I wasn't shown the fourth floor, where some of the house servants lived, nor was I taken "below the stairs," which was occupied by upper rank servants, the wine cellar, food pantries and the main kitchen.

During the tour, I'd stayed silent, learning, observing and nodding, impressed for sure, but scared to death, and wishing I had a friend. Any friend. Mr. Hopkins glanced at me once, as we left the ballroom, and I commented, without thinking, "Wow! That was totally awesome."

As soon as I said it, I wanted to grab the words and force them back into my mouth. I had to stop it with the slang! Among these formal-speaking people, I sounded stupid!

Mr. Hopkins looked at me with kindly contempt, as if I were a child to be tolerated. "How utterly descriptive," he said dryly, an obvious insult.

With the tour complete, Mr. Hopkins escorted me to a white and gold private dining room, where I sat at one of four, linen-covered tables, set with primrose teacups, linen napkins, and a rose-colored vase with sprigs of evergreen and pine. The cathedral style windows offered a stunning view of a nearby carriage house, snowy trees, and distant mountains.

It was so quiet that I was startled when a young, tuxedoed footman, named Edward, appeared from a side door, carrying a tray with a silver teapot. Once the tea was poured, he drifted to a side table and brought a tray of assorted tea sandwiches: ham and mustard, cucumber, butter and jam, and smoked salmon.

"Will there be anything else, Miss Adams?" he asked in a soft, formal voice.

"No, thank you. It all looks..." I was going to say, "awesome," but this time I caught myself. "Everything is lovely. Thank you, Edward."

As I nibbled on the butter and jam sandwich, I thought, *Why am I being treated like royalty*? Gannon hasn't even met me. I could only conclude that he'd already made up his mind and, as crazy and sickening as it sounded, I was going to be his wife.

At 12:50 p.m., Mrs. Grieve appeared, wearing the same black, dreary dress as the night before. She also wore the same sour face and stern, accusing stare, as if I were a thief who was about to steal them blind.

She crossed to my table and stared straight ahead. "Mr. Gannon will see you now."

As soon as my napkin touched the table, the footman glided over and courteously pulled back my chair while I stood up. I thanked him and steadied myself. The time had come to meet the Big Boss.

I followed the "charming" Mrs. Grieve from the

dining room, down a long hallway, which led to winding stairs, which led to the second floor, which led along another curving hallway, where servants were cleaning mirrors and dusting side tables and lamps.

We turned left, passed through a card/game room and another Victorian parlor, styled in emerald green and gold, and, finally, we arrived at a large, impressive, oak door. Inside was John Gannon's private office. Inside my chest, my heart was thumping, and blood surged hot to my face.

Mrs. Grieve knocked firmly, twice.

I heard a deep baritone voice from inside. "Yes... Come in."

Mrs. Grieve opened the door, stepped in, backed away and nodded for me to enter. On rubbery legs, I did so, stepping into a spacious, dark wood room with barrel-vaulted ceilings, towering bookcases, and an outsized window with expansive views of a forest of snow-heavy trees and towering mountains, bathed in a wintry, western light.

"This is Miss Rosamond Adams, Mr. Gannon."

And then Mrs. Grieve withdrew, closing the door. My left eye twitched when I viewed John Gannon. He stood behind a massive oak desk, a taller man than I'd imagined, a younger man than I'd imagined, and a more handsome man than I'd ever imagined. I guessed his age at between forty-five and fifty.

He wore a black frock coat, with a hint of a blue hue, and matching fabric-covered buttons. His white silk shirt was impressive, the black silk string tie knotted formally, and his burgundy vest was a perfect fit, revealing a man who was in good shape. I also noticed a gold watch chain visible across his vest, leading to a gold watch, tucked into a vest pocket.

His bearing was stiff, his features sensual, his black hair flecked with gray and curly over his ears. John Gannon had a strong face that seemed chiseled from rock, with a workman's body and a muscular neck.

We stood in silence as his narrowed, blue-gray eyes looked me over, and my heart jumped a little. And then he gave me a deep, probing look. He made a gesture toward an armless walnut chair with a beautifully shaped carved back. I was grateful it was armless, otherwise I would have never been able to sit in the thing with my bustle dress.

"Please sit down, Miss Adams."

I moved to the chair and eased down, leaning a bit forward, placing my folded, clammy hands in my lap. I wanted to appear like a still-life painting, not moving, not breathing, and not scared.

He didn't sit, but he kept his steady gaze on me, and I was sure he was going to point an accusing finger and bellow out that I was an imposter. And then he picked up the sepia tone photograph of Nellie, which The Rose Daisy Agency had mailed to him.

Gannon studied it, and my racing mind conjured up lies and excuses, but then I thought better of it. Wouldn't it be better if I told the truth? After all,

I had nothing to hide, at least as far as Nellie was concerned.

As John Gannon's attention remained on the photo, I thought, *But what if he doesn't believe the truth?* He'll toss me out, and I'll have nowhere to go, no family or friends. Nothing.

My face and neck burned hot. I felt sweat on my back, my butt, my legs.

And then he placed the photo on his desk and sat, making a pyramid of his fingers, looking at me over the top of them.

I was about to blurt out the truth and tell everything. I was about to beg for help, and tell him I was a victim, when Mr. Gannon rose and walked to the beautiful sandstone fireplace on the left side of the room.

Above the mantel, hanging on the paneled wall, was an oil portrait of a young woman—an attractive young woman. And then I saw it. The woman in that portrait looked a lot like me! Something about the cheekbones and the eyes. Yes, a similarity. How was that possible?

CHAPTER 14

J ohn Gannon locked his hands behind his back and stared up at the portrait, as I shifted to my left to examine the painting more closely.

The woman was a slender beauty, captured by the artist in strokes of muted color and cream-colored light, against a background of a gold and deep burgundy curtain. She stood beside a Greek style column, fingering her pearls; her features elegant and soft; her lush, blonde hair drawn up and styled in waves and supported by combs. It was a startlingly clear rendering of the face, with a tender mouth and lucid blue eyes, alive, as they gazed out into the room.

Her full-length gown featured a dazzling array of white fabrics of varying textures: satin, lace, and chiffon, and the broad stroke highlights on her off-the-shoulder, pink and white, opulent cape were vibrant, adding to the romance of the portrait.

John Gannon released his hands as he slowly turned to face me, looking absorbed and worried. Returning to his desk, he reached for the photo and, once again, studied it. Then he lifted his eyes and studied me, and I felt like a specimen under a microscope.

I waited, in an agony of dread, wondering what in the hell was going on.

He lowered into his chair, turned his head, and stared out the windows with an air of bewilderment. When he said, "You may go, Miss Adams," he didn't look at me.

My eyes flickered. *Go?* I thought. *Had I heard him clearly?*

I sat for a moment, confused, and then flinched when, in a more forceful voice, he barked, "I said, you may go. Now!"

I shot to my feet, trembling, turned, went to the door, opened it, and swept out of the room, closing the door. I stood in the hallway, my mind completely befuddled, unsure where I was, where my room was, what had just happened, and what I was supposed to do.

A moment later, Mr. Hopkins appeared, his ice-gray eyes lowering on me. "I will escort you back to your room, Miss Adams. Please follow me."

At the door of my room, Mr. Hopkins said, "Will you prefer dining in your room this evening or in the private dining room?"

I felt the irrational impulse to tell him to go to hell, but I didn't. I didn't want to eat alone in my room. At least in the dining room, some person would serve me.

"I'll eat in the dining room. Will I be eating alone?"

"That is correct, Miss Adams."

And then he glided off.

Inside my room, I didn't know what to do, so I paced and stared at the trunk, and I thought about the money, and I wondered if I could take that money and the jewels and make a run for it. But run where? Back to the train? How would I get to the train? No idea.

Okay. I'd figure something out. I was smart enough to figure something out, wasn't I? Surely, there was enough money in that purse to get me to New York. It would be 1880 in New York, of course, but so what? It might be fun. It would be scary, and I would have to adjust, but, again, I'd figure something out, even how to make a living, and I'd have to make a living. The money and the jewels wouldn't last forever.

I moved to the windows and gazed out. In the distance, I saw Thomas Dayton leading a team of horses toward the carriage house. I wondered, if I paid him enough, would he take me to the train?

I had to do something. Standing around waiting for John Gannon to pull the strings was not going to work. Maybe it worked for women in 1880, but not for me. I couldn't just sit around and wait... for what? Who knew what John Gannon was thinking or what he'd do?

And then I had the exciting thought that he'd told me to leave his office because he was going to send me away. Maybe I looked too much like the woman in that portrait. His wife? Did I look more like her than Nellie did in her photograph? Is that why

Gannon was so surprised, and so troubled? I hated it when there were just too many damned questions. My head couldn't process them all. My thoughts kept getting tangled up.

Just as I turned from the windows, there was a knock on the door.

"Yes…"

"It's Mr. Hopkins, Miss Adams. May I come in?"

I sighed. Now, what did he want? "Just a minute," I said, walking to the door.

The door opened, and he took two steps into the room. "If you please, Miss Adams, Mr. Gannon would like to see you."

"See me? I just saw him, and he told me to leave. I did leave and here I am. So, in answer to your question, maybe I don't please."

Mr. Hopkins' face betrayed nothing. Not impatience. Not irritation. Not interest. "I will escort you."

The bustle dress was hot and uncomfortable, and I hated feeling trapped and treated like a servant. Childish emotions bubbled up. "You can tell Mr. Gannon that if he wants to see me, he can come here," I said with defiance.

Mr. Hopkins' eyes flicked about, and for the first time since I'd met him, his calm, confident authority melted into disbelief. "I beg your pardon, Miss Adams?"

I didn't even try to stop my sassy mouth. "Tell him he was rude, and that if he wants to see me, I'll be here, waiting."

Mr. Hopkins' mouth twitched into scorn. "Miss Adams, perhaps you do not understand. Mr. Gannon is the master of this house. It will be in your best interests to understand that, and then to comply with his wishes."

"No, thank you, Mr. Hopkins. I will not comply, but I'll be waiting here," I said, stubbornly. "In case he wants to apologize for his rude manner."

Mr. Hopkins' frosty eyes focused on me. "Are you certain of this, Miss Adams?"

I wasn't certain, of course. Maybe Gannon would have me beaten or thrown out into the snow. Maybe he'd threaten to kill me, but I stiffened my spine. "I'll wait for him."

Mr. Hopkins' mouth formed a bitter frown, but even in his utter disdain for me, he offered a little bow, turned, and left the room, closing the door softly behind him.

"Stupid!" I said aloud, and then kept hearing my voice repeating, "Stupid!"

The waiting was hell. It seemed an hour before I heard another knock on the door, and by then I was trembling and sweating. "Yes, come in."

The door opened and, to my astonishment, John Gannon stood there, staring at me, silent, yet imposing.

I was going to say something—anything—like, *Would you like to come in?* But my tongue felt stuck, and my lips were numb. I couldn't tell if he was angry or confused or what. I hadn't been able to read these people's faces. They all seemed to be holding something back, suppressing, hiding. They all had poker faces. What did they know that I didn't? A lot, it turned out.

Mr. Gannon tugged down his vest and cleared his throat. "Miss Adams, would you please join me in my office? I think it would be a more appropriate venue for what I have to say to you."

I heard my unsteady voice. "Yes... Sure. Of course."

He turned and made a gesture toward the hallway. "If you please?"

I started forward, left the room, and entered the hallway, following close behind him until we, once again, entered his private office. With a gesture, he invited me to sit in the same chair, and as I did so, he rounded his desk and sat, placing his folded hands on the desktop.

He lifted his gaze toward the ceiling as if to gather his thoughts, and then he slowly lowered his eyes, resting them on me.

"You are not the woman in the photograph, Miss Adams."

I turned cold. He knew I was an imposter. Of course he did. Nellie and I didn't look that much alike. I'd have to tell him the truth.

I was about to speak when *he* did. "Let me be clear, Miss Adams. The photograph does not capture you. Not in the eyes. Not in the shape of the mouth. It is apparent you are not the same woman. So, perhaps you will pardon my earlier behavior, as I was somewhat lost in surprise and reflection."

His gaze slid away toward the portrait of the young woman hanging above the mantel. "Marie was my dear wife, and I think you can see for yourself that you favor her in some distinctive ways. Not in all ways, of course, but in many ways. You can see that, can't you?"

I nodded. "Yes, sir."

He looked directly at me and continued. "I did not expect that. I was... well, I was a bit overcome, and I needed to compose myself. First, because of the photographic image, and second, because..."

He sighed and lifted a hand toward the portrait. "... You see, Miss Adams, Marie was only twenty-seven years old when she was thrown from a horse and killed."

"Oh... I'm sorry, Mr. Gannon."

He didn't seem to hear me. "When I saw you walk into my office looking as you do, well..." and then his voice trailed off into silence.

In that awkward silence, I didn't know what to say.

Mr. Gannon reached for the photograph and held it up, his expression troubled.

"This woman does not favor you or my deceased wife, Miss Adams. That is blatantly obvious. The woman in this photograph has neither warmth nor a genteel nature. One can see that plainly in the depth of the eyes, and in the pert set of the mouth. I sense a hungry materialist; a woman seeking any means and prospect to rise in station. I have seen such a look many times in the eyes of miners and miners' ladies panning for gold. So, I ask you, in all candor, how is it that you are here... appearing as you do? Appearing with the ghost of a face that favors my dear, deceased wife?"

I fumbled about, searching for words. First of all, if Gannon thought so negatively of Nellie, then why did he send for her and spend ten thousand dollars with an offer of marriage?

My jaded, suspicious little mind tossed out a possible reason: maybe he wanted someone who didn't remind him of his wife. Maybe he didn't truly want a "genteel" woman at all, but a miner's-lady-type, panning for gold in the figurative sense, a soulmate, someone ruthless like himself. Obviously, my showing up, reminding him of his wife, completely freaked him out.

How much should I tell? How much should I not tell? Nellie had told me he was ruthless.

I inhaled a little breath, deciding to tell him the truth—not the time travel truth, of course, but the truth about Nellie and Percy and what had happened on the train.

Would he believe me? Would I believe myself if the roles were reversed?

CHAPTER 15

When I completed my story, Mr. Gannon sat frozen, and the room fell into a cave-like silence. While I was talking, he didn't stir, but his eyes were fastened on me, his expression moving from curiosity to disbelief to anger. Finally, he gazed at me as if he were struggling to comprehend my words.

When I finished, I stared down at the floor and waited, my heart thrumming.

It seemed a good minute before Mr. Gannon responded in a controlled, somber tone.

"So, your name is Cynthia Downing and not Rosamond Adams?"

I didn't look up. "Yes."

He slowly got to his feet and began pacing from the window back to his desk. When he spoke, I heard the seething resentment in his voice. "Well, I suppose it makes perfect sense, since you are not the woman in that photograph. It would seem that the actual Miss Adams is not particularly blessed with even average intelligence if she believed that her silly plot would succeed, and I would be fooled.

Although you, Miss Downing, and Miss Adams have some slight similarities in appearance, as I said before, it is obvious to anyone with a discriminating eye that you and she are not the same woman."

He shoved his hands into his pockets as if a final decision had been made. "All right, then. So be it. I will deal with the woman in due course."

I raised my eyes. "She was afraid you would send men to search for her."

"And so I *shall* search for the conniving vixen, and I will find her, and so she should be afraid. I am not a man to be trifled with. If this little scheme of hers was to be made public, I would be the target of jokes and ridicule, from the mining camps to the ranches to Denver society, and beyond. And so, yes, I will indeed search for her, and I will locate her. She will then pay a steep price for her clumsy and misguided deception. And I will demand the return of the fee which I paid to that useless and poorly managed New York agency."

He faced me squarely. "Do I have your word that you will keep this deceitful and sordid business confidential, an exclusive secret held only between the two of us?"

I nodded. "Yes, Mr. Gannon. I will keep it a secret."

He ran a finger along his lower lip as he pondered the situation anew. "And you were traveling alone, Miss Downing? Is that correct? No lady friend? No sibling? No chaperone?"

"No... I was alone."

I saw it in his face. He wasn't entirely convinced

that I wasn't part of Nellie's plot.

"Where did you begin your journey, Miss Downing, and where is your final destination?"

I readjusted myself in the chair, my mind wrestling about for any believable answer. "I left from New York and, I too, was traveling to San Francisco."

"Miss Downing, it is unusual for a lady to travel so far a distance without a companion, is it not?"

What could I say? Gannon was smart, suspicious and perceptive, and he was waiting for my response.

The survivor in me lifted her head; the street-smart girl who'd learned about lying in jail, also knew I needed to mix in a little truth to help support the lie.

"I wanted a new life, Mr. Gannon. I traveled by myself because there was no one else to travel with. I have no family and none of my girlfriends wanted to leave New York for San Francisco. I'm going because I want a fresh start. Am I scared? Yes. Could I have ever imagined meeting Nellie, or Rosamond, and Percy, and being forced into this situation at gunpoint? No. So, perhaps your point is a good one, Mr. Gannon. Maybe I shouldn't have been traveling alone, but I was, and I am."

I was surprised by my conviction and strong voice. I think he was a bit surprised too.

Considering my words, he sat down, pulling his gold pocket watch from his vest pocket. He clicked it open, checked the time, snapped it closed, and replaced it. And then he reached for a carved wooden box, lifted the lid and removed a cigar. He twirled it between his fingers while his mind worked, finally placing the cigar between his lips. He struck a long wooden match against the box striker and lit the cigar, puffing gray smoke toward the ceiling.

Finally, he looked at me, his penetrating eyes boring into me, and his voice held a warning. "I will only ask you once, Miss Downing. Did you and Miss Adams dream up this little scheme because she had a change of mind, and you saw an opportunity for, as you put it, a fresh start and a new life?"

I sat up, hoping I was projecting an honest, mild outrage. "No, Mr. Gannon. No way... I mean, no, I didn't. I'd never met Nellie or Rosamond before or spoken to her before. Never."

He puffed the cigar, pulled it from his mouth, and stared at it. "I'm not a fool, Miss Downing," Gannon persisted. "Perhaps you learned, by some devious means, that you favor my late wife in appearance, and you saw an opportunity to play on my wounded affections and become the wife of a wealthy man. Is that true, Miss Downing?"

"No. It's not true! I'd never seen that portrait before today. I had no idea she and I looked alike, and I definitely do not want to be anyone's wife."

I rose. "Look... if someone will take me back to that train station, I'll leave on the next train to San Francisco, Mr. Gannon, and you'll never see me again."

His face was impassive. "I presume you have friends in San Francisco?"

My mind went into overdrive. "Yes. I have a friend. A girlfriend who lives with a respectable family."

Mr. Gannon straightened, giving me a sharp, searching look. "Are you running away from something, Miss Downing? I continue to believe that your flight, all alone, from New York to San Francisco, is the exceptional act of a frightened woman, or a desperate one."

I seized on that, beginning to feel like I was on the witness stand being accused of something I was innocent of. It wasn't the first time.

A light in my head blinked on. "Frankly, yes, I am running away," I said, telling a slice of the truth. "I've had some bad luck lately. I left a man... a gentleman in New York, and he doesn't know I left for San Francisco."

Mr. Gannon's forehead lifted, and his self-satisfied smile said it all. "I thought as much. An attractive woman like yourself would surely not be traveling alone unless, as you just said, you had some bad luck, or you were forced to flee for reasons that involved the law. And what will you do in San Francisco?"

"I don't know yet, but I'll figure it out, and my friend and her family will help me."

Did Gannon believe me? I couldn't read him. He leaned back in his chair and studied me.

"You do not have to leave, Miss Downing. I am not throwing you out. Surely, you must consider my point of view in this matter. You appear from out of the night, and you are not the woman who was expected. And then you enter my office, and I am astounded by your close resemblance to my late wife, whom I loved with all my heart. You did not reveal the truth of your situation until after I had confronted you. Do you not understand the reasons for my many suspicions, Miss Downing?"

Our eyes made contact, and, in that moment, I saw his attraction to me—or was it for his wife? I didn't like it, and I shrugged off a shiver. Could things possibly get any weirder? If this was a nightmare, then it was the most real and strangest I'd ever had. At least now I knew why everyone in that house was giving me the poker face. For whatever bizarre reason, Marie Gannon and I did look somewhat alike.

"Let me put it another way, Miss Downing. May I request that you stay here, at least for a few days, for a complete recovery from your ordeal? Will you consider it?"

Leave? Stay? If I left, or more accurately, when I left, where would I go? And I was still tired from my ordeal with time travel and with Nellie. If I stayed, at least I could rest, buy some time, and come up with a realistic plan. Thanks to Nellie, I had cash, jewels to hock, and some clothes. Those gave me a sense of safety and comfort, and I was relieved now that Gannon knew the truth, or at least enough truth that I didn't feel the immediate pressure to run for it.

Mr. Gannon waited for my answer.

"Thank you, Mr. Gannon. I accept your invitation to stay, but only for a few days, and I promise not to be a bother."

"I'm sure you will not be a bother, Miss Downing. We haven't had a guest in this house since the death of Marie. It will be pleasant."

"If I may ask, when did your wife pass away?"

"It has been nearly a year."

Gannon rose. "Now, Miss Downing, you must contact your friend in San Francisco. There is a Western Union Telegraph office in Denver."

That startled me. I hadn't thought of it. Ignorant-about-history me, I didn't even know people could send telegrams in 1880. "Oh, I don't want to trouble you, Mr. Gannon. I'll just send her a letter, then I can explain everything in more detail."

"But she must be frantic with worry, mustn't she, since you didn't arrive at your appointed time?"

He had me. I had to go with it. "Well, yes, you're right. Of course, she must be concerned, but again, I don't want to trouble you."

"It is no trouble at all, Miss Downing. We are modern here in Denver. We'll take your written message to the Denver telegraph office to be transmitted by electric telegraph. It will take no more than five or ten minutes. At the other end, the transcribed telegram will be delivered by messenger to your friend."

I smiled with gratitude, with clinched teeth. "Oh, well, how nice... I mean, how kind of you."

"Just write down your message, along with your friend's address in San Francisco, and I'll have Thomas Dayton take it into Denver. I believe you have met Mr. Dayton?"

How was I going to fake this one, since I didn't know anyone in 2022 San Francisco, let alone in 1880?

CHAPTER 16

So, there I was, sweating, still in Gannon's office.

Who could I send a telegram to in 1880 San Francisco? Nobody. *Stay calm, Cindy, just stay calm*, I told myself. With a sunny little smile I said, "Thomas... Oh, yes, he brought me here from the train station."

"And I trust your accommodations are to your satisfaction?"

"Oh, yes, Mr. Gannon. You have a magnificent home and estate."

He was pleased. "Thank you. I am quite proud of it, and I'm happy to hear you are enjoying your visit."

I stood up, thinking we had concluded our conversation, but Gannon had more to say. "Now, if you would be so kind as to give me just a few more minutes of your time, Miss Downing, I would like to tell you a little about myself. Please sit down."

I felt my lips make a smile, but my heart wasn't in it. I wanted to get out of there. Instead, I eased back down in the chair, hoping to appear interested.

"Yes, Mr. Gannon, I would enjoy that."

"Since you are not from this area and have no knowledge of me or of my many ventures, I would like to introduce myself in a proper manner."

His dark, suspicious mood had shifted, and he was more relaxed. I nodded politely, aware that he was out to impress me.

"I was a mining engineer, best known for my work in the smelting industry in and around Denver and the Leadville area, which was first settled back in 1859. That's when placer gold was discovered in the California Gulch during the Pikes Peak Gold Rush. I was a young man, and an ambitious one, and so I set forth to make my fortune."

I glanced around and thought, *You've certainly succeeded, if this house is any indication.* And then, as a real estate agent, I had the crazy thought, *I wonder if the house still stands in 2022. If so, it would make a great luxury hotel.*

John Gannon smiled modestly. "But that is of no importance except that I eventually settled here with Marie. I met Marie in Colorado City. I, of course, was older than she and we courted a year before we married. By that time, I had already created the Gannon Smelting Company in Denver. Although I realize I am boasting, the company has the tallest furnace stack in the United States, and I am also invested substantially in real estate, the coal industry, and railroads. In fact, Miss Downing, I own forty percent of the railroad that you arrived on."

Gannon turned his sober gaze toward the

windows. "But I don't want to bore you, and I fear that is what I am doing. All that aside, in 1874, I built this house for Marie, completing it in 1875. Unfortunately, she spent only a few years here before her untimely death."

"Again, Mr. Gannon, I am so sorry."

His eyes came back to mine, and he squared his shoulders. "Perhaps you think I'm a fool for what I did, that is, paying for and then entertaining the possibility of marrying a woman I had never met, procuring her from a mail-order agency in New York?"

I answered him with a shake of my head. Why was he being so upfront with me? He didn't owe me an explanation. I hoped it wasn't part of his come-on.

He smiled wistfully. "You don't have to say anything, Miss Downing. Denver society found out about it, even though I have yet to discover who leaked the news. In any event, those *Psalm* singers on Sunday were appalled, as you must have surmised. It has been a great scandal," he said largely, and then chuckled.

He reached for his cigar and took several thoughtful puffs before continuing.

"I am to be ostracized for sending for a mail order wife from New York. All the gossiping ladies said, 'Why doesn't he marry one of our fine ladies?'"

And then Gannon's expression changed, his eyes moved, and I sensed secrets hiding behind those eyes, despite his candid conversation.

He stared at his cigar and his voice dropped

into reflection. "I must be honest, Miss Downing. In Rosamond Adams' attractive face, in that blasted sketch and in the photograph, I'd hoped to start a new life with someone I'd never met and knew nothing about, and I suppose some of the old prospector in me, the gambler, took hold. It was uncharacteristic of me, of course, and perhaps it was foolish, but I longed to forget the tragedy of my wife's death and start anew. Throw the dice, as it were, and start fresh."

After a stretch of silence, he said, "And then you appeared, and... well, how do I say it? Your countenance is startlingly similar to Marie's."

I was perspiring again, and that corset was tight, and that dress was hot, and I wanted to scurry back to my room and rip them both off, fling them away, and dance around naked.

Gannon lifted a hand in a vague gesture. "So, yes, it was a sudden impulse, and I was having a rather difficult time of it when I contacted that agency in New York."

He placed the cigar in the ashtray, and looked at me, frankly. "Perhaps I'm being excessively honest with you, Miss Downing, and that, too, is uncharacteristic of my nature. I hope you understand?"

The man had totally pushed me off balance. What did he want me to say? What should I say to all that?

I smiled down at my hands, not wanting to meet his gaze. "Yes, Mr. Gannon, I think I understand. We all have our hard days when thoughts and emotions get the better of us. Yes, I do understand."

And did I ever. Isn't that how I'd ended up there? Bashing Cliff Prince in the head with a heavy clock and killing him?

He nodded in satisfaction. "Miss Downing, I assure you, I am a man of the highest moral character, and not given to rash action. But here you are, and that is fine."

He clasped his hands together and nodded. "And now, I have said quite enough."

I thought, *Wait a minute! You had lots of time to cancel Nellie's contract, if you had any second thoughts. And you paid for a photograph of her. That doesn't seem rash to me. That took long-term planning.* Of course, I wasn't going to say all that. And what does "But here you are" mean?

He rose. "Now, I'm sure you want to compose your message to your friend in San Francisco, and I will have Thomas rush it into Denver for you."

I thought fast. I had no name or address, did I?

"Mr. Gannon, would you mind if I went to Denver to write the message myself, and send it?"

One of his eyebrows lifted. "Well… no, I suppose that will be all right. If you are up to it."

"The fresh air will do me good, and I would like to see something of Denver."

His face opened to the idea. "Well, yes, of course. That will be fine. I will contact Thomas immediately, and you can travel right away. But you should leave soon, as darkness settles in early on these winter days, and the snows are unpredictable."

At least, as we traveled to Denver, I'd have time to think up something or fake something.

"Thomas will stay with you at all times, Miss Downing. Denver is a growing town, and it is gaining culture, but there are still rough elements to be watched and avoided. We do have a fine marshal, who has a no-nonsense reputation, and he keeps a good measure of law and order, but fine ladies, like yourself, are still somewhat of a rarity, and they must be protected."

"I'm sure I'll be fine, Mr. Gannon. Thank you."

I stood up, smiling. "And thank you for your kindness and generosity."

"Not at all, Miss Downing. Thank you for listening to my ramblings."

His eyes softened on me, and he stood a little taller. "Finally, as I'm sure you understand, based on our earlier conversation, I respectfully request that you return to using the name Rosamond Adams. I'm afraid that trying to explain the situation to others would prove both awkward and complicated. Will that be agreeable?"

"Yes, of course. I am Rosamond Adams."

There was a telling pleasure in his eyes. "I am delighted that you will be staying with us for a time. Will you grant me the pleasure of dining with me this evening when you return from Denver?"

"Well... yes. Thank you. I will."

I thought, *What else could I say but yes? Be careful, Cindy. This could get really weird, if things weren't already weird enough.*

CHAPTER 17

The carriage ride to Denver took about an hour. As we drove along Lawrence Street, I saw unpaved roads, horses and buggies, hitching rails and horse crap. It wasn't the romantic town I'd been expecting. It was rustic and stark, with framed buildings and false fronts, with vacant lots and stacked barrels and piles of coal ash. Some of the brick buildings had brown or blue awnings, plain fabric pulled over wooden frames.

There were many saloons; a sprawling general store; hunters in buckskin clothing with revolvers tucked in their broad belts; horsemen in fur coats and caps and buffalo-hide boots. As we passed yet another saloon, I saw two men pushing and shoving near the curb, their hard, bearded faces set in a challenge.

There were also Native Americans astride small ponies, the men wearing buckskin suits sewn with beads, and, by weird contrast, there were well-dressed white men in fine long coats and bowlers, sauntering along as if they owned the place.

There were very few women, but the ones that

strolled the wooden sidewalks wore long skirts and lavish feather hats, their hands clapped down on top of them to keep them from flying away in gusts of wind.

We passed a bakery, a gun shop and a tobacco shop, and next door to the John Deere Plow Company, Thomas pulled to the curb near the Western Union Telegraph office.

Thomas leaped down from the driver's seat, tied the two horses to a wooden hitching rail, then approached and opened my door.

"We have arrived, Miss Adams. I'll escort you inside."

Since I wasn't going to send a message, I didn't want Thomas with me, looking over my shoulder. "It's okay, I can go alone."

Thomas looked stricken. "But Miss Adams, Mr. Gannon gave me the hard orders to stay with you at all times, to accompany you inside, and then to pay for the wire."

"I have money, Mr. Dayton, and I'll be fine. Don't worry. Thank you."

I left Thomas worried, turning in a circle.

Inside the square, smoky room were two men in white shirts and dark pants, one wearing flaming striped suspenders, the other black suspenders, both sporting bushy mustaches and green visors. They were about the same age and the same body type, so I figured they were probably brothers.

The black-suspendered clerk was standing behind the wooden counter scribbling down a message from a middle-aged man, who had a fat cigar between his lips, and who was wearing a long black overcoat with a fur-lined collar.

The sound of the rapid, insect-like chirp of the telegraph came from the red suspenders guy seated at a desk, his finger chattering away on the telegraph key.

I felt a little catch in my chest at the strangeness of the place, with the dusty-looking floor, the flaring yellow oil lamps and the weird smells of cigar smoke, damp wood, and body odor.

The customer and the clerk paused what they were doing and glanced at me. Both looked me over, studying my long winter coat, my hat, and my face. Did I look like I was from the twenty-first century? I nodded at them, but they didn't respond, and returned to their work.

I looked around. There was a wonderful rolltop desk and chair, a spittoon that was disgusting, and a large 1880 calendar, hanging on the wall near the picture window and featuring an image of a stern George Washington.

A black-and-white mutt dog was curled up at the base of a four-foot-high, cast iron black heater that I guessed was fueled by either kerosene or coal. The dog's eyes fluttered, and his tail twitched. He must have been having a hunting dream.

Through the window, I saw Thomas' troubled eyes looking back at me. I waved, smiled and sat down behind the desk, reached for a piece of paper and pencil, and pretended to write.

The door creaked open, and in walked a tall, lean, and strikingly handsome man. As soon as he laid eyes on me, he removed his black cowboy hat and shut the door. I figured he was in his mid-thirties. He wore a black frock coat, dark pants, a blue and white striped shirt with a short, dark string tie, and a smart-looking, navy blue vest.

I loved his scuffed and muddy boots, and the pewter marshal's badge pinned to the left lapel of his coat was identical to those I had seen in movies.

From his open coat, I saw buckled around his waist a black leather holster, holding an impressive, ivory-handled revolver. In twenty-first century vernacular, the man was hot. No other word would do.

His thick, gleaming black hair was combed smoothly back, and he stood erect, with broad shoulders and a confident gaze. It was a strong, earthy face, a bit brooding and a bit sad, and that instantly turned me on.

And he was a virile man, with a good, clean jawline, the shadow of a beard, and dark blue eyes. Those piercing eyes met mine, and in his, I saw energy and intelligence. I also saw an immediate attraction that flashed with desire, then swiftly vanished.

As he stepped further into the room, I sensed the cool air of a worldly, experienced man that nothing could surprise or frighten.

For a few seconds, I was lost in his stare, and I forgot everything else: time, place, past and future.

"Hello, Marshal Vance," the clerk from behind the counter called.

"Afternoon, Carl," the marshal said, in a rich baritone. And then he waved at the red suspenders telegraph guy. "Eli, how are things?"

"Fair to middlin', Marshal. Yep, just fair to middlin.'"

"What can I do you for, Marshal?" Carl asked.

"Need to send a wire to Laredo."

Marshal Vance looked at me and offered a little bow. "Good afternoon, ma'am."

I swallowed and smiled. "Hello."

The slightest indication of concern passed over his face. "I suppose Thomas Dayton is waiting for you?"

"Yes…"

"Then you'll be staying out at the Gannon Mansion?"

"Yes…"

"Just come to town?"

"Yes…" I said, sounding like an echo.

He took a step toward me. "Well, then, ma'am, allow me to introduce myself. I am Marshal Bryce Vance."

I almost blurted out Cindy Downing, but stopped, swallowed back the name, and said, "It's nice to meet you, Marshal. I'm Rosamond Adams."

He nodded, thoughtfully. "I hear you are from parts East?"

"Yes. New York."

"Big town, I hear."

"It is, yes."

The man had a penetrating glare that was attractive and probing, and I felt a sexy magic in the air, an instant attraction that I'd seldom, if ever, experienced before in quite the same way. There was a dignity and power about Marshal Vance, a natural and confident masculinity that the men I'd dated never had.

There I was, all shy and a little dreamy as I stared at him, and I'd never been shy or dreamy around any man before.

And then I knew what he was thinking. I was the mail-order bride John Gannon had bought and paid for. That's why he'd asked if I was from parts East. Of course, he knew who I was, or thought he knew who I was.

For something to say, I said something stupid. "So you're the marshal of Denver?"

"Yes, ma'am."

I woke up from my dreamy spell and realized he was waiting for me to finish writing my message so he could write his.

I stood up. "Oh, I'm sorry. Do you need to write a message?"

"That's quite all right, Miss Adams. You go right ahead. I am in no hurry."

"No need to wait, Marshal," Carl called out. "Come on over and I'll take it down for you."

Marshal Vance gave me another head bow. "Good day to you, Miss Adams. I hope you'll enjoy your stay here."

At that moment, a dapper man and a fashionably dressed woman entered, and I glanced over. They were both in their forties. The woman, not a beauty, gave me a once-over. Then she cast her gaze out the window at Thomas and the carriage, then snapped her attention back to me, huffing out a dramatic, annoyed breath.

She took a few steps toward me, her stare accusing and indignant. "That is Mr. John Gannon's carriage out there and his man, Thomas, is it not?"

Startled by her tone and rude expression, I said, "Yes, it is."

She made a snorting sound. "Well, I'll be a crow in a coal pile if you don't look just like her, and I, for one, do not approve of what is going on around here. I'll just betcha a hog for a hare that you are…"

The man cut her off. "… Gladys, that's enough now. Don't you start this here in a public place."

Gladys ignored him, keeping her steely little eyes on me. "And so you must be that woman from New York. And, yes, I see now why he has taken to you. You favor her, don't you?"

The man said, "Gladys, come on now. This is none of our business."

Once again, Gladys disregarded his comment. Her sharp nose seemed to grow sharper as she glared at me. "You should be ashamed of yourself. I hope you know what you are getting yourself into—ready and willing that you must be, and a silly goose, to boot, to come here and marry a man like that. A murderer. Yes, I accuse him! John Gannon is a murderer!"

CHAPTER 18

H er words stunned me. "I'm sorry... Who are you?"

Marshal Vance and the other men in the room turned alert, the marshal taking a step toward Gladys.

She sniffed. "It does not matter who I am, you hussy! And so you will get what is coming to you, and I hope you have the stomach for it."

"Stop it, Gladys!" her companion demanded. "Stop this, right now!"

But Gladys didn't stop, and her stormy eyes widened. "No one in that grand mansion of a house, nor anywhere else in this town, will tell you the truth. But, by God, I will, and I'm proud to say it!"

And then Gladys turned to the marshal, pointing a finger at him. "And you know just what I'm talking about, Marshal Vance. Yes, you know the truth of it!"

Her male companion seized her elbow to tug her away, but Gladys yanked it free. "Marie was one of the sweetest and kindest souls on God's earth, and one of the best friends I ever had, and John Gannon killed her."

And then Gladys burst into tears, throwing a hand over her mouth, fighting choking sobs. Her companion grabbed her free hand and tugged her across the room and out the door, closing it firmly behind them.

Rattled, I eased down in the chair while Marshal Vance brought fists to his hips, watching the couple's retreat. The other three men had their eyes glued to me.

And then Thomas burst inside, his body tense, his eyes round with fright as they found me. "Are you all right, Miss Adams?"

I glanced away, confused, troubled, not speaking.

Thomas removed his hat and glanced at the marshal. "Hello, Marshal Vance. Miss Adams and me will be leaving now."

Marshal Vance gazed at me soberly. "Perhaps Miss Adams needs a few moments to gather herself."

I didn't look up. The woman had freaked me out. What the hell was going on? I shot up, ignoring the marshal, feeling embarrassed and anxious.

I looked at Thomas. "Let's get out of here."

"Did you send your message?" Thomas asked meekly.

"No! Let's go!"

Outside, the sun was lowering and there was a bite to the air. Thomas held the carriage door for me, but I hesitated.

"What is it, Miss Adams?"

I shot him a hard stare. "How did Marie Gannon die?"

Thomas turned his face away. "Miss Adams, I... I can't... Well, I mean to say, I can't be talking about that. Nothing about that."

"Why? Mr. Gannon said she was thrown from a horse and killed. Is that how it happened?"

Thomas' eyes shifted left and right. "We should be leaving, Miss Adams. It's getting late and there's a chill in the air."

"Tell me, Thomas. Tell me the truth, or I'll stand here all night."

Thomas pulled on his hat and licked his lower lip. "Mrs. Gannon fell from her horse and broke her neck. That's how she died. Yes, that's the truth of it."

I saw he wasn't telling the truth or, at least, all the truth. "And that's it?"

"Yes, Miss Adams."

"Did you see her, I mean, after the accident? After she was dead?"

He looked down at his boots and scratched his cheek. "We really do need to be leaving now, Miss Adams."

"Do you know that woman... the one who was in the telegraph office?"

"Yeah, I know her. Her name is Mrs. Gladys Frome."

"She said she was friends with Marie, and that Mr. Gannon killed her. So, one more time. Is it true? Did he kill her?"

Thomas' blunt face turned hard. "I can't be talking about this no more, Miss Adams. Now, if you will, please get into the carriage. We are being stared at by Marshal Vance, and Mr. Gannon ain't gonna like it none if he gets bad reports about all these goings on. There is much gossip in this town and the truth of things can be twisted. Please, Miss Adams, it is getting late in the day and darkness is coming."

A stagecoach arrived, with a jangle of energy, clotted with mud, rocking on its springs, pulled by four horses.

There was nothing more I could do. I stepped up and into the carriage, sitting down before Thomas closed the door and climbed up into the driver's seat.

As the carriage bumped and swayed, I sat back, considering my first full day in 1880. It felt like a week, and the anxious tension in my gut was getting worse. It was obvious that something more than being thrown from a horse had happened to Marie Gannon, and many people suspected that John Gannon had killed his wife.

What did the handsome Marshal Vance think? What did he think of me? He probably thought I was a whore. Isn't that what the Old Wild West called women like me? I learned later that they were called "soiled doves" and "sporting women." Terrific.

I wished I'd been quick enough to get the truth from Gladys or, at least, learned the Denver gossip about Marie Gannon's death.

How would I ever learn the truth? No one in that house would tell me, that was for sure, even if they knew. They had good jobs, and if Gannon was as ruthless as Nellie had said he was, then he had the money and the power to shut them all up, one way or the other. No doubt he also had the money to pay off the marshal and maybe a judge or two.

I stared hard at nothing. What black hole, or hell hole, or whatever, had I fallen into?

Sitting there, still hearing the echo of that woman's words in my head, I made up my mind that I was going to leave the Gannon Mansion as soon as I could come up with a plan. I'd leave, but maybe I'd stay in Denver for a few days. Maybe I'd visit Marshal Vance and maybe he'd tell me the truth. Maybe he wouldn't. Either way, I had to see him again. That one-of-a-kind attraction didn't come along every day, did it?

Had the marshal found me attractive? Yeah, I thought so. I saw it in the depth of his eyes. I saw curiosity, and I saw desire come and go in fleeting seconds. But it was there. I was sure of that.

But if he thought I was a "soiled dove," would he even want to have anything to do with me? And anyway, right now, I had bigger problems than dreaming about the handsome Marshal Vance. I had to get away from that "grand" house.

CHAPTER 19

I t was dark when we returned to the mansion. Thomas opened the carriage door and I stepped down; he lowered his head and spoke in a low voice.

"Miss Adams, maybe you won't say nothing about what happened in town?"

"You mean about Gladys Frome?"

"Yeah... and about not sending the wire. Mr. Gannon won't take kindly to me if he knows I didn't escort you."

"Will he fire you?"

"He has a horse whip he uses."

I stared, disgusted. "A horse whip?"

"Yes."

"Then I won't. Of course I won't. It will be our secret." *Yet another secret*, I thought to myself.

"I'm obliged to you."

"And thank you for taking me to town, Thomas."

I hesitated, my old jail-girl mind working. "Thomas... If I don't tell Mr. Gannon what happened today, will you tell me the truth about what happened to his wife?"

Thomas winced and looked away, pocketing his hands.

And then I silently cursed myself for still being the street-smart jailbird who was always looking for an angle or an opportunity. I quickly said, "Never mind, Thomas. Forget it."

Mr. Hopkins was waiting as Thomas escorted me to the front door, said goodnight, and walked back to the carriage.

As Sidney Hopkins closed the door behind us, he said, "Mr. Gannon asked me to tell you that dinner will be served at eight o'clock."

There was no way I was going to eat dinner with that man, not after what I'd heard, and not after what Thomas had told me about the horse whip. "Mr. Hopkins, will you please tell Mr. Gannon that I am not feeling well, and that I won't be able to join him for dinner?"

Mr. Hopkins' voice held disapproval, as did his eyes. "Are you quite sure of your decision, Miss Adams?"

"Yes, Mr. Hopkins. I'm sure. I'm going to my room and then straight to bed. Goodnight."

Inside my room, as soon as I'd taken off my hat and kicked off those tight-fitting shoes, I heard a knock on the door, and Alice's voice.

"May I come in, Miss Adams?"

I wanted to be alone, but I didn't want to make an enemy, and I wanted to ask Alice what she knew about Marie Gannon, even though I was certain she wouldn't tell me. But maybe I could read the truth in her eyes or hear it in her voice. "Yes, Alice, come in."

She entered, closed the door, and looked me over. "Shall I ask the kitchen to bring you something? Some broth, perhaps, or a slice of minced pie? I hear you're not feeling well."

"Maybe just some tea and toast, if it's not too much trouble?"

"Not at all, Miss Adams."

Alice moved to the bellpull, located a few feet from the mantel, tugged on a woven textile pull cord that rang a bell in the servant's hall, and then she turned back to me.

"I will help you undress."

I hadn't used the bellpull, not sure what the thing was for, and even though I'd seen something like it in movies, this one was near the fireplace, so I thought it might be used as a fire alarm.

"I think I'll take a bath, too," I said. "If that's all right."

Alice's eyes opened a bit wider. "Another bath, Miss Adams?"

"Yes… is that okay?"

"Yes, of course."

I detected hesitation in Alice's tone.

"Don't people in this house take baths every day?" I asked.

"It is unusual, Miss Adams, but I will run the water for you as soon as you have undressed."

While Alice helped me out of my dress and petticoat, I asked, "Were you Mrs. Gannon's lady's maid?"

She gathered up the dress and took it to the closet. "Yes, Miss Adams."

"What was she like?"

"She was a fine lady."

"Did you like her? ...Never mind," I added quickly, realizing she wouldn't answer any question truthfully anyway. "You must have been shocked when she was thrown from that horse and killed."

"Yes, it was a terrible day for us all. The house has not been the same since."

"Mr. Gannon must have been devastated."

"Yes, he was."

"Do you think I look like Mrs. Gannon, Alice?" I asked casually.

Alice hesitated for a moment, then returned to remove my corset. She worked quietly and didn't speak again until after she'd placed the corset in a closet drawer. When she returned, I suspected she had used the time to think up a safe answer. "People often have similar features, Miss Adams."

"I saw the portrait of Mrs. Gannon in Mr. Gannon's office. I think we have more than just similar features."

"Perhaps, yes."

And then Alice changed the subject. "Did you enjoy your trip to Denver?"

"Yes, I did. It was interesting. Do you go to Denver often?"

"Not often. There are ruffians about, you know, and I will only go when a man accompanies me."

I wanted to mention Gladys and the gossip about

Mr. Gannon and Marie, but I didn't because I'd promised Thomas, and I was going to keep that promise. I might need his friendship at some point. Why burn a bridge?

I was in the tub, with the door partially open, when Tara arrived. Alice gave her my food order, and she left. While I soaked in the tepid bath water, Alice straightened the room, banked the fire, and turned down the bed.

I left the tub wearing a cotton gown, wrapped in a luxurious robe and slippers. After Alice cleaned the tub and touched up the bathroom, I told her she could leave, and she did so.

I was seated on the love seat before the fire when Tara arrived with hot tea, a slice of toast, mince pie, and some cheese. With a small smile, she placed the tray on the serving table and began to serve.

"How are you, Tara?" I asked.

"I am doing well, Miss Adams, thank you," Tara said, while she reached for the teapot and began to pour the steaming black tea. The cup and teapot were a matching blue and cream-colored floral design that featured beautifully dressed colonial ladies and gentlemen in an outdoor setting.

"I hope you're feeling better, Miss Adams."

"Yes, I'm better. Thank you, Tara, and thanks for the food and the fire. It's cozy and warm in here."

"Mrs. Grieve asked me to tell you that Mr. Gannon has called for the doctor. He will arrive first thing in the morning."

I didn't expect that. "Well... I don't really need a

doctor. I'm just a little tired."

"Mr. Gannon thought it best, Miss Adams."

I shrugged. "Well, okay then…"

After Tara set the teapot on a tray, covering it with a cozy, she straightened. "Will there be anything else, Miss Adams?"

"No, Tara, thank you." And then I quickly added, "Did you know Mrs. Gannon, Tara?"

She smoothed out her apron, turning her eyes from me. "I attended Mrs. Gannon, Miss Adams."

"Do you think she and I look a little alike?"

Tara blinked several times. "I don't know about that, Miss Adams. I should go before they come looking for me."

"Okay, Tara."

Tara was at the door, about to leave, when I called to her. "Tara… Do you miss New York?"

Tara's hand was on the doorknob, her head down. "Yes, Miss Adams. I had friends there."

"It must get lonely here sometimes."

She didn't speak.

"I'm from New York, you know. I have friends there, too."

"Yes, Miss Adams. I did hear that you are from New York."

I spoke softly. "Tara… I can use a friend. We're both a long way from home."

She slowly turned to me, but her eyes were cast down. "Forgive me for saying so, Miss Adams, but you do favor Mrs. Gannon… in some ways, but not in others."

"Do I?"

"There is kindness in you... And pardon a silly girl who doesn't know so much, but I believe you are more beautiful than Mrs. Gannon, though I don't mean no disrespect to the poor lady, who met such a tragic end."

I seized on that. "How did she die?" I asked, although I shouldn't have.

Tara clammed up.

"It doesn't matter, Tara. Forget I asked. I hope you sleep well."

Tara bobbed a bow.

"Oh, by the way. What's in this mince pie?"

Tara brightened a little. "Mrs. Dockery lets me help her sometimes, and I helped with that pie," she said, lifting her eyes, and they shined with small pride. "She used venison, apples, cinnamon, raisins, cherries, and brandy. There are other things in there, too, but I don't know them. I couldn't linger when Mrs. Grieve came searching for me."

"Well, it looks great, and it smells totally awesome. Thank you, Tara. Have a good night."

"I'll return for the tray, Miss Adams, in about forty-five minutes' time, if that meets with your approval?"

"Don't worry about it. Go on to bed. You can always get it in the morning."

"Oh, no, Miss, that wouldn't do. I'll return for it tonight."

After she'd left, I tasted the warm mince pie and was amazed at how delicious it was. The crust was light and flaky, and the flavors were blended to perfection so that none over-powered the other. I'd never tasted anything quite so unusual and flavorful. I sipped the strong black tea, picked at the cheese, and then leaned back and stared into the fire.

Tomorrow, I'd tell John Gannon I was rested and ready to continue with my journey to San Francisco. I'd say, "I'm anxious to begin my new life there. Why wait?"

I didn't trust Gannon or Mrs. Grieve, and the house had a gloomy, depressing quality to it, despite all the lavish rooms and beautiful objects.

Later, Tara returned for the tray, looking very tired. She gathered it up and said goodnight. I was sitting on the edge of the bed when she left, feeling weary myself, but I couldn't imagine the long hours Tara worked every day.

The girl touched me in some way, and I felt the impulse to do something to help her. But what? She deserved a better life than this, didn't she? Would she be stuck working in this house for the rest of her life?

It was after eleven o'clock when I switched off the lamps, and the peaceful glow of the fireplace made me sleepy. In bed, I burrowed myself under the warm quilt, shut my eyes and tried to sleep, but flashes of bad memories and distorted faces flitted in and out of my head and kept me awake.

Despite the drowsy discomfort, I must have finally fallen asleep. I awoke at some point in the night, feeling hot and feverish. My back and legs ached, and my stomach churned. Had I eaten something bad? Had I caught an 1880 bug?

For the rest of the night, I tossed and groaned and grew worse. Thank God the doctor was coming. But feeling as I did, there was no way I'd be able to leave the Gannon Mansion unless I miraculously improved by morning.

CHAPTER 20

E arly the next morning, I was as sick as I could ever remember being. My entire body ached and was on fire. I was so sick that I was sure I was going to die, convinced that I'd caught some Old Western disease that I had no immunity against.

Dr. Harlan Broadbent's face was bland as he looked down at me. He was the same doctor who had treated me on the train, and even in my semi-conscious state, I saw his look of disapproval.

He'd taken my pulse and my temperature, and thumbed up both eyelids, the corners of his eyes crinkling as he studied me.

Mrs. Grieve stood by, stiff and watchful, and as cold as an ice sculpture.

"Dr. Broadbent, you should report to Mr. Gannon regarding Miss Adams' condition right away," Mrs. Grieve said formally. "He is quite eager to hear from you. Meanwhile, what can we do to nurse Miss Adams back to health?"

Dr. Broadbent straightened, tugged down his charcoal frock coat, and looked at Mrs. Grieve, wisely. "Miss Adams has autumnal fever. I have seen a lot of this in the last few weeks. At 102 Fahrenheit, her temperature is not worrisome. If it rises, give her cold baths and summon me. Meanwhile, I recommend beef broth, three times a day, along with a cold wet cloth on her forehead, also three times a day. I have a powder, composed of willow bark and meadowsweet, which should be mixed with tepid tea and administered once in the morning and once in the evening."

Through the thick fog of my buzzing head, I heard him whisper to her.

"The resemblance of this woman to Mrs. Gannon is uncanny, Mrs. Grieve. I noticed it when I first treated Miss Adams on the train. There are differences, of course, but..." He lifted a hand as his voice trailed away.

Mrs. Grieve's voice rose above a whisper, and it had a note of surprise in it. "You have met Miss Adams before, Doctor?"

"Yes. She fainted on the train some hours before we arrived in Denver, and the conductor summoned me to examine her."

"She fainted, you say?"

"Yes, and she had a friend with her."

"What friend?" Mrs. Grieve asked, her suspicious voice louder, easy to hear.

"Isn't her friend staying here in the house?"

"No, Dr. Broadbent. Miss Adams arrived here quite alone. She had no friend with her. Do you remember the friend's name?"

"Yes, I do. I've always had a good head for names

and numbers. Her name was Nellie Cummins."

Feeling a wave of nausea, I noisily released a breath. They both stopped talking and glanced down at me. Their faces seemed out of focus and weird, like the distorted faces in a carnival mirror.

Mrs. Grieve said, "You must go now, Dr. Broadbent, and speak with Mr. Gannon. He is waiting in his office."

For some reason, in my weakened and sick state, I thought "he is waiting in his office" was funny, and so I laughed. It must have been a scary laugh, because Mrs. Grieve took a few steps back.

"Start the broth immediately, Mrs. Grieve," Dr. Broadbent said, reaching into his black leather medical bag and retrieving a small, brown envelope. "This is the powder, and I would administer it post-haste."

I lost track of the days, each one blurring into the next. Tara brought me the broth and fed me, and she placed the cool cloth on my forehead, and she gently lifted my head so I could drink the tea. Sometimes she hummed to me, a sweet, lilting song, in her sweet, lilting voice. Other times I awoke and found her slumped in a chair next to my bed, sleeping.

Once, I stirred, hardly conscious, and I heard Tara singing to me in a feathery, light voice, while she placed a cool, damp cloth on my burning forehead.

"What's the name of that song?" I asked, struggling to speak.

"*Beautiful Dreamer*," Tara said. "My mother used to sing it to me when I was little, but I don't remember most of the words. So I sing some and I hum some."

"How nice. You have a pretty voice, Tara," I said in a raspy whisper.

"It's not as beautiful as my mother's voice, Miss Adams. She had the voice of an angel."

"And so do you, Tara... Keep singing. I love it."

"You mustn't talk so much, Miss. Sleep is what you need now. You must sleep, Miss Adams, and get well... You are my friend."

****

I awakened early one morning, and my head wasn't throbbing, I wasn't sweating, and the aches and pains were gone. Turning my head left, I saw Tara was once again asleep in the chair next to my bed, her arms crossed, her chin on her chest, her breathing soft like a child's.

I glanced at the clock on the nightstand; it was a few minutes after 6 a.m. Had Tara been sleeping next to me all night? I struggled up to a seated position, leaned back against the headboard, and watched the sweet Tara sleep—gentle breaths, a little whistle in her nose, and her little cap bonnet leaning to the right.

At that moment, the young girl broke my heart. Had I ever been as thoughtful and sacrificing and kind as she? No. I'd lived only for myself. I'd wanted the rich man, the most fashionable clothes, the expensive jewelry. Since my sister, Casey, had died, I'd never let myself feel much of anything for anyone. To me, the world was a selfish, unpredictable and nasty place, and I was going to get what was coming to me, one way or the other. It was Cindy Downing against the mean, get-out-of-my-way-or-I'll-mow-you-down world, and I was going to win.

My soft eyes remained on Tara, and they misted up in appreciation and admiration. With all the work she had to do, how much time had she spent nursing me back to health? How many nights had she slept in that chair?

A knock on the door jarred me and startled Tara awake, alarm on her face as she jumped to her feet and adjusted her cap bonnet.

The door swung open and Mrs. Grieve entered with the posture of an indignant general, her hard stare falling on Tara.

"What are you doing in here, Tara? Mrs. Dockery is furious! And the fireplaces need cleaning! Now, get out of here and go do your work. You'll work through breakfast!"

Tara gave me a frightened glance, and in her eyes, I saw a vacant fatigue. She ducked her head and scurried out like a frightened mouse.

A flare of anger gave me new strength. "She was here with me, Mrs. Grieve. She was taking care of me all night, and she fell asleep. She shouldn't be treated like that."

Mrs. Grieve kept her face under tight control, although I knew she wanted to tell me to shut up and mind my own business. But she couldn't, could she? Mr. Gannon wouldn't like it, so she forced an even tone, as she stepped deeper into the room.

"Tara has her chores to do, Miss Adams, and others in the house depend on her and she must learn responsibility. I'm sure you can appreciate that."

Before I could respond, she gave me a tight twitch of a smile. "I see that you are sitting up, and your color has improved. This is pleasant to see, Miss Adams."

"It's thanks to Tara that I'm feeling better."

Mrs. Grieve ignored my comment, but I could see she was smoldering. "Mr. Gannon will be very pleased, Miss Adams."

And then she put her business face back on. "I will have Alice come up and help you to bathe and dress. Are you strong enough to have your breakfast in the private dining room, or would you prefer to have it here?"

I thought of Tara having to climb those stairs and serve me. "I'm sure I can make it to the dining room. Thank you."

"Very good, Miss Adams."

"How long have I been here? I mean, how long have I been sick?"

"Four days."

I'm sure my mouth fell open. "Four days?"

"Yes... Dr. Broadbent visited you twice and assured us your fever would break sooner than later, and that his powder would be most efficacious. Mr. Gannon has faith in him."

"Will you thank the doctor for me?"

"He will visit today or tomorrow, and you can thank him yourself. Now, let me leave to apprise Mr. Gannon of your improved condition. Alice will arrive promptly. Good morning, Miss Adams."

The bath felt wonderful. Alice helped me wash my hair and then dry it near the fire while I sat, still feeling a little woozy, but determined to make it to the dining room. A good breakfast and a cup of coffee would totally help me feel better.

Thankfully, Alice brought a simple, bottle-green, black trimmed day dress, with only petticoats underneath, and button boots with buttonhooks. I was relieved when the boots didn't pinch my toes, but I missed sneakers, jeans, and off-the-shoulder sweaters, and my cellphone. I missed being free in New York City, to wander and shop, and to work out in the gym. I missed working, and my friends, and the diners and the delis, and, yes, I even missed the subways.

I sat before the vanity mirror, while Alice patiently styled my hair. She piled the hair loosely atop my head in wavy locks, and then she finished the style with curled bangs. I studied her face in the mirror. She was friendly, but aloof.

"You're an artist, Alice," I said, smiling. "I love your hairstyles. Where I come from, you could open your own hair salon and make a fortune."

"Thank you, Miss Adams, and, as I said, I am so happy that you are feeling better."

"Did you style Mrs. Gannon's hair?"

"Yes."

"In a similar style?"

"Somewhat similar. Your hair is thicker than Mrs. Gannon's was."

"Did you have time off when I was sick?"

"A day, yes."

"Did you do anything fun?"

"It was pleasant to have the day to myself. I did little except clean my room and read a book."

"How is Tara?"

"Tara?"

"Yes, she works hard. She took care of me when I was sick."

"Tara is a sweet child," Alice said, patting my hair and checking her work in the mirror.

"Yes, she is. I think you all work very hard," I said.

"We are grateful, Miss Adams. Grateful to work in such a good house that is run so well."

I couldn't read Alice, and I had always been good at reading people. I didn't know if she liked me, hated me, or couldn't give a damn either way. I decided to try to shake her a little.

"I guess I'll be leaving soon."

For only a couple of seconds, Alice halted, then continued combing and shaping.

"Leaving, Miss Adams?"

"Yes... Leaving."

"But I thought..." she stopped.

"What did you think?"

"Oh, well, nothing, Miss Adams."

"Go ahead. Say it."

"It's just that... Well, I thought you might be staying."

"Why would you think that?"

"I've said too much, Miss Adams. Forgive me."

"Maybe *I've* said too much," I countered.

Alice's mouth buttoned up.

"People talk in riddles in this house, Alice."

"Oh? Do they?"

And then she stepped back with a practiced, polite smile. "You are most beautiful, Miss Adams. I think Mr. Gannon will be pleased, and perhaps he will tell you so at breakfast."

My stomach growled from hunger, a good sign. The growling stomach was also a bad sign. I didn't care if Mr. Gannon was pleased or not, and I was not looking forward to seeing him at breakfast. What was I going to say to him? "I'm outta here? Hasta la vista, baby?" What would he say? "You look like my dead wife that I murdered. Please stay?"

CHAPTER 21

Inside the private dining room, I sat by the windows at one of the linen-topped dining room tables, staring out into a snowy day. There must have been six inches on the ground, blowing into mounds of creamy white and clinging to the evergreen trees. It was a Christmas card setting, and it was beautiful.

The footman, Edward, brought a plate of two sunny-side-up eggs, skillet fried potatoes, sausage, biscuits, gravy, and a pot of strong coffee. It may have been the best breakfast of my life, and I was grateful that John Gannon hadn't dropped in, because I was so hungry that I ate like a wild animal.

After I finished and Edward removed my plate, I relaxed in the chair, feeling refreshed, strong, and nearly my old self. While I sipped the last of the coffee, the dining-room door opened and John Gannon entered, with calm authority, wearing a dark suit, dark vest and burgundy string tie.

I shrank a bit in dismay, but I recovered as he approached my table, putting on a polite, little smile.

"Well, Miss Adams, I must say I am pleased to see

you up and around and looking so well. Edward said you ate a substantial breakfast and Dr. Broadbent informed me yesterday that he was confident in your full and complete recovery."

I kept my polite smile. "Thank you, Mr. Gannon, for all your kindness. I'm afraid I've been a burden."

"Not at all, Miss Adams. I hear you've been a model patient and no trouble at all. Absolutely no trouble."

I doubted that, and I was sure Mrs. Grieve hadn't thought so.

He indicated to the chair opposite me. "May I join you for coffee?"

"Of course, Mr. Gannon."

He sat, and Edward promptly appeared with a gold-rimmed cup and saucer, then returned with a silver coffeepot. After he'd refilled mine and poured Mr. Gannon's cup nearly full, Edward withdrew, and we were alone.

Mr. Gannon pointed at his cup of coffee, the steam rising from it. "I like black coffee, Miss Adams, and I see that you do, as well."

"Yes, and this coffee is very good."

"I am delighted you approve. It is from San Francisco, and it is roasted. It is not the belly wash or brown gargle I used to drink when I was out with the miners."

And for something to say, I asked, "Did you like your work as a mining engineer?"

"Yes, very much. I love the outdoors and I like feeling the earth in my hands, and I continue to make frequent visits to Leadville, to parts further west, and to Denver, to oversee my interests. I was in Denver for two days while you were recovering."

A tremor of alarm froze my hand on the cup. He was in Denver? Had he stopped at the telegraph office and checked up on me to see if I had truly sent that telegram to San Francisco? Surely he knew most everyone in town and, since he was rich, they knew him. Wouldn't I have visited the telegraph office if I was in his place? Oh, yeah.

I invented a question to distract my mind. "You previously mentioned that you were involved with smelting. I actually don't know what smelting is."

He laughed a little. "It is a very boring subject for the ladies, Miss Adams, and most, I dare say, would never ask, nor have the interest to want to know. To keep it simple, smelting is done to extract metals from their ores. Smelters separate gold, silver, copper or iron from the quartz rock that is hauled from the mines. I worked for nearly ten years as a mining engineer. Smelting is Denver's largest industry, and as I have said, my stack is the largest of the eight stacks. Sometimes those stacks do darken the skies, but they enrich the residents, so the residents seldom complain."

I nodded. "Yes, I did notice an odd odor when I was there."

He seemed pleased by that. "Yes, and it is a good odor, an odor of ambition, and labor, and progress. It is the fine odor of prosperity."

"So you're a practical man, Mr. Gannon," I said,

curious how he would respond.

He brought his cup to his lips, blew the steam away, and sipped at it. "I like to think I'm a man who appreciates the finer things of life and I don't mind working hard to get them. But enough of boring business subjects, Miss Adams."

He faced the windows, gazing out with pleasure. "Just look at that winter scenery. It's a lovely view, is it not?"

"Yes, it's beautiful. I've been admiring it."

"This view is another reason why I built this house, Miss Adams. I wanted the convenience of easy access to Denver, but I did not want to live in the city, as many do. I love the outdoors and I love privacy, and I like to be away from prying eyes and gossipy mouths. I'm sure you can understand that?"

"Yes, Mr. Gannon. You have the best of both worlds."

"Speaking of Denver, I haven't seen you since your little journey into town to send a telegram to your friend. Thomas told me you were successful."

I kept my eyes on the snowy view. Was this a trap? I needed to come up with a quick and cagey answer because I was sure it definitely *was* a trap. And I was sure that Dr. Broadbent had told Gannon that he'd treated me when I'd fainted on the train. The doctor would have also mentioned that I wasn't alone. I was with a woman friend, named Nellie Cummins. But, of course, Gannon knew that, because I'd told him. Maybe he didn't believe me?

CHAPTER 22

I stared Gannon directly in the eye as I'd learned to do from a tough old woman named Fancy-Lynn, who'd spent time in jail for multiple offenses. She once told me, "When the cops, or the female guards, or the dirty lawyers ask you somethin' and you know they're out to trap you, always look'em full in the eye, girl, and don't you blink. Give'em a stare that dares them to doubt you."

That was the stare I gave Gannon. "Yes, the journey to Denver and to the Western Union Telegraph Office was successful."

He nodded before responding, not taking his eyes from mine. "I hope and trust, because of your unfortunate illness, that your friend is not once again unduly worried that you haven't yet appeared in San Francisco... or been able to contact her."

I lowered my gaze and reached for my coffee cup. "I wrote that I would contact her when my plans were made."

"Very good. I'm glad to hear it."

Mr. Gannon took another thoughtful sip of his coffee. "By the way, I also heard that you met our marshal, Bryce Vance, at the telegraph office. Is that so?"

I wasn't prepared for that, but I kept my composure, feeling a little tickle of delight at the mention of the marshal's name, which I hoped didn't show on my face. "Yes, I did. He was polite and friendly."

"Well, don't think him so polite or so friendly, Miss Adams. Marshal Vance has had to take on many a drunken lout, miner, outlaw, and cattle rancher, who came to town looking for trouble."

"Where is Marshal Vance from?" I asked, casually.

"Some small town in Illinois, I think. He ended up on the Wichita Police Force and developed a good reputation as a lawman, but he was let go after getting into a shootout with a politician's son. He shot him dead, along with two of his pals, when they ambushed him."

"Ambushed him?"

"He'd caught them cheating at cards and, forgive me for saying so, Miss Adams, but they'd also beat up some of the girls who worked at one of the local houses. I'll say no more about that. So Bryce Vance clapped them into jail for a spell. When they got out, they plotted to kill him."

My attention was acute. "And the marshal killed all three?"

"Yes, he did, although he took a bullet in his shoulder, and one grazed his skull. So, after he mended, the town counsel thought it best if he left town, and he did. Denver's lucky to have him. He's a good lawman, and he keeps pretty much to himself."

"Do you know him well?"

"As well as anyone, I suppose. As I said, he is somewhat of a loner. But enough about these unpleasant things, Miss Adams."

When he looked at me, the blue-gray warmed in his pupils and his face became lively with anticipation. "Miss Adams, while you were ill, I did some thinking about... well, about certain aspects of your arriving here as you did."

I didn't like the sound of that. Earlier, over breakfast, I'd formed a partial plan. It was time to go, but not to San Francisco. It occurred to me that if I caught a train east, heading back to New York, there was a slight possibility I might pass through that same train tunnel and the same strange, electric current that had somehow jolted me to 1880.

It was a long-shot, for sure, but I had a weird feeling that if I put myself back on that train, something might happen. Was it a crazy thought? Yep. But I was here, wasn't I? And that was crazy.

And if nothing happened, the idea of returning to New York, even in 1880, appealed to me more than traveling to San Francisco. How I'd survive and make a living, I had no idea, but I was a survivor. I'd figure it out.

John Gannon pulled me back from my thoughts. "Miss Adams, I'm a direct man, a man of few words, once my mind is made up."

He cleared his throat, slid his saucer and coffee cup aside, and folded his hands on the table.

"Would you consider staying at the Gannon Mansion for a time? Perhaps for a month? Perhaps until after Christmas and the New Year? Now, before you give me your answer, I would like to add that the ballroom hasn't been used for some time and I believe that a Christmas ball, here at the house, would be welcomed and well-attended by most of Denver society. Not all will attend, of course, but those I have business with will come, and the society that delights in such Christmas events will also attend. They will come, if for no other reason than for the lavish banquet, the festivities, the dancing... for giving the ladies the opportunity to wear their best ball gowns and, let's face it, they will come for curiosity's sake. I would be honored if you would remain here as my guest and attend the ball. You will, of course, be fitted for a new gown and jewels for the occasion and, if there is anything else you wish, if it is within my power, it will be granted."

My first reaction was to say, *No, thank you. I'm getting the hell out of here*. But I counted to ten, and I took a drink of coffee, and I wasn't sure how much longer I could hold my mannequin smile. And then I thought it was best to stall, to gain more time. I needed to think.

"Mr. Gannon... You have been so generous and kind. I don't know what to say."

"I hope you'll say that you'll stay and attend the Christmas ball."

I held the smile, but it was hurting my face. "It's just that it is so sudden. May I think about it?"

"But of course you may think about it, Miss Adams. I see I have caught you off guard. By all means, take as much time as you need."

I had no intention of staying, but I needed to build my case as to why I was leaving. There were many things left unsaid, and I didn't know if that's the way people communicated in 1880, or if it was particular to Mr. Gannon, while he was evaluating and investigating me.

It was also a strain to match the mode of speech of the 1880s, so formal, with few contractions and no modern slang. I'd practiced in my room before the vanity mirror, but my voice still seemed pitched too high, and my words contrived.

Staring out into the snowy day, I decided to begin my case as to why I shouldn't stay until Christmas.

I said, "Mr. Gannon, perhaps I should not speak about it, but I am here under false pretenses. I mean, we both know I am not the woman you were expecting. Second, aren't people talking, I mean... aren't they? I don't really know the right word, but aren't they upset? Don't they disapprove of me being here, since I'm single and because, by some strange chance, I resemble your wife? I have seen surprised expressions from the house servants, as well as from people I met in Denver. People must be talking, and it makes me uncomfortable."

I didn't look at him, so I couldn't read Mr. Gannon's expression.

He surprised me, quick with his answer. "Miss Adams, I don't give a good blacksmith's damn about what people think. That's the first thing. Second, since we are speaking rather frankly, I will do so in kind. I know that Gladys Frome insulted you in the telegraph office. I heard about the entire unpleasant incident from Carl, one of the telegraph operators. So now, you must think I'm a murderer and that I killed my wife."

His blunt words yanked my head right, to face him. His face betrayed nothing, but his eyes held a gleaming, steely grit.

"Miss Adams, I do not fit into society, so I am an outcast, at least to some. And, yes, I knew when I contacted the Rose Daisy Agency for a mail-order bride, many more society ladies would—shall I say it politely? I knew I would be further ostracized. I did not think they would stoop so low as to call me a murderer, but it doesn't surprise me. The world strikes you hard where it can strike you, and then you must fight back."

I considered his words, his strong, square face, and his rigid posture. I couldn't tell if he was telling the truth or not, so I gambled and decided to come out with it, to see how he responded.

I inhaled a quick breath. "Did you kill your wife, Mr. Gannon?"

He blinked. Once. Twice. Three times, and then he stared at me long and hard, just as I'd done to him earlier, the Fancy Lynn stare. "Yes, Miss Adams. Yes, I did kill my wife."

CHAPTER 23

I t was kind of funny the way my conversation with John Gannon ended. That is, if you have a twisted sense of humor. After he'd stunned me by declaring that he had killed his wife, he rose, tugged on his vest and stared over my head at the far wall.

"Miss Adams, you did not send a telegram to your friend in San Francisco. Perhaps you don't have a friend in San Francisco or perhaps your friend, so called, is one and the same, the true Miss Rosamond Adams, and you are both playing at a game, with me as the fool? Perhaps you are after my wealth, and all that it offers, after all. Well, I must say, you are clever. So, I think you are not who you say you are. I think you are not even Cynthia Downing. Frankly, I don't know who you are."

Before I could speak, not that I could find any words, he continued, and, as he spoke, I grew cold to my bones.

"And since we are being frank, I will play your little game, Miss Adams. Despite your many mysteries, I am considering you to be my wife, so you may well achieve the wealth and status you seem to crave. Meanwhile, I have asked Marshal Vance to find out who you truly are and where you came from. The marshal is a skillful man at his job. As per his own instructions, he thought it best if you remained here until his investigation has been completed. If you are truly in some sort of trouble, Miss Adams, I can help, and I will help. But, if you continue to lie to me, and if you are out to swindle me in some female way, I will break you, just as I will break that trollop who broke her contract and ran off with her lout of a gambler to San Francisco."

Mr. Gannon offered a courtly bow. "Good day, Miss Adams. We had a candid conversation, and I am pleased about it. I must say, I admire your clever, bold courage and your plain-spoken manner. I do believe we could make a good match, and I assure you, you would not regret being my wife in any aspect. You will have wealth, position, and a virile partner, who will satisfy your every whim and wish."

He stood with his hands at his sides, looking at me with stern appraisal. "I do not think we are much alike, Miss Adams, but I believe we will be compatible in our differences."

With that, he turned and exited, no doubt pleased that I was too shocked to speak.

Back in my room, I paced. My head was empty, my stomach in knots, and my heart kicking hard against my ribs. Gannon had trapped me, and I hadn't seen it coming! Well, I'd been sick, hadn't I, or was that just a lame excuse? In any case, it had given Gannon plenty of time to go to Denver to check me out and, of course, he was the kind of man who *would* check me out. If I hadn't been sick, I definitely would have been on a train heading East, and, by now, maybe I'd be in New York, starting a new life.

Maybe I would have re-entered that time portal, or time tunnel, or whatever it was, burst through it and returned to my own time. Would that have been a good thing? Only if I'd managed to return to the twenty-first century, before I'd accidentally killed Clifton Prince.

I didn't want to think about why, or how could this happen, or what caused this. What good would it do? I'd always taken action. I'd never thought of myself as a victim, and I wasn't about to be a victim now. So what were my options?

I sagged down onto the loveseat, seeking answers and possibilities. My mother used to say, "Just when you think you're done for, if you give yourself a good kick in the ass, something will move, even if it's just your own ass."

Taking stock, I had to admit my options were limited. I couldn't call Uber to take me to the train station. If I stole a horse, I didn't know how to saddle it, and I couldn't ride. And, anyway, weren't these people good at tracking things? Animals and bad guys? They'd find me in a heartbeat, before I could gallop off to the train station, wherever that was. And, if they didn't find me in the snow and cold wind, I'd freeze to death.

I had no connections whatsoever, and since

Gannon discovered I didn't send that telegram and that Thomas Dayton didn't escort me inside, who knew what happened to poor Thomas?

He would have been my only hope. I may have been able to convince him to drive me to the train station in the dark of night. But not now. I hoped the big guy was still alive, and that Gannon hadn't beaten him up with a whip—or shot him.

I pushed up and paced the length of the gorgeous room, darkly amused that I was in the most luxurious jail I'd ever seen, being waited on like a queen and eating delicious food. I was living in a mansion and dressed in stunning clothes, although wearing the bustle dresses made me feel like a balloon in the Macy's Thanksgiving Day parade.

The thought of Thanksgiving brought a cold loneliness I'd never experienced. It hurt, and it brought a sinking, hopeless ache that sent me to the windows to stare out at drifting snow flurries. Yes, it was a beautiful jail.

How ironic. I had always wanted to be married to a wealthy man, be waited on hand and foot and have the finest of everything. Well, Cindy, guess what? If you want that wish, you've got it.

It was time to face it, at least for now. I was trapped, and two thoughts I'd been pushing away finally clanged in my head like alarms. Marshal Bryce Vance was investigating me, and he'd find nothing. Absolutely nothing, because I didn't exist in 1880. So what would he think and what would he do?

Second, John Gannon had admitted to me that he'd killed his wife. Was he telling the truth, clearly aware that there was nothing I could do about it, or anybody could do about it? Was he toying with me, purposely trying to scare me by menacingly suggesting that the same thing could happen to me?

I'd been in some deep shit in my life, but nothing, and I mean nothing, like this. I was stuck in time, playing by rules I didn't understand, in a house controlled by one of the wealthiest and most powerful men in the state, maybe even in the country.

Still, I had to come up with a plan. Anything to move the needle on this 1880 game board, even just a little, in my favor.

As I saw it, I had one not-so-good advantage. John Gannon was attracted to me, and I resembled his wife. From his expressions, and from what I'd seen in the depth of his eyes, he had loved her. I'd seen brief seconds of vulnerability and regret when he'd spoken of her, and when he'd viewed her portrait. So, whether he'd killed her or not, I had some power over him and, if I played it just right, I was certain I'd eventually find the opportunity to escape.

And I had another potential advantage, slim as it was. When Marshal Vance gave me the once-over, he'd liked what he'd seen, and I'd seen a lively curiosity in his eyes. Although he'd tried to hide it, I'd felt a crackling electric energy between us that was immediate and obvious. His sensual mouth had opened slightly. His eyes had shined with warm interest. As I said before, being pretty was sometimes good and sometimes not.

Marshal Vance's investigation would come up empty and that would confound and frustrate him, and hopefully, make me even more mysterious and attractive. I could use that to my advantage if I was clever enough, and if I managed to time it just right.

I was reasonably sure that eventually, Marshal Vance would come to the Gannon Mansion for a visit. His reason? To question me. For survival's sake, I'd make the most of that visit, and I'd play the oldest card in the romantic triangle deck.

John Gannon would be jealous of me flirting with the marshal. Depending on the type of man Marshal Vance was, perhaps, when the time came, and my life was in danger, he'd be a dashing, heroic cowboy and come to my rescue. In the nick of time, he'd save me from the lethal, jealous and strong hands of John Gannon, just as his fingers tightened around my throat.

Hey, if Gannon killed a woman once, a woman he apparently loved, he would do it again, wouldn't he?

CHAPTER 24

The next morning, Mrs. Grieve stopped by to tell me that Mr. Gannon was away on business, and he wouldn't return for two weeks. "But he'll be here for Thanksgiving. You can be sure of that, Miss Adams. No doubt," she said, with inflated zeal, as if she'd received the inspired news from the same mountain top where Moses had received the ten commandments.

"He gave me strict instructions that you are not to leave the house for any reason," she said, with a touch of malicious glee in her voice. "I'm certain you will not give me or Mr. Hopkins any trouble in this matter."

I was grateful Gannon was gone, but his instructions were clear: Keep Miss Adams locked up.

During the following week, I read, did Hatha yoga, thought, and paced. Often, I stood before my bedroom window and watched it snow, and snow, and snow, and sometimes it was a frenzied snow, driven by high, squealing winds. I welcomed that squealing wind, and I talked to it for something to talk to. And sometimes it talked back to me. From the wind, I heard voices, voices from the past.

My mother said, "Cindy, God made you pretty, and you'd better make good use of it, or you could be punished, and it could all be taken away."

I heard my father say in his hoarse, drunk-slurred voice. "Ain't no man ever gonna want you for nothing but a play toy, baby doll, because that's just how we men are. You remember your own daddy's words, 'cause they are as true as this world is evil."

From the moaning wind, I heard my sister say, "Not many things scare me, Cindy, not Daddy and his punches, and not even dying. But one of the few things that really does scare me is dying before I get to make a good difference in this world."

And then the howling wind asked, "What about your sister's words, Cindy? Have you ever made a good difference in this world?"

It was the quiet that started to get to me. A quiet so loud I could hear every damned bad thought I'd ever had. A quiet that skillfully picked the lock of my mind and released imprisoned memories, forcing me to confront who I'd been, who I was, and how I'd become trapped in a mansion in 1880. Thoughts circled the air above, like hawks looking for prey. Why was I here? Was there a reason? A purpose?

In my restless sleep, Mr. Gannon's voice often wormed its way into my dreams, his face tight with a threat, his words angry and sharp. "I'll kill you if I have to, Miss Adams!"

Alice came every day and helped me dress. She cleaned the room and made the bed, but she was stingy with her words. They were mostly "Yes" or "No."

When I'd tried to engage her in any conversation about Denver, or about her life, or any news about her coworkers, she'd answer pleasantly, and with a pasted-on smile, "I don't know much about that, Miss Adams," or "My life is not so interesting, Miss Adams."

To get out of that room, I ate alone in the dining room, or hung out in the library, hoping someone would come by and want to talk, but no one did. I longed to start a journal, and it would have been the perfect opportunity to document my bizarre and fantastic story, but what if someone found it? Mrs. Grieve or Alice? And then, what if they handed it off to John Gannon? No, I couldn't write anything down. Not then, anyway. That would come later. Much later.

Tara came to clean out the fireplace and build another fire. She, too, didn't have much to say, and I finally realized that the servants had been instructed not to talk to me any more than they had to.

I thanked Tara again for her kindness and for nursing me back to health. She was kneeling on the tiled fireplace hearth when she said, "I wanted to help. You were very sick."

"I hope you didn't get into any trouble because of it," I said.

She was silent, keeping her back to me.

I went to my trunk, lifted the lid, grabbed the

change purse and opened it, removing two silver dollar coins. I crossed the room to Tara and, standing a few feet away, I said, "Tara, I want to give you something."

Her head turned, and she looked up. I lowered my open hand, revealing the silver dollars. "I want you to have these. It's not much, I know, but I want you to have them."

To my disappointment, Tara turned away from me, lowered her head, and returned to her work.

"Tara... please take them."

She spoke in a near whisper. "Thank you, Miss Adams, for your kindness, but I cannot accept your gift."

"Why?"

"They will be found, and Mrs. Grieve will have me dismissed for stealing."

"But I'll tell her I gave them to you."

"It won't matter, none, Miss Adams. She won't believe you. I need my job. I've got nowhere to go, and no one to go to. I'm on my own."

She turned again and looked up at me with grateful eyes. "I thank you, Miss Adams, but I can't take the money, and I wouldn't take the money anyhow. What I did for you... well, I did it because I wanted to, and not for any other reason or for money. Ain't we both from New York, like you said, Miss Adams? Well, friends don't take money when a friend is sick. At least, that's how I see it."

After Tara was gone, for long minutes, I didn't move from the fireplace. As much as I tried to stop them, tears formed, stinging my eyes, and they ran down my cheeks. I seldom cried. I couldn't remember the last time I'd cried.

That young girl had more kindness and generosity at thirteen years old than I'd had in my entire selfish life. Sure, my childhood hadn't been ideal or easy, but neither had Tara's life been easy, had it? And it still wasn't easy. And yet, I sensed no bitterness in her, and she had a beautiful, loving spirit.

It was as if she'd held up a soul-searching mirror before me, and for the first time in my life, I truly saw the authentic me, the selfish me, the scared me, the pretty and the petty and the devious me.

Sure, I'd given the woman at the train station in 2022 twenty bucks, but that was easy; just pull a bill, hand it to her because she reminded me a little of my mother, and then walk away. I'd never sacrificed for someone, nursed someone back to health, helped someone get out of a jam. No, I had never made one good difference in the world. And, if I was honest, and I guess it was a day to be honest, I'd made the world a little more nasty and a little more selfish.

On Thursday night of that very long second week, I'd had it. Obstinate and determined, I made up my mind that I wouldn't stay couped-up in my room any longer. I put on a woolen day dress, found a pair of heavy, lace-up boots with a heel, and shouldered into a long, cashmere winter coat. I found a pair of heavy woolen gloves, and the fur hat I'd taken from the closet shelf fit tightly over my ears.

I was ready. If Mrs. Grieve or Mr. Hopkins wanted to chase me down, let them. I was younger, in better shape, and I had run track in high school. So, snow or no snow, I would easily out-slip and slide them, and give them a run for their money. Wouldn't that be fun?

I left my room, stepping into the hallway, tossing furtive glances left and right. No one was about, so I walked briskly down the hall to the winding, wrought-iron back stairs and descended, careful not to trip over my skirts.

The back door wasn't far, and I quickly closed the distance, reaching for the heavy doorknob, twisting it, and giving the door a little shove. It creaked open into the night, and a rush of cold wind swept across my face.

Closing the door behind me, I ventured across the snow-shoveled path, moving gingerly, searching the stone walk for ice. The back door lamps spilled feeble light upon the walkway, but it was enough to see and, if I walked a bit further, I'd be in the shadows and not easily spotted from upper windows and spying eyes.

Feeling a thrilling lift of freedom, I inhaled the cold night air deep into my lungs and blew a cloud of white vapor into the night. The sky was a midnight blue, with a crystal clear quarter moon and a hazy mass of gleaming stars so dense and so bright that I stood for a long time staring up at them, grinning like a kid. I'd never seen so many stars.

I ambled down the walkway, with my gloved

hands deep into my coat pockets, not venturing off the path into the eight inches of undulating snow spreading out in all directions.

As the winter wind whirled and wrapped around me, I didn't care that I was cold. In the face of all that had happened, I experienced an immense joy at being out of that house and in the small freedom of a glorious winter night. The crisp, clean, moving air was intensely quiet, and I encountered a peculiar peace, without electric lights and motors, without the murmur of traffic noise or jets flying over.

I grinned with pleasure as a big night wind burst over me, kicking up snow, stinging my face and stirring the evergreen trees.

Just as I stepped into the shadows, away from the light, I heard a voice. A man's voice! I froze.

CHAPTER 25

"YOU SHOULDN'T BE OUT HERE, Miss Adams," Thomas Dayton said.

I jerked my head left and saw his silhouette—his large silhouette—near a mound of shoveled snow.

"Son of a bit..." I stopped, grabbing a startled breath, putting a hand to my heart. "You scared the shit out of me!"

Real ladies in this period of history didn't curse, so I swiftly recovered. "I mean, I didn't know you were there."

"Mr. Gannon said you wasn't meant to leave the house."

I saw clouds of vapor puffing from his mouth.

"Yeah, well, I couldn't stay locked up in that house another hour. I had to get out. It's not like I can run away, right?"

"Still, that's what he said."

"And do you do everything Mr. Gannon says?" I asked, in a defiant tone. "Every single thing?"

"He pays me my wages."

I lifted my shoulders and settled them, trying to shake off the fright. "Yeah, well, I guess that's how the world works, isn't it? You kiss ass so you can get money."

I shook my head, instantly regretting the words. "I'm sorry. I shouldn't have said that."

Thomas remained still. "You're right, Miss Adams. That's the way of it, all right, until a man's had enough. And then, maybe he ain't gonna take it anymore."

I wasn't sure what he meant. "Did you get into trouble when Mr. Gannon found out I didn't send the telegram and that you didn't escort me inside?"

"I was wrong about that. I should have gone in with you."

"No, Thomas, I was wrong, and I'm sorry, and I'm sorry if I got you in trouble, and I'm glad you're still here."

"Do you know what he said to us all? Mr. Gannon said, 'Don't talk to Miss Adams. You leave her be.'"

"And why do you suppose he said that?"

"Don't know. None of my concern."

"But you're talking to me now," I said, suddenly aware he was up to something.

"And I've got my reasons, don't I?"

"I don't know. Do you?"

"I just said so, and I'm sure you heard me."

"Did Mr. Gannon threaten you when he found out about Denver?"

"He whipped me."

"He did what?"

"Horsewhipped me."

"And you didn't fight back? You're a big guy."

"One of his old miner pals held a 45 Colt on me while Gannon whipped me. Either I take it or I'm dead and buried, and won't ever be found. I took it, standing. I didn't go down. So my back's sore, and my face took some licks, but I didn't go down no matter how he slashed at me."

My stomach twisted. "That's sick. Gannon's just sick. I'm so sorry Thomas."

His laugh was low, moist and dark. "Yeah… sick's the word, and it's right for the like of him."

"And what if he finds out you're talking to me now?"

"He said next time he'd kill me."

I blew out a jet of vapor, frustrated, not wanting to get Thomas killed. "And would you let him kill you just because he pays your wages?"

He was quiet for a moment, as he kicked at the snow. "I was a weedle before I came here looking for work."

"I don't know what a weedle is."

"A roamer, like the seeds from the creeping jenny, an Oklahoma Territory weed, where I'm from."

"And so, you were tired of roaming?"

"I was then, and that's why I settled here, but not so much now, after what I've seen. After what Gannon done to me."

"And what have you seen?" I asked, anxious to know, and maybe not wanting to know.

"I've seen things I shouldn't have seen, and nobody knows I've seen. So, maybe I'm waiting for the right time before I spill my guts to the marshal."

His vague hints and runaround were irritating me. "Okay, Thomas, then I guess I'm curious. Why are you standing out in the snow on a cold night like this? I mean, are you like a security guard or something?"

"I don't guard nothing after my chores."

"Okay, then, why are you out here?"

In the darkness, I could feel his eyes on me. "'Cause things have turned and come about, and I've been doing some thinking, and so I've been walking and thinking."

"And that's why you're standing out here in the cold wind? Were you waiting for me? Did you know I'd come out?"

A puff of wind blew up a funnel of snow and Thomas turned his face from it, as I lowered my head.

When he spoke, his voice had changed to a low accusation. "You must have hit the skids back East for you to try your luck out this way."

"And why do you keep stalling, Thomas? Why don't you just tell me why you're out here?"

His voice grew louder and held mild contempt. "And now I know you didn't come out here to be Mr. Gannon's bride."

I stilled, narrowing my eyes at him. "Do you, now?"

"Yes, ma'am."

"And how do you know, or are you going to keep talking in circles?"

"I know, because I found her."

"Found who?"

"The real woman. The real Rosamond Adams."

My mind locked up and my shoulders tightened. "What?"

"She was about froze to death. I found her when I was out hunting, three days ago."

My thoughts thrashed about as I grappled for words. "Three days ago?"

"Yes, ma'am. You ask why I was out here. I don't read and write so good, so Rosamond wrote a note for Tara. She was coming out to get it from me, and then give it to you."

Fear struck like a hammer. "Where is Tara?"

"She won't come now. She's seen us. That one is as smart as a whip and twice as clever as a fox. She took to you, and she don't take to nobody. She told me you was in danger, so I worked it all out and I was going to give her the note."

"Where's Rosamond?"

"She's safe now. Still sickly, with the fever."

"Is she alone?"

"Yeah. She's alone, when I have to leave the place."

I spoke with urgency and determination. "Where is she, Thomas? Tell me."

"I don't tell nothing more until you and me work things out."

My first thought was of escape. Of course it was. Self-preservation had always been my first thought. "Thomas, can you get me out of here? Can you get me to the train station so I can catch a train back East? I can give you money. I'm a prisoner in that house, you know that now. My real name is Cindy Downing. Rosamond is Mr. Gannon's mail-order bride, not me."

"I know about it," he said proudly. "I know all about it. She told me. The real Miss Adams came clean about it all, because she thought she was going to die."

I suddenly thought of Tara, and something inside shifted. My selfish, get-the-hell-out-of-town thoughts stopped when an image of Tara's innocent face froze me to the spot. I flashed back, remembering her asleep, slumped in a chair next to my bed, and she'd sat there night after night, after working fourteen-hour days. I thought about what she'd said to me.

"*What I did for you, I did because I wanted to, and not for any other reason or for money. Ain't we both from New York, like you said, Miss Adams? Well, friends don't take money when a friend is sick. At least, that's how I see it.*"

Thinking of someone else other than myself— thinking about Tara—sent me into confusion, and I stared blindly. Shouldn't I get Tara out of that house, too? I didn't know where we'd go, or what we'd do, but at least the girl, like me, would be free. With our shared shaky backgrounds and learned survival skills, we'd make it one way or the other. I was sure of that.

But if we did escape the house, I had a lot of planning to do. And, if I was caught, I had no idea what Gannon would do to us.

CHAPTER 26

Thomas' harsh voice jolted me back to the present. "That no-good gambler Rosamond took up with, beat her up and left her with nothing except a train ticket. Rosamond says you have her trunk with money and jewels in it. That's why that gambling son-of-a-bitch beat her. Beat her because she was fool enough to mix the trunks up and give her trunk to you. That was going to be his gambling stake. You see it now, don't you?"

His big silhouette moved a few steps closer, as he kept talking. "So, as I see it, it's time for me to get back to roaming, and away from John Gannon and his evil ways and this house."

"What's going on, Thomas? What do you want?"

"You ain't a stupid woman. What do you think I want? I want Rosamond's money and her jewels. What else?"

"Then what?"

"Then me and Rosamond will hightail it back to the Oklahoma Territory."

"Gannon will go after you, and he'll find you. He paid ten thousand dollars for Rosamond to be his wife."

There was a long silence as the wind whistled through the trees.

"Ten thousand dollars for Rosamond?" Thomas finally said, in a wonder. "And she wants to run off with me, a nobody? Ten thousand dollars?"

"Yes, so you know Gannon will go after you both. He'll want revenge because, you know as well as I do, that's the kind of man he is."

"Yeah, well, let him. I've got two brothers. Caleb, my older brother, tracks game and Indians for the Army. If Gannon gets close, we'll shoot him, and bury him where he'll never be found, and there won't be no man or woman on God's good earth who will care. That's what I want. I want Rosamond, the money and the jewels, and I want to run for it. Maybe I want Gannon to give us chase because I want him dead and buried. Nobody comes at me with a horsewhip and keeps his life. My Pa didn't raise me to take that from no man. The day Gannon struck me, with a man pointing a Colt at me so I couldn't fight back, was the day Gannon signed his death in blood. If I stay, I'll kill him. If he comes for me, I'll kill him."

Trembling from the frigid air and from Thomas Dayton's threatening words, I decided to seize the moment and ask the big question, while he was chatty, angry and wanting revenge.

"Thomas, did Gannon kill his wife?"

Thomas didn't hesitate. "Yes, ma'am, he killed her, all right. He caught her with the groom, Jubal

Banks, out in the carriage house back in a horse stall. Jubal was handsomely made, and with a shiny eye for the ladies, and Mrs. Gannon took to him right off. They was closer in age, and they was closer in temperament, them both being more bold than smart."

I crossed my arms tightly against my chest, suddenly sensing danger everywhere. Could I believe Thomas? If he had stepped out of the shadows into the light, I would have been able to read his face and his eyes. But then, maybe I didn't need to see him to believe him. I heard the truth, and I heard the rage in his voice.

Thomas blew on his hands, stuffed them back into his sheepskin coat pockets, and continued.

"So, Gannon caught them, all right. He ordered all hands to ride off, and they did. All but me. I mounted my horse and rode a-spell, then I moved into the trees and waited. I heard two gunshots. Gannon shot Jubal Banks twice, and then he strangled his wife. Broke her neck, he did. Then he laid her across her favorite horse and took her to a far field. He didn't know I saw him, but I did. I swung down, tied my horse aways out, then moved back through the trees, silent like a ghost. Gannon left his wife there on the ground near her horse. He just walked away and didn't give a care if the buzzards got to her. I left the trees, crouching, and went to her. That's when I saw she was strangled. Neck broke."

"What about the marshal?" I asked, my pulse high. "Did he come to the house?"

"Yes, he did. The marshal was sent for, all right, and he found the dead woman just lying there. When Gannon was called to come to the scene, he was in his office. He fell into grief, play-acting out his sorrow and his distress, and I don't know if Marshal Vance suspected a bad deed or if he just took it for what it seemed to be. The marshal don't talk so much, and he don't show so much on his face, so I don't know what Marshal Vance thought about it."

My mind flashed back to 2022, to Cliff Prince's dead body and to the antique clock gripped in my shaking hand. I had been a killer, too, and the awful memory made me nauseous.

I cleared my throat. "What happened to Jubal Banks' body?"

"One of Gannon's miner pals buried him in some hidden ground. Never was found. Never will be found. Gannon told the marshal the man had run off."

"And did the marshal believe that?"

"Had no reason not to believe it, did he? Hired hands go running off all the time."

I stared down at the snow, feeling more frightened than I could ever remember.

Thomas' voice took on conviction. "You get me Rosamond's cash and jewels, Miss Adams, and we'll be gone in short order."

I looked up. "Can you take Tara and me to the train?"

"I will, once I have the goods from Rosamond's trunk, but we'll have to do it before Gannon returns, and he's back in two days."

I nodded, a glimmer of hope rising. "Okay... Okay. How do we do this?"

"You get the goods to Tara, and she'll get them to me. That's what the note Rosamond wrote was all about, the one in my pocket, the one I was going to give to Tara. I don't need to do that now. I've told you directly."

"How do I know you won't leave before you take us to the train station?"

"Now, I'll call you rightly, by your given name, Miss Downing. I am a man of my word. That's the way my Pa raised me. You get me the goods and you'll get to the train. After that, you're on your own."

I wanted to jump up and scream into the sky. I'd soon be free, and so would Tara!

CHAPTER 27

J ust when everything was going my way, and I was about to flee the place, it all went to hell. John Gannon returned early the next morning, having traveled all night across bad roads and through high winds.

That killed any chance I had to give Rosamond's jewels and money to Tara, and for Tara and me to pile into a carriage, with Thomas at the reins, and make a run for it. And what was worse? Tara was sick. It was probably the same illness that had clobbered me. She didn't arrive at her usual time to clean the fireplace and make a fresh fire.

An older servant girl named Hilda showed up in Tara's place, wearing a tight, troubled face, a baggy blue dress and a tight blonde bun. It was the first I'd heard that Tara was in bed with a high fever.

My anger and frustration about Gannon's sudden return immediately melted into concern for Tara. "Is she okay? Can I see her?"

Hilda went straight to work, distracted, kneeling before the fireplace, mumbling in German as if to herself. "Frau Grieve lässt niemanden in die Nähe des Mädchens, damit sich das Fieber nicht auf uns alle ausbreitet."

"I don't speak German. Can you please say that in English?"

Hilda turned about, her face wadded up with fatigue and worry. "Frau Grieve, don't let nobody see Tara. Says, fever could spread in the house."

"Well, I'm going to see her," I said firmly, and then asked Hilda where Tara's room was. With a shake of her head, Hilda muttered incomprehensible German.

I left the room, marched down the hallway and up the stairs to the fourth floor. Tara's room was the third door on the left. I knocked lightly and waited. Hearing nothing, I opened the door and peered in. The curtains were closed against the light, but I saw two beds, one neatly made and unoccupied. On the other was a still, gray mound.

I entered softly, closing the door behind me, and approached the bedside. Even in the weak light, Tara's sleeping face was visible, her breath labored. I leaned, and with the back of my hand, I touched her damp forehead. She was burning with fever.

I didn't know what to do. Had the doctor been called? I knew they didn't have antibiotics.

At that moment, the door opened and Mrs. Grieve appeared, wearing her usual funereal black dress and scowling expression.

"I gave strict orders that no one was to come into this room."

I straightened my back in defiance. I'd had it with

these people and their weird ways and sour faces.

"Have you called the doctor?" I asked, ignoring her declaration.

"Leave this room, Miss Adams!" Mrs. Grieve demanded.

"Or what, Mrs. Grieve? What will you do? Stop your bullshit and call a doctor for Tara. She's sick with a high fever!"

My crude language and demands set the woman back, but only for a few seconds. Her spine stiffened, her sharp little chin lifted. "If you do not leave this instant, I will be forced to call Mr. Hopkins."

"So call Mr. Hopkins, and while you're at it, call the doctor, too, because I'm not leaving Tara until I know she's being cared for."

Mrs. Grieve's eyes were angry, narrow slits. "You impudent hussy, entering this house and making demands. I run this house! Do you hear me?"

I'd had it with her, and I'd had it with the entire ridiculous situation. Anger rolled off me in hot waves, just as it had when I was a rebellious teenager. "Shut up, you stupid, arrogant bitch, and go get the doctor! Do it now—or so help me, I'll punch you in the face!"

Mrs. Grieve took a shaky step back, her stunned eyes blinking fast, her face twisted in shock.

Tara cried out, and I turned, lowering to my knees beside her. "Tara, it's me, Rosamond. We're going to get you a doctor, okay? Are you hungry or thirsty? Can I get you anything?"

Tara's eyes fluttered open, and they struggled to

focus. "Miss Adams?" she asked, in a wheezing voice.

"Yes, I'm here."

"I'm sorry... Sorry I didn't come..."

"Shh, Tara. Don't worry about that. Can I get you anything?"

"Water... Please."

I glanced back to the open door, and Mrs. Grieve was gone. I pushed up, found a pewter pitcher of water and a glass on a side table, poured the glass full and took it to Tara. As I held it to her dry lips, she lifted her head and took small sips, finally dropping back down onto her pillow and falling to sleep.

I found a high-backed wooden chair, carried it to her bedside, sat, and waited, worried about Tara and speculating about who was going to show up next.

A moment later, I stood up and found a basin and sponge in the snug servants' bathroom. I poured some water into the basin and took it and the sponge back to the narrow bedtable.

For the next half hour, I gently dipped the sponge and blotted Tara's feverish forehead, hoping I was doing for her what she'd done for me when I'd been sick.

About an hour later, I heard heavy footsteps approach, and I braced for battle. I didn't turn to look when those footsteps entered the room.

"Miss Adams..."

I turned. It was John Gannon's deep, commanding voice.

With the sponge in my hand, I gave him a cool stare. I don't know why, but I wasn't frightened of him. I should have been, knowing what he was capable of, but at that moment, I was calm and determined.

He stepped further into the room. "Miss Adams, you need to leave this room, as Mrs. Grieve requested. She is the matron in charge of the housekeeping, the maids, and the kitchen servants."

"I won't leave Tara until the doctor comes," I said firmly.

"Miss Adams, we don't call the doctor for the servants unless it is a life-or-death issue."

"And how do you know it isn't a life-or-death issue? Are you a doctor? She's burning up with a fever."

"These things come and go. She's a young girl and she will survive it."

"And what has caused the fever?"

"I do not know," he said impatiently.

"I don't know either, and that's why the doctor should examine her."

"Miss Adams, I have had a trying few days and I am weary from travel. Marshal Vance will arrive early this afternoon, and I have much business to discharge before he does. Therefore, I request that you leave and let this servant girl recover from her illness, as I am confident she will."

I did not back down, although his information about Marshal Vance coming was disturbing. I hoped he saw in my expression an unmovable determination. "I'll stay here until the doctor comes, Mr. Gannon."

He sighed heavily, with irritation. "She is a servant girl, Miss Adams. A servant girl from an orphan train. I give her work, her lodging and her meals. Please do not try my patience further in this matter."

I stood up, facing him squarely. "She is a beautiful young girl who works fourteen-hour days for you. She deserves care when she's ill, Mr. Gannon. She needs a doctor, and I won't leave her side until the doctor tells me she's okay and will improve."

In a burst of sunlight that briefly lit the window curtains, our eyes met. His were burning. I hoped mine showed conviction.

"You are too bold, Miss Adams."

"Yes, sir, I am, and I'm not likely to change. I beg you, please... Will you send for the doctor? I will greatly appreciate it."

His jaw tightened. His mouth twitched, and when he spoke, there was a raspy tone of a threat. "I will summon Dr. Broadbent, but this is the last time you will make demands of me, Miss Adams. Do you understand?"

The rebel in me wanted to say, "Kiss my ass!" But I managed to tamp down the words. "Yes, I understand."

He pivoted and stormed out of the room.

I stood there, shaking, my right toe tapping the floor like a tap dancer.

It was close to noon before Dr. Broadbent arrived, looking weary and annoyed, his medical bag in hand. I acknowledged him, but he only grunted a "hello" at me as he went to Tara's bedside.

She remained asleep, and I stood in the shadows, out of his way, while he took Tara's temperature and pulse, and checked her tongue.

"Has she vomited?"

"Yes. Twice, but not much. I don't think she's eaten much in the last two days."

Dr. Broadbent nodded and made a blurred noise of irritation. "Her fever is high."

"Does she have the same illness I had?"

"It's difficult to say. How long has she had the fever?"

"I don't know... A day or two, I guess."

"She should drink elderflower tea. Make certain that whoever brews it, mixes two teaspoons in a cup of boiled water. Let it steep for fifteen minutes and then strain out the elderflower. She should drink it three times a day as long as the fever continues. Also, keep applying the cool compresses. Ensure she stays in bed and does not work. I'll stress that point with Mrs. Grieve. Activity can raise the body temperature, so rest is especially important now."

"Shouldn't she eat something?"

"I'll ask the kitchen to send up chicken or beef broth. When the fever breaks, give her porridge and sausage."

"So, she's okay... I mean, it's nothing serious, is it?" I asked.

He removed his spectacles and looked at me. "The fever will break in response to her young body's ability to fight it off."

I folded my hands at my lap. "Thank you for coming, Dr. Broadbent."

He scratched the end of his nose and considered me. "Miss Adams, the young girl is too thin. Can you see to it that she eats more and works a bit less?"

I was surprised when I saw concern and kindness in his eyes. "I don't think Mrs. Grieve will listen to me. We don't get along very well. Maybe she'll listen to you."

He looked down. "I examined this girl when she came from the orphan train some years ago. She was too thin then, and she's too thin now. I will speak to Mrs. Grieve about it."

I was pleasantly surprised and grateful. "Thank you again, Dr. Broadbent."

He closed his medical bag, placed his spectacles inside his frock coat pocket, and looked at me with warm consideration. "I have two daughters of my own, Miss Adams. Their names are Beatrice and Mary."

I waited for more, but he didn't offer more.

"I will confirm the girl's needs with the kitchen," he added.

"Her name is Tara, Dr. Broadbent."

He nodded. "Just so. Tara. Yes, a pretty name it is. A good day to you, Miss Adams."

When the doctor was gone, I drew back the curtain and gazed out into the white sheet of the day. More snow. Not heavy, but persistent and blowing.

I hated feeling helpless and unable to take any

action. Did Thomas and Rosamond know what was happening? Would they dash off for the Oklahoma Territory without the cash and the jewels, leaving Tara and me trapped in this place?

As I returned to Tara's bedside, I vowed to find some way to break free from the Gannon Mansion, with or without Thomas, and I'd take Tara with me.

Now, I had to worry about what Marshal Vance had learned—or, more accurately, what he hadn't learned about me.

CHAPTER 28

I spent the next three days caring for Tara, getting little sleep and having frequent spats with Mrs. Grieve, who complained about Hilda bringing the broth and tea three times a day. From Hilda, I learned, in broken German and English, that the nasty woman complained to Gannon that I was spending "too much time with the girl," and that "Tara should have returned to her duties by now. Work will do her more good than any broth or tea."

Mr. Gannon did not visit Tara's room or ask to see me, and that was great news, but I wondered what he and the marshal had discussed three days ago.

Each day blurred into the next, and I lost all sense of time until the day Tara awakened, with a weak smile and glazed eyes. "Hello, Miss Adams," she said. "I'm feeling so much better."

Two days later, Mrs. Grieve put Tara back to work, and three days later was Thanksgiving Day.

I hadn't heard from or seen Thomas, so I had no idea what was going on, and no way of contacting him to learn if Rosamond had recovered from her illness. No one had mentioned that Thomas had left, but then, no one in that house ever told me anything, so who knew? Meanwhile, everything was on hold.

So, what could I expect on Thanksgiving Day? Again, I had no idea.

While Alice dressed me in a stunning, black and green gown, I asked her. "I've only heard bits and bobs, Miss Adams. It will be a lovely spread, no doubt. Mrs. Dockery has been cooking for days, and Mr. Hopkins has brought the finest wine from the wine cellar. Mr. Gannon's old Aunt Cora will attend, and perhaps a businessman and his wife. Mrs. Dockery was all a flutter when she heard that Marshal Vance was coming as well."

My eyes widened. "Why is Marshal Vance coming?"

"I don't know, but that's what I've heard."

As I strolled to the dining room, I could feel the adrenaline affect my breathing, especially with the corset feeling tighter than usual. Had I gained weight or had Alice wanted me to have a twenty-six-inch waist?

Just before I entered the grand room, I thought, *What in the world am I about to walk into?*

The formal dining room was broad, with a deep red carpet, mahogany paneled walls, high beamed ceilings and ornate crown molding. On the walls hung heavy, gilded-framed oil paintings, one portraying a muscled, determined farmer at the plow, bathed in golden light, trudging along a furrowed field.

Another painting featured a sundrenched battlefield containing defenses of timber with projecting spikes, and stalwart Civil War soldiers shouldering into battle, with rifles raised, bayonets glinting.

The enormous painting above the stone fireplace depicted two bearded men, wearing western outfits and cowboy hats, astride chestnut horses. They gazed reflectively into distant, dark mountains during a crimson sunset.

The paintings seemed odd choices for a formal dining room, but they certainly projected masculinity, which was surely John Gannon's intention.

Parlor oil lamps, with painted floral glass bases, added a warm glow to the room. Polished heavy oak furniture and a massive roaring fireplace gave me the impression of stepping into an historical exhibit at the Metropolitan Museum of Art in New York.

I had arrived late, on purpose, so I was stiffly introduced to Aunt Cora, and to John Gannon's business partner and his wife, Otis and Martha Webster. I was then reintroduced to Marshal Vance; our eyes met only briefly as we nodded and smiled.

All but the marshal were dressed in formal attire. He wore a black suit, white shirt and black string tie. In the glow of the fireplace, I thought he was even taller and more striking than the last time I'd seen him in Denver.

Everyone had been seated by the fire with a glass of sherry in hand, except for Marshal Vance, who sipped a whiskey from a cut-crystal old fashioned glass.

Gannon's partner, Otis Webster, was about sixty years old, with steel-gray eyes, bushy white muttonchop sideburns, and a walrus mustache. His dark frock suit coat was a loose fit over his large frame. The granite jaw and deeply lined face gave him ruggedness and determination; he was a man who appeared ready and able to accept any challenge and overcome it.

His wife, Martha, was a mousy woman, with a round, very white face, thin lips and little mouse eyes that shifted nervously. Her voice was soft, her manner meek, her hair styled tight to her head, with a whisp of bangs.

John Gannon's aunt, known as Granny Cora, plodded toward the table, cane in hand, poking and pointing it like a weapon at any person, place or thing.

"Let's get on to eating, John," she demanded. "I don't like eating too late in the day because the food don't sit so well when I put these old bones to bed."

Cora looked like an old warrior, with a long, black dress and a little, black top hat that I loved. She had wiry white hair, dark, agitated eyes, and a stubby body. Her twitchy mouth uttered grunts, blew out deep sighs, and produced a high, strident voice that sounded like a dog's squeaky toy.

The six of us sat at a twelve-seat mahogany dining table, covered by an off-white linen tablecloth and an extravagant arrangement of blooming flowers of red, orange and yellow. Crystal glasses gleamed, the porcelain China was gold rimmed, and the silverware was ornate and heavy. There was a golden, three-tiered chandelier overhead that was dazzling, and it gave off a muted glow that added warmth to everyone's face, except for maybe Granny Cora's.

John Gannon sat at the head of the table, and Granny Cora sat at the other end. Otis and Martha were seated to John's left, and Marshal Vance and I were seated to his right, with me closer to Gannon, and the Marshal closer to Granny Cora.

Clad in white tie and tails, Mr. Hopkins emerged from the door of the servants' dining room, bearing a silver platter with a large, brown turkey, embellished by an assortment of nuts and cranberries. Two women servants and Edward followed, carrying trays of crusty sliced bread, boiled potatoes with butter, creamy butternut squash, stewed prunes, and a chicken pie.

Granny Cora put her hands together in prayer and closed her eyes. The guests followed. After she'd wheezed out a mumbled grace, everyone but me whispered "Amen." I didn't, because when I was a girl, our family had never prayed over a meal. My father forbade it. "Ain't nobody but me put food on this table," he'd once said, "so if you're going to pray, you sure as hell better pray to me."

We snapped out our linen napkins and prepared for the feast, with the smells of turkey and freshly baked bread scenting the air. At a sideboard, Mr.

Hopkins sliced the turkey, and then Edward served us from a tray that featured both white and dark meat.

While we ate, John Gannon stole looks at me, while the conversation at the table was mostly about the weather and everyone's health.

Marshal Vance turned to me. "I hear you were ill, Miss Adams. I hope you have entirely recovered."

"Yes, I'm feeling very well," I said cordially.

Since weather and health were hot topics, I decided to join in. "And you, Marshal, have you been well since I last saw you?"

"I am fortunate in that I seldom succumb to illness, Miss Adams."

I looked at him with a small, flirtatious smile, drawn by his lean face and muscled neck. And there was something in his voice and in his quiet, confident manner that flipped a switch inside my fluttering heart and turned me on. Did he see it in my eyes? Did John Gannon? I hoped he did because I was ready to turn on my charm and focus it on Marshal Vance, putting my "let's make John Gannon jealous" plan into action.

"Do you like being a marshal?" I asked, wanting to hear more of his sexy voice.

"Yes, Miss Adams. It is agreeable to me."

I thought, *Agreeable? These people speak so politely and yet they say nothing.*

And then Granny Cora talked about her heartburn and rheumatism. Otis and John talked business, and demure Martha said nothing as she took small bites of the turkey—but loaded up on the bread and fresh creamy butter.

John Gannon stared at me until I turned away, putting my attention on Marshal Vance.

"What do marshals do all day long?" I asked.

Marshal Vance reached for his white wine glass. "Simply put, Miss Adams, I keep the peace, provide security and enforce Federal laws."

"Sounds like an exciting job," I said, overdoing my flirtation.

I didn't have to glance over to Gannon to feel his jealous irritation, but I did.

CHAPTER 29

I looked at Gannon, smiled sweetly, and avoided getting my eyes entangled in his.

And then Otis turned his attention to Marshal Vance. "Marshal, I came across an article in the *Kansas City Gazette* some days ago. It spoke of your Civil War encounter at Perryville, Kentucky."

I had not been a particularly good or interested history student, so I knew little about the Civil War.

Marshal Vance swallowed some turkey and took a sip of his wine. "That was a very long time ago, Mr. Webster, and I was a very young man."

John Gannon spoke up. "I knew you served the Union cause, Marshal, but you have never spoken about it."

Before the marshal could speak, Otis continued. "The article stated that the marshal here was a hero of sorts. As a young captain, he fought battles at Mill Springs and Perryville. According to the article, when engaged strengths and casualties are considered, Perryville was one of the bloodiest battles of the Civil War, and the marshal here was instrumental in turning the tide."

"Mr. Webster," the marshal interjected, "I was one of many men who helped turn the battle in our favor," he said modestly. "I'm afraid newspaper men are employed and encouraged to inflate and dramatize events for the purpose of increasing readership."

Otis continued on. "But it was the largest battle fought in the state of Kentucky, and it was said to be fierce and terrible."

Marshal Vance nodded. "I will say, sir, that it was a day for the devil, if you ladies will pardon my use of the word. The Reb leader, Colonel Bragg, finally withdrew deep into the night, retreating through Cumberland Gap into East Tennessee. It was the darkest day and the darkest night of my life, and for we who survived, we honor the dead, and we give thanks to Providence for our lives."

Cora said, "Well, you are to be commended, Marshal, yes indeed. And on this day of Thanksgiving, it's good to give thanks to God that the war is long over and, although I had a nephew killed at Gettysburg fighting for Lee and the South, I say, we should have no more war talk tonight."

The room fell into silence for a time, and then Cora blabbered on about her bad stomach, her right deaf ear, and the "interminable" rash on her upper left arm, which no salve, ointment or herb had been able to heal.

After a dessert of cookies, custard, mince and apple pies, all delicious, the men retired to the den for cigars and brandy, and I was stuck with Cora and

Martha in the parlor, where we were served coffee and port.

As I sat on a red velvet, tufted sofa, positioned next to an upright piano, Cora opted for an armless chair situated by the fireplace. Meanwhile, Martha couldn't resist the lure of the card table, settling into a nearby chair with glittery, eager eyes, undoubtedly envisioning herself as the triumphant winner of a poker game, raking in piles of cash.

Cora drained her first glass of port and shook it at Edward to pour her another. I didn't know what to say, so I said nothing. Cora said the port "lacked something" and Martha surprised me by saying, "Shall we play cards, Granny Cora? I am so fond of cards."

"I don't play at cards," Cora boasted, putting her admonishing eyes on Martha. "The road to perdition is paved with the likes of playing cards."

Martha's round face fell a little and her tight mouth pursed up into a mild insult.

And then I thought of Nellie and her gambling friend. And I thought of Thomas Dayton, and I thought of John Gannon. What would he think if he knew that the real Rosamond was living somewhere nearby, and that Thomas was hiding her and taking care of her? And what would all these people do if I told them I was from the future, from 2022? Well, that's what a bit too much wine and a glass of port will do.

Cora faced me. "Do you play the pianoforte, Miss Adams?"

"No, I don't."

"I think all young women should learn to play the piano, or the violin, or some musical instrument. I myself played until my rheumatism took hold. Yes, I played Chopin, Mozart and Brahms waltzes. Yes, all young women should play. It adds charm, romance, and mystery to any relationship."

And then Cora lifted her cane and jabbed it at me. "Miss Adams, my nephew tells me you are from New York."

"Yes, I am."

"And he says, candidly, and rather vulgarly, that you are a mail-order bride. Is that so?"

Mrs. Webster's little eyes swelled with vivid interest as she took quick sips of her port.

I wanted to tell Granny Cora the truth. All the truth. I wanted to blow the lid off the entire absurd situation, make Gannon angry, and have him toss me out of that house.

But before I could say anything, Cora leaned her head forward, her eyes flashing.

"Well, I find it preposterous, and eccentric in the extreme, that you and Marie have such similar facial features, although I will add that you possess a more refined manner and deportment than Marie ever did. She lacked the finer graces, but then she was from Colorado City. Frankly, I never liked that girl, and, if the truth be told, and I will tell it, few people in Denver did like her. She came from a dirt shack, and as soon as she wed my poor nephew, lovesick as he was, she began putting on airs, like she was the

Queen of Sheba. Well, the mysteries of life go as they go, don't they? And we mere mortals have little or no say about it."

Cora eased back, momentarily satisfied with her opinions. But with a lift of her head, she was ready to fire another round. "And I will say this: it seems to me, Miss Adams, that perhaps Providence has deposited you here in order to help heal my nephew's wounded heart over the tragic loss of his young wife, common as she was."

Martha Webster spoke up. "Oh, dear, what a tragedy it was, too, the poor pretty thing, to be thrown from a horse like that."

Cora shook her head. "Now, don't mishear what I said, Miss Adams. I don't approve of this sort of thing, that is, John taking it upon himself to purchase a wife through the mail. Why, it is utterly primitive. Something from one of those sordid dime novels, like the series *Deadwood Dick*."

I was about to blurt out the truth about myself and Nellie when Marshal Vance entered the room. He bowed to us ladies and looked at me with a pleasant smile.

"Miss Adams, will you do me the honor of speaking with me in the library?"

CHAPTER 30

I sat on a brown, patterned sofa, and Marshal Vance lowered himself into a golden fabric armchair with carved front legs and scroll arms. I remember the chair because the marshal seemed uncomfortable in it.

The gleaming fire from the brown marble fireplace warmed the room, which was lined with floor-to-ceiling cherry wood bookshelves, stocked with hardback books. Hanging on the walls were sketches of famous writers, Shakespeare, Washington Irving, Sir Walter Scott and Daniel Defoe. I knew who they were by the engraved gold nameplates attached to the bottom center of each frame.

The marshal crossed his long legs, ran a hand over his jaw, and then fixed his eyes on me. "Miss Adams, Mr. Gannon has reported to me the somewhat unusual events which brought you here. As you might imagine, he is concerned that perhaps the entire truth of this matter has not been fully communicated."

I sat still, knowing where the conversation was

going.

"Frankly, Miss Adams, at his request, I did send some wires back East to discover if you are who you say you are."

I looked him straight in the eye. "And we both know that I'm not who I say I am."

He didn't move, and his probing eyes stayed focused on me. "You say you are Cynthia Downing, or at least that's the name you gave to Mr. Gannon."

"That's right."

"And is the story you told to Mr. Gannon the truth?"

"Yes. The truth."

"So, you were a victim of the actual Rosamond Adams?"

"Yes, the victim of Rosamond and her man friend, Percy Blackstone, if that was his true name."

"That is one of his names. He goes by many."

That surprised me. "Then you know him?" I asked.

"He is a swindler and card cheat, and he is wanted in two states for armed robbery."

I settled back into the sofa. "Okay... Did you find anything on Rosamond?"

He drilled into me with his eyes. "More to my interest, Miss Downing, I want to ask you a frank question, and I'd appreciate an honest answer. Are you and Rosamond Adams working together in any capacity?"

I folded my hands, not pulling my eyes from his. "No. I'm not working with Rosamond. I told you the truth, and I'm sure you have spoken to Dr. Broadbent, who will confirm that he saw Rosamond and me on the Denver train."

"Yes, I spoke with the doctor, and, yes, he confirmed your story, or what he knew of it. He said you'd fainted."

"Yes."

"Why did you faint?"

"I don't know. The heat? The chill? Something I ate?" I shrugged. "I don't know."

He ran the tip of his tongue across his upper teeth.

I kept talking. "To Dr. Broadbent, Rosamond claimed we were friends. We were not. I'd never seen her before, and that's the truth."

Marshal Vance uncrossed his legs and sat up. "Then who are you, Miss Downing, and where were you traveling from and traveling to?"

"From New York to San Francisco. I would be back in New York by now if Mr. Gannon, on your advice, hadn't kept me here against my will."

"But he has treated you well, has he not?"

"That's not the point. I want to leave."

"And not continue on to San Francisco?"

"No... I want to go home to New York."

His expression changed, relaxing with curiosity. "Do you have a family in New York? A husband, perhaps?"

He was fishing. There it was again, the gleam of attraction in his eyes.

"I have no family and I'm not married."

"And you were traveling alone?"

"Yes, there's no law against that, is there?"

"No, ma'am, there is not, but it is uncommon for a lady of your... well, of your attractive looks, to be traveling alone, especially out in these parts, where outlaws and desperados roam and attack trains, coaches and towns."

"What is the difference between an outlaw and a desperado?" I asked, truly not knowing the answer.

Marshal Vance tilted his head, checking me out anew. When he saw I wasn't mocking him, he smiled. "An outlaw applies to any person who is wanted by the law. A desperado commits acts of violence against innocent people, and generally behaves in a reckless and unpredictable manner."

I nodded, allowing my happy eyes to feast on his very handsome face. "Well, now I know, don't I?"

Marshal Vance's eyes seemed to gleam with perception, and I wondered what he was thinking.

I stood up. "Marshal Vance, I want to leave this house. I'm not the woman, the mail-order bride, Mr. Gannon paid for, and I'm not working with Rosamond in any way. I have done nothing wrong, and I want to get out of this house."

"And return to New York?"

"Yes."

Marshal Vance rose. "Then I see no reason why you cannot do as you wish, Miss Downing."

My shoulders relaxed. "Really? Just like that?"

"Yes, of course."

"Will you tell Mr. Gannon that? Will you tell him that I'm not working with Rosamond Adams and that I never was, and I have no reason or wish to stay?"

"Yes, if that is what you want. Yes, I will tell him."

I sighed with relief. "Thank you, Marshal."

He gave me a long, searching look. "Miss Downing, might you consider staying in Denver for a few days before you return back East?"

Well now, I thought, *was this the 1880 version of 'Why don't you hang around for a few days, so we can get to know each other a little better?' How tempting, because I'd really like to get to know Marshal Sexy Vance a lot better.*

Our eyes made contact while he waited for my response. I had to do some quick thinking. Thomas and Rosamond were still hiding some place, waiting for her cash and jewels, so they could get away. But if I gave them the cash and jewels, I'd have no money whatsoever, which meant I couldn't take Tara with me back to New York. Tara was my little sister now, and I had made a vow I'd get her away from John Gannon and Mrs. Grieve.

Should I keep the cash and jewels and run for it? Should I keep *some* of the cash and a ring to hock, stay in Denver for a few days and then purchase two fares back to New York? Or should I stop wasting time and not take any chances, grab Tara and get the hell out of Dodge? Or, to be more accurate, Denver?

Marshal Bryce Vance was a nineteenth-century man, a real fantasy that I wanted to explore. He was sensual, dangerous and irresistible. But then I heard that still, loud voice in my head that I'd seldom ever listened to.

"Don't do it, Cindy! For once in your life, listen to me! This is not the time to fall in love."

I had made bad decisions my entire life, and most of the time, those decisions had centered around a man. Not this time. If I didn't grab Tara and run for it, things would turn ugly. John Gannon would see to that.

No, it was time to go. Now.

CHAPTER 31

The silence between the marshal and me lengthened, and it was exciting, and the desire was exciting, and I saw it on his face that he felt the same for me.

But… this time, it wasn't just about me. It was also about Tara. I had to think about Tara.

I faced the marshal, my mind made up. "As much as I'd like to stay, Marshal, I'd better not. I'd better catch tomorrow's train and start back to New York."

Marshal Vance's crooked smile suggested disappointment. "Then we will miss you, Miss Downing."

At that moment, the door swung open, and John Gannon entered, a brandy in one hand, a big, lighted cigar in the other. He stepped in, closed the door and moved toward us, his tentative expression suggesting he was evaluating the mood and the outcome of a conversation he had requested.

"Well… It appears as though I have arrived at the conclusion of the… shall I say, interview?"

The marshal nodded. "Yes, Mr. Gannon, Miss Downing and I have concluded our discussion."

Mr. Gannon looked first at me, and then his curious eyes shifted to the marshal.

Marshal Vance said, "Miss Downing wishes to leave on the next available train back East to New York."

There was resistance in Gannon's face. "I don't understand. Have you made your conclusions so quickly, Marshal, that Miss Downing's intentions are entirely legitimate?"

"Mr. Gannon, according to my investigations and conversation with Miss Downing, there is no basis to suggest she has any involvement with the actual Rosamond Adams other than what she has stated. Now, she wishes to leave, and I see no reason why she should not."

Gannon lifted his chin and threw back his shoulders, giving me a hard stare. "After all I've done for you, and all I have offered, you want to leave this house, Miss Downing?" he said, rather harshly.

I tried to smile, but I'm not sure I did. "I'm grateful for all you've done, Mr. Gannon, but it's time for me to go."

"And if you never intended to travel to San Francisco, then why did you lie to me about it? What possible reason can you offer for that blatant lie, Miss Downing?" he said, raising his voice, his face flushed from booze. I knew that face well. I'd seen it in my father, and I'd seen it in Cliff Prince. I didn't want to say anything else to the man. I was finished.

Gannon swung his fiery gaze toward the marshal. "Did you question her about that, Marshal Vance?"

I spoke up. "I lied because I didn't know you or trust you, Mr. Gannon. I didn't know what you intended to do or what Rosamond might do. Fear and self-preservation were the reasons I lied, and anyone in my situation would have done the same."

"And what if I say that your feeble explanation is nothing more than balderdash!?" Gannon countered.

We stared eye-to-eye.

"Then, I'd say, I don't give a damn what you think," I said sharply. "I want to go home to New York, and that's just what I'm going to do."

Gannon shot the marshal a look. "She's lying. She's hiding something, I know it. I smell it. I feel it. She's after something."

"I'm not," I protested. "I'll leave tomorrow, and you'll never see me again."

He took two threatening steps toward me, jabbing a finger at me. "No, you will not leave. I'll tell you when you can go! This is my house, and you will do as I say!"

Marshal Vance said, calmly, "Mr. Gannon, Miss Downing is not a prisoner. She is not charged with any crime, and she is free to go as she wishes."

Gannon's stormy eyes widened as his face strained to understand. And then the dawn of his worst fear tightened his features. "Wait a minute here. I know what's going on! You want the woman for yourself, don't you, Bryce Vance? Yes, I saw it at dinner. I saw the two of you, whispering and plotting. I'm not a fool, you know."

Marshal Vance dropped his voice, speaking in a firm tone. "Mr. Gannon, thank you for a pleasant evening. It is getting late, and it's time I started for home."

I whirled to face the marshal and blurted out, "Take me with you!"

The room fell into an icy, hostile silence.

John Gannon finally spoke, his voice low and strident, the note of a threat in it. "Take the trollop with you, Marshal. Take this low, flimflam woman and get her out of my sight. Take her and leave my house! Leave this instant! I can't stand the sight of her!"

Gannon turned on his heel, marched to the door and stopped, not turning around. "But I warn you, Miss Downing, I will not be mocked. You have not seen the last of me."

When he was gone, I stared at the far wall, stunned, my breathing coming fast. A log shifted in the fireplace, and it hissed and popped, drawing the marshal's eyes.

"Mr. Gannon has had a glass too many. By morning, he will be himself, I suspect."

We stood there, awkwardly.

I found my shaky voice. "I guess I shouldn't have been so impulsive, but..." I shrugged a shoulder. "Can I go with you, Marshal? I don't think Mr. Gannon will be himself in the morning, and I don't want to be here in the morning."

The marshal cleared his throat, and I could see he was suppressing a smile. "Well, Miss Downing, it seems that you are taking me up on my offer to stay in Denver, after all."

"Yes, I guess I am. Did you come on a horse? I mean, will I have to ride a horse?"

The marshal smiled. "No, ma'am, I came in a one-horse open sleigh."

I almost blurted out a laugh, thinking of the Christmas song *Jingle Bells*. "I'll pack my trunk. It won't take long."

"Miss Downing, there will be no room in the sleigh for the trunk. It will have to be brought tomorrow."

I thought about it. I just wanted to get out of there. "Okay... fine."

"Of course, you will need some time to pack a few necessary items."

I heaved out a sigh, my head spinning. "Yes... I won't be long."

Then I thought, *What about clothes? What about the cash and jewels? What about Tara? I couldn't leave Tara to those vultures, could I?*

CHAPTER 32

M arshal Vance waited in the library, while I bounded up the stairs to my room. Thankfully, Alice arrived soon after, her face alive with questions, but she didn't say anything.

I asked her to pack the trunk with the underwear and dresses I'd come with. For seconds, she stood staring at me with blinking eyes, and then I told her I was leaving.

"Leaving, Miss Adams?"

"Yes, Alice. I am, and as we say where I come from, I'm like, totally outta here!"

"I don't understand, Miss Adams."

I put my hands on my hips. "I'm sorry, Alice, I don't have time to explain. I'm not the woman you think I am, and Mr. Gannon wants me out of the house. Can you please start packing? I'm going to stay in Denver for a few days, and I'll have to find someone to bring the trunk tomorrow. There's no room in Marshal Vance's sleigh for it, and he's downstairs waiting for me."

Alice's face, which had always been under control, came apart. Her mouth fell open, and her eyes were amazed. "The Marshal, Miss Adams?"

"Yes, I'm leaving with him. While you pack, I have to run upstairs and talk to Tara."

Alice's head lowered in dazed obedience, and then she moved to the chest of drawers to start packing.

I slipped inside the closet, grabbed the purse that held the cash and the jewels and stuffed the thing into my hidden dress pocket. For now, I'd keep all of it, and later, find some way to get the rest to Thomas and Rosamond.

I hurried across the room to the door and called out over my shoulder, "I'll be back in a few minutes."

The adrenaline was pumping through me like crazy, as I rushed down the hallway to the stairs and ascended to the fourth floor. I gently knocked on Tara's door and waited, fighting for calm.

The door slowly opened, and Hilda's sleepy eyes peered out from a dark room. "Yah... what is it, Miss?"

"I need to speak with Tara."

"Tara? Tara not here."

"Is she still working?"

"Not working. Not here. Gone."

I stiffened. "What do you mean, Tara's gone?"

And then I remembered. Tara hadn't shown up that morning to clean my fireplace. I'd been so distracted I'd figured she'd slept in or something. When I'd asked Alice, she'd said Tara was all right as far as she knew, but then Alice always held things back, didn't she?

Hilda sniffed and said, "Yah, gone from this

place. I tell you what I know. Tara gone from here yesterday night. She pack. She gone. She crying. Gone is all I know."

I struggled not to shout at the woman. "Gone where? Tell me!"

"No one talk. Not tell me nothing. I working when Tara gone. Mrs. Grieve don't say and she tell me to shut up or she send me off into the night. So, I shut my lips."

Rage geysered up. I was going to strangle Mrs. Grieve, that witch of a woman. Hilda closed the door, and I stood there, trembling with anger, confused as to what I should do.

At first, I thought I'd march downstairs and demand to see Mrs. Grieve, but then I thought better of it. If Gannon was still around—and of course he was in a drunken state—he might pull a gun on me.

I hustled back to my room and found Alice by the bed, the trunk nearly packed.

I stormed in, my voice tight with emotion. "Alice, where is Tara?"

She didn't look up. "I don't know."

"Tell me, Alice! Please, just stop the bullshit and tell me!"

Alice fixed me with an icy stare. "It's not for me to say, Miss Adams."

"Why are you doing this, and why didn't you tell me this morning? You know I care about Tara. Why? I don't understand you people."

Alice's voice seethed with resentment. "I need my job, Miss Adams. My mother is ill, and my brother has left us for Alaska. I must work, and it has not been easy in this house since you came. Mrs. Grieve is watching us all, looking for the slightest infraction. Honestly, I do not know where Tara has gone, and I have many other important issues that have to be dealt with. So ask Mrs. Grieve, though I can say for certain that she will not tell you."

We stared at each other, neither speaking. Alice was trapped, too. I saw that now, and I softened my voice.

"Alice... I'm sorry. I'm sorry for all I've put you through. I didn't want to come here. It was all a mistake, and I'm sorry. When I'm gone, I hope things will be easier for you."

Without another word, Alice returned to packing the trunk.

I struggled to contain my panic as I realized that Tara being sent away was entirely my fault. It was clear that Mrs. Grieve and John Gannon had orchestrated her departure in retaliation against me. Unfortunately, Tara was the victim.

Where could they have sent her? Had they put her on a train and sent her off to God only knew, to San Francisco or Alaska? How would I find her?

While Alice hastily packed, I paced the room, massaging my forehead, fighting a pounding headache. One thing was certain, I wouldn't give up searching until I found Tara.

I stopped when Alice closed and fastened the trunk. Something was happening to me. I was feeling compassionate and emotional. I wanted to take Alice with me, too. Get her out of that gothic, dysfunctional house, and I knew all about dysfunctional homes and families.

I stopped pacing, faced Alice, and released my breath slowly. "Alice... I truly am sorry. Thanks for everything."

She crossed her arms and stared down at the floor. "I hope and trust all will be well with you, Miss Adams."

"Alice, my real name is Cynthia Downing."

Alice snapped me a look.

"I wanted you to know. Thank you for all your hard work, and I hope your mother gets well soon."

Alice glanced away. "Thank you, Miss Adams... that is, Miss Downing. If there is nothing else, I will leave and tell Mr. Hopkins where your trunk is to be forwarded. And where will that be?"

"I don't know. I suppose the marshal will know, and he will tell Mr. Hopkins."

Alice nodded. "I'll see to it."

I looked down at my very extravagant dress. "If anyone asks, tell them I'll return this dress, the shoes and the hat as soon as I can."

Alice bowed and left the room.

I eased down on the edge of the bed, uncomfortable in the bustle dress and feeling nauseous at the thought of Tara being some place alone with strangers. She must be terrified. What was the matter with these people?

CHAPTER 33

A beautiful, strawberry roan horse named Baron pulled Marshal Vance's one-horse open sleigh.

"I won him in a card game, from a real German Baron," the marshal said. "Baron and me have become fast friends. He knows he's royalty and I'm not, but he doesn't hold it over me so much," he said, with the slant of a grin.

And just like in the song *Jingle Bells*, little, clear ringing bells, tied to Baron's bobbed tail, sang through the snow-white, peaceful night. After the tension of the day and the past few weeks, dashing away from that awful house into a Christmas-card night was like a dream. It helped cool my nerves, distract my worrying mind about Tara, and give me a well-needed mood lift. *I was free! I was free!*

The sleigh glided gracefully on its runners as we journeyed past tall, snowy trees, into the black of night. There was only room for two people, so we had to sit close, which was fine by me. I saw a rifle stored in a leather scabbard attached to the inside of the sleigh, near the marshal's left leg, and

I wondered if he'd ever had to use it when he was sledding.

A thick woolen blanket covered my knees, a woolen cap was tugged low over my ears, and I'd buttoned my coat at the neck. The marshal wore a long greatcoat, a red and black woolen scarf, and a fur hat that made him look a bit Russian.

We moved along the snow-covered road, under a dazzling, diamond-studded sky. I thought the sleigh must have been the sports car of its time. It was small, light, responsive and smooth-riding, as the runners crunched over snow and ice instead of bumping over rocks and ruts, as the wheels of a carriage did. When we crested a hill, the wind whipped across my face, and I felt the sting of snow. I laughed.

"It's a blustery night," the marshal said. "That's a mountain wind, coming from the west."

"I love it. It's a beautiful night," I said, hugging myself against the cold, as we traveled through the drifting, white snow.

"Miss Downing, you understand that the hour is late," Marshal Vance said. "The Hotel Denver is filled with Thanksgiving guests and parties, so you'll have to stay at my place tonight. I trust you are agreeable to that?"

"Isn't there another hotel where I can stay?"

"They are not so respectable, Miss Downing, and they are not as clean as the Hotel Denver, and because of the day, there will be much celebration and imbibing. I fear it would not do for you to stay anywhere else."

"Okay... Then, whatever. I mean cool," I said, unconsciously, because I was nervous and tired.

The marshal passed me a curious glance, but he said nothing.

I asked, "Won't you be needed to... I don't know, be on duty, with the celebrations going on?"

"I have deputies who are more than capable of keeping the peace or tossing any law-breakers into jail for the night."

I inhaled several deep breaths of the cold air and blew them out toward the sky. "I don't care where I sleep as long as I'm out of that house."

"I have four rooms, and you'll have the back bedroom to yourself," the marshal said. "You will have privacy and, I am hopeful, comfort, but you will not have the luxuries of the Gannon Mansion, I'm afraid. There will be no private bath or lady's maid."

"That's fine with me."

"Most women would not say so."

"Well, I like doing things myself."

I looked at him. "And where will you sleep?"

"In the parlor, near the fireplace, is a lumpy old sofa I often fall asleep on. We understand each other. It gives me a crick in my neck, and I give it another loose spring. I suppose you could say it is a marriage of sorts."

I smiled at that. The marshal's sense of humor was quirky, and I liked it.

"Have you ever been married, Marshal Vance?"

"No, ma'am."

"Ever close?"

"Once, right after the war, but I thought better of it when her father fired his Kentucky long rifle at me. The lead ball grazed my left ear, and I ran off and never went back."

It probably wasn't the truth, but I let it go. I thought it ironic that I was with a marshal in 1880, after killing a man in 2022. It was yet another moment that seemed more fantasy than reality, but the sleigh was certainly real, and so was the cold wind biting into my face.

"Tomorrow morning, I will take you to the Hotel Denver," the marshal said. And then he clicked his tongue at the horse, gently tugging the reins as we slid out of a curve. "I will cover your bill."

"You don't have to do that, marshal. I have some money."

"It's all right, Miss Downing. They'll give me a discount. As I said, it's a clean hotel, no fleas or bedbugs, and they've got a new zinc bathtub which the maid will fill for you. I told Mr. Gannon's butler, Mr. Hopkins, to have your trunk sent there."

I glanced over. "Thanks again for getting me out of that house."

His attention was fixed ahead. "Mr. Gannon has been under a strain of late. Losing his wife in that tragic manner was a blow to him, I suspect. And then that business with the mail-order bride further vexed him, no doubt. It seems you were caught in the middle of a bad situation, Miss Downing, and that was unfortunate for all concerned. I'm sure Mr. Gannon will come out right in the end."

I had lots of questions, but I had to be careful. I didn't know how much Marshal Vance truly knew about Gannon killing his wife. He might have been well paid to look the other way.

"Did Mr. Gannon tell you he was looking for the real Rosamond Adams?"

"He did. He's hired two men to find her."

"What will he do when he finds her?"

"I do not know."

"But aren't you afraid he'll, I don't know, kill her or something?"

"At this time, Miss Downing, it does not concern me. I hear the woman is in San Francisco, and she may not be so easy to find. If she is on the run, I'd wager she's clever enough not to remain in San Francisco, and most likely she will make her way north to Sacramento, to Canada, or even to Alaska."

I sat back, wishing I didn't know where Rosamond was. I hadn't seen or talked to Thomas since before my illness, but I'd heard he was still working for Gannon, so he and Rosamond hadn't left for Oklahoma. Obviously, they needed her money and jewels to start a new life.

I was concerned that the longer they stayed put, the greater the odds they'd be found. I was also certain that when Thomas heard I had left the house, he'd come looking for me, and that wasn't a pleasant thought. I had no doubt he'd arrive the next day with my trunk. How much would I give him?

How much *could* I give him? I'd need money to live on until I could find Tara.

When we finally arrived in Denver, Marshal Vance nudged the sleigh down a quiet, tree-lined street with modest, Victorian style homes. We drew up to the curb, and he pointed to a dark house that sat next to other dark houses. I had no idea what time it was.

Inside, the house was cold, with high ceilings, throw rugs on wood floors, and basic furniture. It was definitely a man cave, with nothing of the woman's touch anywhere.

He removed his hat and led the way to the bedroom at the rear of the house. I waited, so cold my teeth chattered, as the marshal built a fire. When the fire caught, crackled and burst to life, the marshal stood, adjusting his fur hat, and turned.

"Warm yourself, Miss Downing, and make yourself at home. I'll be returning the sleigh and Baron to the stable. I want to make sure he gets brushed down and has plenty of hay. There's a bed pan under the bed, the privy is out back, and a pitcher, basin and sponge are over there," he said, pointing to a rickety-looking table near the window. "If you need another blanket, there's a woolen one in that chest at the foot of the bed. It's clean, and so is the bed. The place isn't much to look at, but I like it tidy."

He gave me a little bow. "Oh, also, there's a coal stove in the kitchen, a well pump, and a pot if you want to make yourself some hot tea. I hope you will sleep good, Miss Downing. At first light, I'll knock on your door, and we'll have breakfast at the Hotel Denver. They put on a pretty good breakfast spread for these parts."

After he was gone, I kept my coat and hat on. White vapor puffed from my mouth as all the tension from the day drained from me. I felt exhausted. I moved to the fire, rubbing my gloved hands together, and sat on a stool, letting the crackling warmth seep into my bones. I cast my wary gaze about the simply furnished room, and I thought, *Well, the marshal was right. This place certainly isn't the Gannon Mansion.*

Before climbing into bed, I removed the dress and struggled to remove the tight corset, but I kept on my petticoat, the bloomers, my coat, my hat and gloves. I was cold. With the patchwork quilt pulled up to my chin, I thought, *1880 certainly isn't for the faint of heart, is it?*

There was a lot to be said for central heating, a cellphone, a wide screen TV, and a bathroom with a toilet and hot running water. I was going to have to use the bedpan because there was no way I was going back out into the cold to use an outhouse.

I patted the velvet purse that held the jewels and money. It lay next to my pillow, giving me the feeling of security. What time tomorrow would Thomas Dayton appear? If it wasn't for Tara, I would catch the first train traveling East. But I couldn't leave her. I had to find her, and I *would* find her.

CHAPTER 34

T he marshal knocked on my bedroom door at 7 a.m., and my head came up with a jerk. Where was I? What had happened? What day and year was it? I hated those seconds of jarring terror when I was yanked from a dream, back to 1880 awareness.

The marshal spoke from behind the closed bedroom door. "We should be leaving in a half-hour or so, Miss Downing. I trust that will be to your liking?"

"Yes, Marshal," I called. "I'll be ready."

The fire in the hearth had gone out, so I forced myself out of bed, took off my coat, hat and gloves—which I'd worn all night—and took a shivering, cold sponge bath. By the time I fastened the corset, not so well, stuffed myself back into the dress, and tried to do something with my hair, it was almost eight.

Of course, I had no makeup, so I pinched my cheeks, yawned, and arranged my bangs so that, hopefully, they enhanced my face. As I stared into the tarnished circular mirror hanging on the bedroom door, I winced. Puffy, tired eyes, a very white face crying out for makeup, and droopy lips.

I forced a smile. It didn't help. I looked like a sad party girl who'd been out nightclubbing till dawn.

When I met the marshal in the drawing room, he was crouched, banking the fire. I was too embarrassed to ask him what I should do with the bedpan, but he seemed to read my mind.

"I have a hired woman, Rose, who comes in once a day and cleans the place, so I hope you didn't tidy up."

"A little... I made the bed."

"Well, that's fine. I reckon most women would do that, being more civilized and thoughtful than men."

I looked at my dress. "I guess I'm overdressed for breakfast, with this formal gown. I hope the trunk will come soon."

The marshal stood and dusted off his trousers, scratched his cheek, and then reached for his well-worn, ammunition gun belt and holster. I noticed the bullets in the belt's loops. He buckled the holster around his slim, taut waist under his frock coat, secured it to his thigh, and then slid the revolver into the holster. I'd seen sidearm holsters in movies, but Marshal Vance wore his snug, not loose, as I had seen on the big screen.

And then he reached for a pocket pistol that lay on the mantel, and he stuck that one under his vest in a front pocket.

"What's that?" I asked.

"It's a 5-shot revolver. I can hide it in my palm, and

it can come in handy in a quick fight."

He looked at me, a slight grin forming. "No need to fret about the dress, Miss Downing. It looks real fine on you, and I will be the envy of every man. We do not see many of these dresses in these parts and, if it isn't quite the dress to wear during the day, neither I, nor none of the men in this town, will give a miner's damn about it."

I smiled at him, my eyes lingering on his face, a sting of desire warming my chest, neck, and face. Did he notice? "But won't people talk if they see us together? Especially the neighbors, as we leave the house?"

"It will surely stir up gossip with the church ladies, but that'll be all right. They don't complain about me much as long as I keep the peace. And Denver ain't so highfalutin, so let's not worry about it."

I had the impulse to ask if he would help me find Tara, but I thought it was best to wait. I'd ask him over breakfast.

****

"Marshal Vance... can you help me find someone?" I asked.

He regarded me with interest. "That depends on who it is and if you are honest with me, Miss Downing."

We sat near a tall window at a wooden table in the small, clean dining room of the Hotel Denver. The marshal had already booked me a room for three nights and insisted on paying, telling the friendly, red-bearded clerk that my trunk should arrive shortly.

The dining room had solid wood floors, soft gas lighting and cream-colored walls. Overall, it was a cheerful room, and it was nearly full, mainly with men dressed in dapper suits. All of them gave me the once-over when the marshal and I entered the dining room.

A woman in her fifties, wearing a chocolate brown day dress and lavish, broad-rim hat with ostrich feathers, gave me a cool glance and a lift of her nose, registering her disapproval of me and my inappropriate dress.

Our table had a good view of the street, and I watched the busy foot traffic: a buggy pulled by a beautiful black horse, struggling through the mud and melting snow; and two men on horseback, wearing fur coats and buckskin hats.

A lanky waiter with a black walrus mustache, wearing a long, white apron, appeared at our table and handed us menus.

"How are you, Marshal?" he asked, with a polite smile, keeping his eyes focused on the marshal, waiting for a proper introduction to me.

"I'm just fine, Dan. How's business?"

"It ain't so bad when the womenfolk come in. Keeps the men more civilized. I hear you had your Thanksgiving dinner at the Gannon Mansion."

"Yeah, that's right."

"Must have been quite a spread."

"Yes, a fine dinner it was." The marshal indicated to me with a hand. "Dan, this is Miss Cynthia Downing, come to visit for a few days and stay here at the hotel."

Dan's eager eyes found me, and he gave a quick bow of his head. "Nice to meet you, Miss Downing. We don't get so many of the pretty ladies here in the winter."

I smiled graciously. "Thank you, Dan. It's nice to meet you."

Dan looked at the marshal. "Coffee for you and the lady?"

"Yes, bring a pot, will you, Dan?"

When he was gone, I glanced at the menu, nosing in closer, amazed by the items.

The menu included eggs and omelets, broiled sweetbreads, chicken livers, and salted mackerel. There were broiled lamb kidneys, veal kidneys, bacon, a plain old mutton chop as well as an English mutton chop. I had no idea what the difference was. There was buttered toast, milk toast, cream toast, and a baked apple with cream. You could even order a glass of cream.

"I've never seen a menu like this," I said, curious about the smoked beef in cream and the broiled honey-comb tripe.

"I imagine you're hungry, Miss Downing?"

"Hungary as a bear."

When the coffee pot arrived, Marshal Vance poured my cup half full and then motioned toward the cream pitcher. "Help yourself, Miss Downing."

I did help myself, delighted to have real cream that had no doubt come from the cow that morning. He poured his own cup full and then he lifted his eyes on me.

"Who are you wanting to find?"

"A thirteen-year-old servant girl who worked at the Gannon Mansion. Because of me, they let her go, and no one will tell me where they sent her."

He picked up the cream pitcher and tipped some of the cream into his cup. He stirred, and the coffee turned a rich brown. "And why do you want to find her?"

"When I was sick, very sick, she took care of me, sleeping in a chair by my bed after working her fourteen-hour days. Her name is Tara. She came here on an orphan train and has worked in the Gannon house for about four years. It was the only home she knew after she was put on that train at nine years old. She must be scared to death. I've got to find her."

"And what will you do when you find her?"

"I'll bring her with me, back to New York."

"Miss Downing, pardon me if I'm too forward, but are you a woman of means?"

I barked a laugh, not very ladylike, I realized, after it came out. "No, I'm not."

"Do you have the necessary funds to return to New York?"

I stared down into my coffee and then took a drink. It was rich and bold and wonderful. "Wow! This coffee is awesome!" I said, not caring about the slang.

Marshal Vance smiled. "Are those New York words? Wow? Awesome?"

I seized on that. "Yes... Yes, I guess they are."

He repeated the words, sampling the sounds. "I have never been to New York. As we discussed at the Gannon Mansion, I was not able to find any trace of you or a family. Do you have family there?"

I paused, but then came out with it, so as not to increase his suspicion. "Yes, I do."

"Your parents?"

I hesitated too long, and that wasn't good. I was an experienced liar, and I knew you should never hesitate when questioned by a cop. It implied guilt or a lie.

"... Yes."

"Not sure, Miss Downing?"

"No, no... It's just that... well, we had a disagreement about me traveling alone, that's all."

"They must be worried about you. I'm sure you've sent them a wire to let them know where you are and that you are doing well?"

This cop was asking too many questions, just as all cops do. I wasn't ready for them, so I abruptly changed the subject, another sign I wasn't being truthful.

"Can you find Tara? I can pay you."

And then Dan the waiter returned, and we ordered, me the plain omelet, boiled ham and buttered toast, and the marshal, two eggs, with broiled calves liver, bacon and buttered toast.

The marshal leaned back in his chair, one elbow

leaning on the arm, and it was obvious he was reviewing everything he knew about me. "Are you running away from a husband, Miss Downing?"

"No... no way."

He was about to ask another question when a stocky, young man in his mid-twenties pushed through the swinging doors that divided the hotel dining room from the hotel lobby, and he glanced about, searching. He wore a frock coat, a red bandana tied about his neck, a vest, and a cowboy hat. He had a six-shooter at his waist, and after he spotted Marshal Vance, he came toward us.

When he drew up to our table, he glanced at me, removed his hat and tipped his head, muttering, "Ma'am."

To the marshal, he said, "Sorry to bother you, Marshal Vance, but Thomas Dayton is in the lobby, and he's been at the bottle, and he's cussin' at the clerk. Says he wants to see Miss Downing, and he knows she's here. Says he won't go till he sees her."

I tensed and shot a glance toward the lobby.

The marshal nodded calmly. "Deputy Clay Fallon, meet Miss Cynthia Downing."

The deputy acknowledged me again with a nod. "Hello, ma'am."

My smile was stiff. "Does Mr. Dayton know I'm in here?"

"He knows, ma'am, but I told him to hold his ground until I spoke to the marshal. He wasn't none too happy about waiting, so I'm thinking we should get out there and deal with him."

"Has he brought Miss Downing's trunk?"

"Yes, Marshal, but he won't give it up to the boy who's waiting to take it upstairs to Miss Downing's room. The man's in an ornery mood and says he won't leave until he talks to Miss Downing. He's got the whiskey breath, blurry eyes and shiny face. I don't like it, Marshal."

"Thank you, Clay," the marshal said, placing his cloth napkin on the table and standing up. "I'll talk to him. Please stay here with Miss Downing until I return."

I pushed up. "I'll go with you."

The marshal leveled his eyes at me, thinking about it. "All right, Miss Downing, but let me do the talking, and stay back from the man. Agreed?"

"Yes, okay."

I wanted to go, in case I needed to cover my lies, and to offer Thomas some of the money, but not all of it. With all that Rosamond had done to me, I deserved some of the cash, and I needed it. I also wanted to know if he knew where Tara was.

CHAPTER 35

The modest hotel lobby had one potted palm, a brown carpeted runner that ran from the door to the front desk, and a corner newsstand displaying a dozen or so newspapers.

Thomas Dayton loomed even larger than I'd remembered as he stood near the front desk, beside the trunk. If Marshal Vance stood over six feet tall, Thomas was at least six-feet-three inches tall, and he was at least thirty pounds heavier than the marshal.

The frightened desk clerk had backed away from the lobby desk, standing in front of the betasseled, metal room keys that hung on a wood panel.

Since our first meeting, I had sensed that Thomas, for all of his "ah shucks" polite manner, was always perilously close to violence, just waiting for a fight. In the bright light of day, I could see that his eyes were red-rimmed and bloodshot, from booze and probably from lack of sleep.

When he saw me, his eyes filled with a gleaming hatred that stopped me in my tracks. I was standing near the swinging doors to the dining room, and I took a step back.

Marshal Vance moved toward Thomas, projecting a hard, brusque confidence. "Hello, Thomas. What's this about?"

Thomas pointed an accusing finger at me. "She knows what it's about, all right. She ain't who you think she is. She ain't what anybody thinks she is."

The marshal's sharp stare didn't leave Thomas' face. "Suppose you tell me why you're here, Thomas, so we can straighten it out and you can get back to your work and we can get back to our breakfast."

Thomas carefully pulled a rolled, lumpy cigarette from his left coat pocket. He struck a match across the lobby desk and lifted it to his cigarette, cupping the match in his left hand. He drew deep and then exhaled, taking his time.

Marshal Vance was wary, with an eye on the man and the room, in case one of Thomas' friends was hiding with a weapon.

"I'm waiting, Thomas," Marshal Vance said. "You talk now, or you walk out, get into your buckboard and ride back to the Gannon Mansion."

Thomas glared at me. "You need to be talking to that piece of calico over there."

"I'm talking to you, Thomas, and only you. Now, get it talked out, or get out of town."

Thomas took another drag on his cigarette, tossed it on the floor and crushed it out with the toe of his muddy boot.

He stared at me with a cold, entranced anger. "She's dead, no thanks to you. Died of the fever in the middle of the night. Couldn't do nothing to save her."

My breath caught. Rosamond was dead?

"Who died of the fever, Thomas?" the marshal asked, his eyes steady, his voice even.

"That gal over there knows, all right. You ask *her*, 'cause she knows all about it."

Thomas pointed another threatening finger at me. "We waited for you. We was ready to go, and we waited for you. Then I hear you was gone, leaving us with nothing! Rosamond suffered over that. It took the strength and the hope from her. It took the fight and the very life from her!"

Marshal Vance flipped me a quick glance as Deputy Fallon took a few steps closer to Thomas, his palm resting on the stock of his holstered revolver.

Thomas noticed the deputy, and he noticed Vance's careful side-glance, searching for a trap.

"I'm playing a lone hand, Marshal. Ain't nobody with me. That I swear."

Marshal Vance's voice rose in tight irritation. "Say what you've come to say, Thomas, then git! It's the last time I talk."

I broke in. "When did she die?"

"I told you. Last night, but it don't matter, now, does it? I said what I said. She went in the dead of night, and I buried her under the trees where the ground wasn't so frozen."

I took a step forward. "What about Tara? Where is Tara?"

Thomas snorted like an angry horse. "Don't know

nothing about where Tara went, and I don't care! She weren't nothing to me."

"What is the dead woman's name, Thomas?" the marshal asked, his eyes on Thomas' shaky hands.

Thomas' eyes misted with tears, but he angrily swiped them away. "Rosamond Adams. The true Rosamond Adams, and not this lying and cheating woman. Rosamond was going off with me," he said, his voice cracking with emotion. "We was going to run for it and make a good life... make something of my life."

Marshall Vance snapped me a side glance, not taking his full attention away from Thomas. "Did you know about this, Miss Downing?"

"No... I didn't know she'd died, but Thomas told me he'd found her."

Vance's full attention returned to Thomas. "Where did this Rosamond expire? Where was she hiding out?"

"At one of Gannon's hunting lodges, out near Pine Bluff."

"Does Mr. Gannon know that the woman is dead?"

"No, and I won't tell him, and nobody else will, unless you tell him, Marshal. And if you tell him, I say he'll have his hired guns with him when he comes into town. He'll be feeling wronged, and maybe he'll be blaming you, Miss Downing, and maybe you, too, Marshal."

The curious dining room crowd had left their tables and crowded into the lobby, hanging back next to the wall. When a patron tried to enter the lobby from the entrance to the hotel, Deputy Fallon waved him off with a warning stare, and then he shouted at the buzzing crowd, "Git back into that dining room!"

The jittery crowd clambered back through the swinging doors, muttering, tossing glances over their shoulders.

Thomas' cold gaze turned back to me, and he rubbed a fist along his unshaven jaw.

"But this scheming gal knew what we were waiting for, didn't you, Miss Downing?" he said, his voice gaining strength and force. "And I hear you gave poor Mr. Gannon the mitten, and he's plenty sore about it. He's been kissing a bottle of whiskey ever since you left, and he ain't none too happy about you neither, Marshal, 'cause he's got it in his head that you stole something that was his. And we know that Miss Downing favors Gannon's wife, don't we? Okay, well, I don't give a damn about any of you. Now, I just want what's mine, so I can ride out and not look back on this hell of a place."

I was shaken, but I recovered, standing firm. "Everything that was in the trunk was Rosamond's, Thomas, not yours."

He angrily thumped a fist into his chest. "It's mine, now, ain't it!? Didn't I sweat for it? Didn't Rosamond promise it to me? Didn't I pay thirty dollars for a horse for her, when I only make twenty-five dollars a month? And I searched that trunk and there ain't no money and no trinkets in there, so you must have them."

"All right, Thomas. Fine. I'll give you half of everything. That's fair."

Thomas launched himself toward me, hands gripped into fists, but the marshal stepped in. Thomas went lunging and swinging at Marshal Vance, trying to land a roundhouse punch on his jaw, but Vance went under the swing, his movements perfectly timed.

As Deputy Fallon pulled his revolver, Thomas took another wild swing at Vance, but he blocked it, his face hard and fierce. Vance's blow to Thomas was quick and vicious, his rock fist landing on Thomas' left jaw. The marshal hooked short and hard, and followed it with a smashing elbow to Thomas' nose, which squirted blood. Thomas stumbled backwards, dazed and wounded. He stared wildly for a moment, staggered, then dropped to his knees, wavering.

"Get the cuffs on him!" Vance ordered, his hands still clenched into fists. Deputy Fallon holstered his revolver and crouched beside Thomas.

It happened in a split second. Thomas cocked, then jammed an elbow into the deputy's stomach. The air burst from Fallon's lungs and as he bent forward, Thomas leaped to his haunches and punched the Deputy into the face, sending him sprawling, crashing to the floor.

With lightning speed, Thomas whirled to his knees, pulled a pistol from his belt, and squeezed off a shot at the Marshal.

Vance jerked to his right, pulled his 5-shot revolver, aimed and fired two shots, just as Thomas fired his last. Struck in the chest, Thomas jerked stiffly, swayed, then toppled to his left, dead, one leg twisted under the other.

I'd never seen anything like it, and it shook me to my soul. I'd seen fights in jail, and even been in a few, but the close, brutal fight and death I'd just witnessed would stay in my memory forever.

Vance crept gingerly to Thomas. He stood over him, keeping his revolver pointed at his head, and dead, staring eyes, and then kicked Thomas' pistol away to the other side of the room.

The marshal released a weary sigh and lowered his revolver. "There was no cause for that, Thomas. None at all."

Deputy Fallon climbed to his feet, dusted himself off and replaced his hat, moving to Vance's side.

"Are you all right, Clay?" Vance asked, not taking his attention from Thomas's dead body.

Clay Fallon stared down at Thomas and shook his head. "Why did he do that, Marshal? It weren't like him to pull a trick like that."

"He wasn't in his right head today, Clay," Marshal Vance said, as he touched his left arm and winced.

Fallon noticed. "Are you shot, Marshal?"

"Just a nick from his first shot. It ain't nothing. I'll wrap it back at the office and have the doc look at it later."

Marshal Vance returned his 5-shot to his pocket and turned to me with a cold stare. "Miss Downing, you go back inside and have your breakfast. We'll talk later."

When I reluctantly returned to the table, my breakfast was waiting for me, but I wasn't hungry. Because of me, Tara was gone, and Rosamond and Thomas were both dead.

Okay, well, maybe I wasn't responsible for Rosamond's death, but if I hadn't come along, perhaps things would have been different. Perhaps Rosamond and Percy would have made it to San Francisco and lived happily ever after. I didn't think so, but it was possible, wasn't it?

As I sipped coffee and nibbled the toast, all the eyes of the room were stuck to me. I had become infamous, and I suspect I hadn't helped Marshal Vance's reputation either.

Surely, Mrs. Gladys Frome, the woman I'd met in the Western Union office, had spread the word that I was John Gannon's mail-order bride.

So these people were surely asking, what was I doing sleeping at the marshal's house, having breakfast with him in a formal dinner gown, and then getting him involved in a gunfight in the hotel lobby, where Thomas Dayton had been shot and killed? It didn't look good. Not good at all. What would John Gannon do when he heard about it?

I shrank a little in my chair. *What weird shit had tossed me into this time, and into this mess, and what were my choices?*

I had to find Tara and grab a train out of Denver before Gannon rode into town looking for me. And he would come. No doubt about it. Someone in that hotel crowd had heard that Rosamond was dead, and they would tell him. Yeah, no doubt.

CHAPTER 36

For the rest of the day, I didn't leave my hotel room. I took a bath in the zinc bathtub, which was pure heaven, and over-tipped the quiet teenage maid who brought ten buckets of hot water that she'd heated on the downstairs kitchen stove. It was humbling to see how hard the people of this time had to work, both young and old.

As the hot water seeped into my bones and relaxed my tense muscles, I closed my eyes, willing my brain to erase the violence I'd seen, and not to think about Thomas' dead body, and Rosamond buried alone where no one would find her for years. Seeking escape, I sank further into the tub, drifting in and out of sleep.

By the next morning, a Saturday, I had a plan. I'd awakened deep into the night with a face staring back at me from a half-remembered dream. It was Dr. Broadbent!

After washing my face in the basin and brushing my teeth with horsehair and agave bristles attached to an ivory handle, I slipped into one of Rosamond's two-piece day dresses, a reddish-brown bodice and skirt made of soft, lightweight silk. The low-heeled, matching shoes were not a great fit, but then none of the shoes I'd worn had fit well.

After piling my hair on top of my head and pinning it as Alice had done, I reached for the modest-looking, chocolate-brown felt hat and put it on, staring at myself in the mirror. Even in the morning light, it was depressing to think of Rosamond being dead and buried out in the middle of nowhere. She didn't deserve that, no matter what she'd done to me.

And it felt weird to be wearing one of her dresses, but I had nothing else to put on. I couldn't buy a stylish dress at the local department store because they didn't exist. Mail-order catalogs were available, and I'd seen shops advertising skilled seamstresses able to create the latest fashions, but they were expensive, and I didn't plan to stay that long. And, of course, there was no online shopping.

Being nervous about showing my face in the dining room, I removed the hat, left the room for the hallway, and found a maid cleaning a room down the hall, and ordered breakfast from her. The busy maid wouldn't meet my eyes, a sure sign that the entire town was gossiping about me.

After gobbling down an omelet, toast and ham, and tossing back two cups of coffee, I was ready. Checking myself in the mirror one last time, I hunched into my coat, adjusted the hat, took a deep breath and left the room.

I descended the broad stairs as butterflies

fluttered in my stomach, in my chest, and in my head. I had no idea what to expect after what had happened yesterday.

The desk clerk saw me, and he dropped his gaze, and his still hands suddenly went into frenetic motion, reaching for keys and then rustling through papers. That wasn't a good sign, was it? Nevertheless, I strolled over.

"Good morning, sir. Would you happen to know where Dr. Broadbent's office is?"

I heard murmuring conversations coming from the dining room, and I was aware of a man standing at the newsstand, reading a newspaper. He was bearded and middle-aged, dressed in a snazzy brown suit and puffing on a stinky cigar.

After I spoke, I heard the crinkling newspaper, and I knew he was staring at me.

The clerk's eyes remained lowered, as he cleared his voice and spoke. "You'll find Dr. Broadbent at his home, on Alcott Street. Out the front door, turn right and walk two blocks. Turn left at the barbershop. Walk another two blocks. The doctor's house will be on your left. It's a brick house. You'll see the sign out front."

"Thank you, sir," I said pleasantly.

As I passed the newsstand, I glanced at the *Denver Courier* and read the headline.

SENSATIONAL GUNFIGHT OVER
WOMAN IN HOTEL LOBBY!
Marshal Vance Shoots Straight and True!

I stopped dead in my tracks and gawked. I, of course, was the woman. Great! I didn't want to read the article.

The man next to me removed his bowler and said, in a low, smooth voice, "Good morning, Miss. It's a fine day. You seem to be quite alone. Shall I accompany you?"

"No!" I said sharply, and left him, pushing through the front door and out onto the wooden sidewalk. I walked fast, following the desk clerk's directions, keeping my head down. Coming toward me were two shabbily dressed miners in floppy hats who made lewd comments and whistled. A tall, thin man, wearing a top hat, drifted by without a glance. He reminded me of Abraham Lincoln, who had been assassinated in 1865, not so long ago.

I stepped around heavy barrels and burlap sacks, and a young couple brushed by me, their expressions troubled, their conversation tense. Both looked bone weary and thin, and their clothes were loose and worn.

The sun slipped in and out of white clouds, the shops were busy and loud, and a young boy and girl fought over a piece of stringy licorice, he slapping at her grabbing hands and she fighting back, shouting.

As I passed a café, it smelled of bacon, coffee and sawdust. Buggies and horses were tied to hitching rails in front of the General Store, and the streets were a tangle of horse and buggy traffic, mud, melting snow, and horse and dog manure, filling the chilly air with disgusting smells. It wasn't romantic, like in the movies.

I found Alcott Street, a lovely, quiet street, with two and three-story Victorian style homes in a variety of colors, blue and white, yellow and cream, and deep red and brown.

Dr. Broadbent's house was an attractive, three-story, red brick Victorian, with a pitched roof, turrets and gables. Two tall, graceful pine trees were sprinkled with snow and a signpost on the front lawn held a green, hinged, rectangular sign that read HARLAN BROADBENT, M.D.

I climbed the stairs, crossed the porch and stood before a beautiful, deep red, oak door, the entire top half patterned in stained glass. I gave the decorative doorbell a turn and heard a soft ring.

A moment later, the door opened, and a middle-aged maid appeared, wearing a black-and-white uniform.

"Good morning, Miss."

"I'm here to see Dr. Broadbent. Is he in?"

"Do you have an appointment, Miss?"

"No, I don't. I'm not sick or anything, I just need to speak with him. It's very important, and if you tell him Miss Adams is here, I think he'll agree to see me."

The maid lowered her eyes. "Come in, Miss Adams. I will ask the doctor."

I was led into a gorgeous parlor with peach and white colored walls, glass-enclosed bookshelves, an ornate, black marble fireplace and an opulent chandelier. The thick carpet had a red and brown pattern. Two magnificent red sofas faced each other across a wide room, which included a white, marble-topped, clawfoot coffee table, and two side tables featuring red and green floral oil lamps.

I sat on one of the tufted sofas and waited, literally twiddling my thumbs and staring into the warming fire.

Ten minutes later, Dr. Broadbent entered the parlor, wearing his wire spectacles, a fine dark suit, white ruffled shirt, and royal blue string tie. His short, gray beard appeared freshly trimmed, but his mustache was bushier since the last time I'd seen him.

I stood, and he straightened his spine, cleared his throat and looked at me warily.

"Good morning, Miss Adams. To what do I owe this visit?" he asked, staring at me with the stern eyes of a warden.

"Good morning. Thank you for seeing me, Doctor. I won't take up much of your time."

He turned to the French doors, closed them, and then faced me with an agitated, impatient manner.

"After what I read in the paper this morning, I should have you escorted to the door. You should not have been allowed into my house. No, not at all. Now, if that is too frank for you, then so be it."

CHAPTER 37

We stood in Dr. Broadbent's parlor, and the silence began to hurt.

Finally, he spoke, his voice low and edgy. "I don't have much time. Please get on with it."

"Yes, thank you, Doctor."

He gestured with a hand. "Sit down."

I sat, and he lowered himself on the opposite sofa, folding his hands in his lap. Despite his obvious negative opinion of me, for whatever reason, I trusted the man, and I liked him, and I wanted him to approve of me and like me. Why? I sensed kindness in him, and that's why I'd come to tell him the truth.

"I am waiting, Miss Adams. I have a patient in twenty minutes."

I nodded and sat up. "Yes... Okay, then I'll be quick, and I'll be direct, so I won't waste any of your time. First, I'm not Rosamond Adams. My real name is Cynthia Downing."

He arched an eyebrow. But that was it. He didn't move or say anything.

And then I leaned forward and told him the entire

story, except for the little saga about time travel. I was so engrossed that I lost track of the time, and when the mantel clock chimed eleven times, I glanced at it. I'd been talking for fifteen minutes, and I still hadn't told him why I'd come.

Dr. Broadbent pursed his lips, removed his spectacles and looked away toward the fireplace. He stood up, faced the fire, and placed his hands behind his back.

"I suspected something, Miss Downing, but I will admit that, in my wildest dreams, I could have never conjured up anything like what you have just told me."

He turned to me, replaced his spectacles and said, "But I will say that I knew there was more to you than met the eye."

I said quickly, "Mr. Gannon wanted me to continue using Rosamond's name so he wouldn't look bad. He didn't want the town to know he had been swindled by the actual Rosamond."

The doctor nodded and nodded, and nodded. "Yes, well, I suppose it was a reasonable request for Mr. Gannon, under the rather disagreeable circumstances."

Dr. Broadbent didn't look at me. "I read the papers this morning. Has this Rosamond woman fled for her life, or is she deceased?"

"She's dead… Thomas buried her."

Dr. Broadbent released a heavy sigh. "And now poor Thomas Dayton is dead as well, shot dead by the marshal and, according to the account in the morning paper, you were present?"

"Yes. I was."

"It's a sad business, Miss Adams..." He stopped and corrected himself. "Excuse me, Miss Downing. And I hear, from a source, that Mr. Gannon feels betrayed by all."

"I didn't betray him."

Dr. Broadbent returned to the sofa and sat down heavily. "Your resemblance to Marie Gannon is somewhat exaggerated, so I believe, but Mr. Gannon sees you in her, and I have learned during my many years of treating patients that we often see in others what we wish to see. Mr. Gannon sees in you the ghost of his late wife, whom he loved deeply, and no one will dissuade him of that impression, I'm afraid."

I shouldn't have said it, but the words just came tumbling out. "Thomas Dayton told me that Mr. Gannon caught his wife with one of the grooms in the carriage house and he killed them both. He shot the groom and strangled his wife, placing her body to make it look like she was thrown by her favorite horse."

Dr. Broadbent fixed me with a hard stare and his jaw clenched, and his chin lifted in shock. "What are you saying? How dare you repeat such lies!"

I swallowed. "Thomas said he saw the whole thing."

Dr. Broadbent shot up and ripped off his spectacles. "I will not stand here and listen to such blatant lies. I will never believe nor countenance your slanderous drivel! You, young lady, have been a thorn in the side of the good and generous people at the Gannon Mansion, and now you have brought scandal down on this town, bringing dark lies and death. I ask you now to leave my house this instant, and don't ever return, or I will have you thrown out!"

His outburst stunned me, but it didn't stop me. What made me say it, I don't know, but I pushed to my feet, standing erect, ready to fight. "Dr. Broadbent, did you examine Mrs. Gannon's body at any time after the horse threw her?"

Dr. Broadbent's mouth twitched. He turned toward the fire, and then he shrank a little. He turned back to me, blinked several times and lowered his voice, struggling to keep his emotions under control. "What are you saying?"

"I think you know, Doctor. I don't think Thomas Dayton made it up. He had nothing to gain by telling me."

Dr. Broadbent stared down at the carpet. When he spoke, it was in a low, worried tone. "I must say, in all candor, that I did not examine Mrs. Gannon's body. I arrived at the mansion, but Mr. Hopkins, who told me Mr. Gannon did not wish to see me or anyone else, turned me away. He conveyed to me that the country doctor, Mathias Hobbs, had examined Mrs. Gannon's body and he'd determined she'd broken her neck when thrown from her horse. But Mathias is a horse doctor, an animal doctor. I let it stand because of Mr. Gannon's wishes to be alone and to mourn in silence. But I should have insisted," he concluded with a regretful shake of his head. "Yes, I should have insisted I see Mrs. Gannon's body."

Dr. Broadbent was silent for a time while he pondered, while he picked a piece of lint from his frock coat and then, once again, put on his spectacles.

He studied me. "I heard rumors, of course, but then one always hears rumors in a town like this, where there is so much ill will over wealth, and progress, and land."

With my hands at my side and in a low voice, I hoped my expression projected sincerity. "Dr. Broadbent, I'm leaving town just as soon as I can. I never wanted to be here. I never wanted any part of Rosamond's con job, and I certainly never wanted Rosamond and Thomas to die. And I never, ever, wanted to be John Gannon's mail-order bride, or any other kind of bride. I came here to speak to you for one reason."

The doctor seemed to brace himself against the words that were to come.

"Dr. Broadbent, do you remember Tara, the thirteen-year-old servant girl you treated at the Gannon Mansion?"

He gave me a concentrated stare, and then nodded.

"Because of me, because I insulted her, Mrs. Grieve either fired Tara or she sent her away. I have to find her. You told me you have two daughters. Can you imagine either of them out in the world, orphaned, with no family or friends, and maybe homeless?

She could be working in some dirty hotel, or God only knows where, with no one to look out for her and help her. Please, is there any way you can find out what happened to Tara or where she was sent? When I find her, I'll take her with me on the first train back East, and you'll never see me again. Please, can you help me?"

CHAPTER 38

Back in my hotel room, I sat on the edge of the double bed and stared ahead at the lemon blossom wallpaper. I'd left Dr. Broadbent in a brooding, anxious mood. At the front door, he'd said, "I will do whatever I can to find this unfortunate young girl, Miss Downing, but I can't promise anything."

As an afterthought, he'd said, "Miss Downing, have you told Marshal Vance about what Thomas Dayton allegedly witnessed?"

"No... Should I?"

The doctor scratched his beard, his sad eyes coming to mine. "There is no evidence, is there? None whatsoever. Now that Thomas is dead, it would be only hearsay, your word as an outsider against Denver's own, John Gannon. No, Miss Downing, I would advise against revealing what Thomas communicated to you. I believe we have trouble enough without adding to it."

A knock on my hotel room door brought me to my feet. "Yes?"

It was a young maid with a high-pitched voice. "Pardon me, Miss, but Marshal Vance is downstairs in the lobby, and he wishes to speak with you."

I felt a twist of angst. I hadn't seen him since the shoot-out with Thomas Dayton the day before.

"Okay... Thank you."

I went to the oval wall mirror, checked my face, finger-placed a loose strand of hair, and turned to the door. What was it with attraction? In the midst of chaos, my tummy did a little flip, thrilled to be seeing Bryce Vance again. My neck and face flushed, and I felt an adrenalin rush just like a sugar donut, coffee-kick.

The fantasy of kissing the marshal brought heat. I didn't want it to, but it did, and what could I do about it? Would the marshal take me to his office and question me again? I could handle that. I was okay with it. I could flirt, bat my eyes and play the victim. I was good at that. Men liked it. At least they did, way out in the future.

Maybe we'd return to the dining room and have lunch; finish the meal we'd never been able to complete because of Thomas.

I descended the stairs with my shoulders back and head held high. He was waiting for me by the front desk, standing tall and dark, seething with the sexy looks of a Hollywood bad-boy movie star. He moved away from the desk and met me, removing his black cowboy hat and offering a little head bow.

"Good afternoon, Miss Downing."

"Hello, Marshal."

I waited while he cleared his throat, glanced about self-consciously, and then looked at me with a hint of a smile. "I was wondering if you would accompany me on a buggy ride so we can talk. The day is bright, the sun warm, most of the snow has melted, and I thought it might be pleasant."

I stared at him. Had he just asked me out on a date? "Well... Yes, Marshal Vance, I would love to go for a ride."

He smiled his satisfaction and waited for me while I returned to my room for my winter coat, hat, and gloves.

The two-seat buggy, with wooden spoke wheels, was waiting outside the hotel, the horse tied to a hitching rail. Marshal Vance helped me up onto the metal step and into the buggy. The wooden seat was hard, but the marshal had added a cushion to make it more comfortable.

He untied the horse and climbed up beside me. He shook the reins, clicked his tongue, and the horse trotted off down the muddy street, falling behind a black carriage.

The sky was a deep blue, and the dazzling, afternoon sun cast a glow over the town, enhancing it. For the first time, I thought Denver was appealing, especially as I gazed into the distance to see the snow-topped mountains.

As the city faded behind us, we moved along a dirt road that led between tall spruce and pine, and I presented my face to the sky, feeling the welcomed sun, inhaling the scented, pine breeze.

Marshal Vance said, "Rosie here is a fine horse, a worker, unlike her sister, Bailey, who's not much for pulling a buggy. Rosie is happiest when she is working, and nothing makes her happier than trotting along outside town. I think she's a country girl at heart."

"She's pretty. Can I say pretty about a horse? To a horse?"

"Of course you can, Miss Downing. Rosie knows what pretty means, and she responds as any woman would do. She adjusts her fashionable hat and smiles modestly."

I laughed, and the marshal glanced over, flashing a slanted grin.

"Miss Downing, if I may say so, you have an engaging laugh, and it is most attractive."

"Then I will laugh all the way to wherever it is we're going. By the way, do you have a place in mind, or are we just out for a Saturday ride?"

"Oh, I have a destination for us, all right. We are going to travel a little over a mile down this old, muddy road to have lunch. Have you had lunch?"

"No, I haven't," I said, looking about. "I don't see anything but trees and mountains and snow. Where are we going to have lunch?"

"Lunch will be with Tappy Guff."

I glanced at him, unsure of what he'd said. "I'm sorry, did you say, Tappy?"

"Yep. Tappy Guff. He runs a food shack out this way."

I couldn't process it. Food shack? Was that a kind

of 1880 diner out in the middle of nowhere, because everywhere I looked was nowhere?

"Tappy makes the best corn pudding and camp bread in a hundred miles. I think you're going to like his food."

"Okay... where is this shack? I mean, there's nothing around here."

Marshal Vance laughed. "Old Tappy comes from someplace in Mississippi, but I don't recall the town. He fought for the Rebs in the war, and he was engaged in some pretty hard fights."

"The Civil War?"

"Yes, the Civil War."

"But didn't you fight for the Union? Weren't you a Yankee?"

"Yes... but that was a long time ago, Miss Downing, and out here is a new world with new lands and new prospects. Old Tappy came out here in search of gold and silver. He didn't find much, but he learned that men needed to be fed, and his mamma was a darn good Southern cook, and she taught him. So when cattlemen started trailing Longhorns up from Texas to graze on Colorado's open range, and loading them on the trains that run through Denver, Tappy... well, he built himself a home and a food shack, tapped into a need, and now he makes himself a good bit of coin."

"A real entrepreneur," I said, without thinking.

"Now that's a big Eastern word I've never heard and will never be able to pronounce."

I laughed nervously. "It just means he's a creative

businessman."

"He is that for sure."

To change the subject, I said, "By the way, how's your arm where Thomas shot you?"

"Just a graze shot. It don't amount to nothing, and I'm doing just fine, thank you."

As we bounced along, I adjusted myself on the hard seat. "You said you wanted to talk," I said, curious, wanting to get it over with, so I could relax and have fun.

Marshal Vance kept the reins loose in his hands as Rosie trotted happily, her head gently bobbing, her tail swishing.

"Miss Downing, I am not a diplomatic man, and sometimes that has put me into bad straits with folks. So, I am going to speak frankly to you, and I hope you are agreeable with that."

I pinched the collar of my coat closer to my neck and braced myself. "I like honesty."

"I was certain of that. Now, you are a woman of mystery, and you are a woman who often finds herself in disturbing, and even dangerous, circumstances. Your answers to questions sound confused or suspicious, and you seem to hold much of yourself back, as if you fear your past will come riding down Main Street at any moment and expose your true identity."

I didn't say anything. The less said, the better.

"Do you not have a comment about what I have just said, Miss Downing?"

"No, Marshal, no comment."

"I see. So, you will persist with your mystery?"

"I am who I am, and nothing more."

"Oh, I think you are much more, and that is another reason I wanted us to talk. I am a blunt man, and I am a truthful man, and I have seen life flee into death as suddenly as I have seen the bright sun swallowed by a dark cloud. Time is a rare and fleeting mystery, Miss Downing. One must act when one is compelled to act, or the moment is gone, never to return. Let that moment go, and it is like a dream upon waking. It soon fades, and it cannot be recovered."

He fastened his very dark, and very appealing, and very probing eyes on me. "Miss Downing, I would like to request that you stay in Denver and consider making it your home. I would like you to stay and put down roots. I would like you to stay so that you and me can get to know each other. You are a beautiful woman, and I surmise you are a strong one, unlike any other woman I have thus far met. Simply put, I would like to court you, Miss Downing, but I warn you, I am not practiced at it. I do not have the manners, the education, nor the unlimited funds of John Gannon, but my work is honorable. I am paid well, and I'm respected."

I stared ahead, stunned. I had to do, or say, something. So, unable to speak, I looked at him and managed a quiet smile that, I hoped, said nothing. *Keep the mystery going*, I thought, *until I can think of some way to respond. Keep him off guard.* That's how I'd always been with men. Keep them off-balance.

Now, I was the one off-balance.

Bryce Vance's declaration produced never-before-experienced feelings crashing in at once: a pressure of desire, a confusion of emotions, and a steamy passion. I was suddenly drunk from a boozy cocktail, high and ready for a hot kiss and more, and terrified that fate was about to clobber me on my head with a judge's gavel and toss me back to 2022, where I belonged.

Bryce Vance was a fantasy man from way back there in the past who I couldn't have imagined, a man who pierced my tough skin with his earthy, courageous cool, in a way no modern man ever had.

The thought of touching the marshal's face, of kissing him and sleeping with him, sent my very lively imagination longing to taste a mixed platter of naughty sensual pleasures.

And the temptation of planting myself in 1880 did have appeal, but it was also a crazy idea, and it was very dangerous. John Gannon was out there.

What would I do if I stayed in Denver? Women in this time were subjugated, denied the right to vote and own businesses. They were culturally shoved into subservient positions, their sole function to be a wife and mother, and although I wanted to be a mother someday, I wanted more out of life than just that. There were too many unknowns, and I still had to find Tara, no matter what I decided.

The road grew rough, and we bobbed and thudded along; a front wheel struck a pothole so hard it jarred my eyeballs.

"You are silent, Miss Downing. It seems I have surprised you, and yet, I think we both felt an easy attraction the first time we met inside Western Union."

A herd of deer burst from a grove of trees and went sprinting across the road ahead, retreating up a slope and out of sight. The brief distraction helped to clear my head.

"Marshal Vance…"

"You may call me Bryce, if you wish, Miss Downing."

"Okay, then call me Cindy."

He scratched his cheek and nodded. "Cindy, then it will be. Please continue."

"I was going to say that I'm sure you are aware that most people in Denver think I'm John Gannon's mail-order bride. And that my being seen with you is… what is the word? Scandalous? And the situation was already scandalous, as I learned, since Mr. Gannon paid for Rosamond to come here, to live with him in that house, until he decided about her."

"Yes, I have considered that. All of that."

"And have you also considered that Mr. Gannon is very upset about the fact that he looks like a fool to the people of Denver? And now that Thomas and Rosamond are dead, no one, except Dr. Broadbent, will ever believe I am not Mr. Gannon's true mail-order bride. That is a very real complication, isn't it?"

Bryce turned, his expression defiant. "I don't give a damn what anyone thinks, Cindy, and I will deal with Mr. Gannon, if it ever comes to that."

"Oh, it will come to that, Bryce, and you know it."

He jerked a nod. "Yes... you are right. I know it. But I say, Cindy, that you are the woman for me, and you are a woman to fight for."

Bryce Vance robbed me of speech. I wanted him.

CHAPTER 39

T appy Guff's Food Shack was made of sun-bleached wood, and it looked to me like a good gust of wind would blow it into sticks. It had two sagging windows, a sloping, rusty tin roof, and a leaning brick chimney, where a thin trail of gray smoke curled up and dissolved in the wind.

Bryce parked the buggy near the rear of the shack, next to a wooden hitching post and two tied horses. He helped me down and then, with a nod, acknowledged two cowboys squatting on their haunches near some pines. They wore red bandanas and cowboy hats, one wearing a short woolen coat, and the other a long duster. They ate from tin plates, dunking bread and chomping on cooked beef and beans.

"The place ain't much to look at, Cindy, but as your nose will bear witness, the smells make up for it."

Three dirty-faced men in tattered clothes were seated at a leaning wood table near the entrance. I smelled their rank body odor, and they stared at me as if I was dessert. Bryce waved to them and told me they were prospectors.

"Not so successful, I guess?"

Bryce grinned. "Well, you never know. By tomorrow, one of those boys might be as rich as John Gannon. There's a miner over in Leadville named Horace Tabor, who made a fortune during the silver boom years of 1877–79. I'd wager he has more money than John Gannon himself."

I glanced back at them with a little laugh. "Maybe I should join them."

Inside was a square, smoky room, with a potbelly stove, sloping floors and a slanting ceiling. Three cowboys sat at a farmhouse table made of rough milled spruce, sipping tins of hot coffee, finishing their meal. Their curious eyes lifted on me for a quick look, but then turned down to their food when Bryce put his eyes on them.

"Hello, boys. How's the day?"

One young, hatless and freckled cowboy said, jokingly, "We'll be coming to town later tonight, so don't be tossing us into your jailhouse, Marshal."

Marshal Vance grinned at them, nudging his hat back off his forehead. "I'll be waiting for you and so will my jail, with its hard bed and bad coffee."

They laughed, and one cowboy said, "Hurrah for that, Marshal!"

In the right corner of the room sat a big man with a cowboy hat, a bandito mustache, dark, watchful eyes, and a rifle cradled in his arms. When he saw the marshal, he touched the brim of his hat in a greeting, then leaned back, balancing the chair on its hind legs.

"That's Big Tom Donner," Bryce said, "the watchman for Tappy. He's a dead-eye good shot and a fighter with rock fists."

"So, he's like a security guard?"

Bryce nodded. "Yeah, I suppose you could say that."

In the opposite corner sat a Mexican man wearing a sombrero, strumming a guitar, a tin cup of coffee placed on the floor next to his chair. Curled up next to him was a brown and white dog.

"That's Nugget," Bryce said. "The dog, that is."

I grinned. "I figured."

"I don't know who that Mexican is, but Nugget is a kind of watchdog. He sort of watches things, and then he goes to sleep. Old Nugget and Tappy have been partners for many moons."

"Can I pet him?" I asked.

"I wouldn't. He's snappish."

I glanced at the cowboys. "Do cowboys move cattle in the winter?"

"Not in winter. Cattle drives usually start in the spring."

"What are these cowboys doing, then?"

"They're kept on to keep track of the ranchers' herds and watch for cattle thieves."

I shook my head in wonder. It was like living on another planet.

Tappy, a grizzled, wrinkled and wiry man in his 50s, wore faded overalls, a long, white apron and a bowler. He stood over a black, cast-iron, coal-burning stove, a skillet of crusty bread resting on the side, a pot of beans and ham hocks on the burner.

"Smells good, Tappy," Bryce said. "I've brought a special guest with me, and she's anxious to sample your grub."

Tappy passed us a quick, I'm-not-impressed glance, looked me over twice and then wiped his nose with the back of his hand. "Go on and sit over there, Marshal," he said, in a thick, Southern accent. He nodded to a lone table against the wall. "I'll bring you over what I got and hope the fine lady don't throw it back at me."

Then he went back to work.

"Do you have any corn pudding today, Tappy?" Bryce asked. "I've been bragging about it to Miss Downing here."

"What kind of a danged cook would I be if I didn't have corn pudding? And, anyway, if I didn't cook it every danged day, those cowpokes over there would string me up and feed my carcass to the buzzards. So, yeah, I've got some, all right, and more on the way. Now, you sit yourself down and let me get on with my business."

We sat, and when I coughed from the thin cloud of smoke in the room, Bryce rose, lifted the window a few inches, and returned to his chair opposite me.

I said, "Thank you, sir. You're a gentleman."

Without us asking, Tappy brought two tin cups of fresh, black coffee, set them down before us and left without saying a word.

Bryce blew the steam from his coffee while he

gazed at me. "I know you're troubled by the servant girl, Tara. I did some nosing around here and there and talked to some folks."

I perked up. "And?"

"Nothing yet. I talked to the ticket clerk at the train station, Samuel, thinking he might recall the girl if she was put on a train to somewhere, but he didn't remember seeing her."

"I went to see Dr. Broadbent this morning," I said. "He treated Tara when she was ill, and he said he'd see what he could find out. I'm hoping he'll go to the mansion and ask Mrs. Grieve. If anybody has a good relationship with that woman, I think Dr. Broadbent does."

Bryce ran a hand across his jaw. "Don't count on Mrs. Grieve telling anyone anything. She's as vicious as a hungry wolf and as venomous as a rattler. It's not commonly known, but she still has an eye for John Gannon, and her hatred of Marie was obvious."

I took a drink of the hot, strong coffee, the strongest I'd ever had, and I tasted whiskey. "Is there booze in here?"

"Oh, yes, of course there is. Rye whiskey. It's Tappy's special coffee. Do you like it?"

"Well, it certainly has a kick."

A moment later, Tappy brought the food on dented, round, tin plates, and the aroma was indescribable. The corn pudding was a rich, golden brown around the edges and slightly jiggly in the center. I tasted butter and cream and sweet corn. It was truly awesome, as was the hot skillet bread and the beans and ham hocks.

"This is fabulous!" I said. "Where I come from, Tappy's would be one of the hottest places in town."

"You mean in New York?"

"Yes, in New York."

"And you are truly from New York, Cindy?"

I glanced up. "You doubt me?"

"It's not doubt, exactly. I suppose I want to know you better, and I want you to trust me."

I swallowed a bite of the bread. "Why should I trust you?"

His eyes were bold and then they were soft. "Because I find myself unable to put you out of my mind for any length of time. Because I want to protect you, and I feel the pull of you, and I feel all those things that a man feels when he wants a woman."

I kept eating, not looking up, but feeling his words throb my pulse in a low, sexy drumbeat.

Bryce continued. "I am going to be as honest with you as I have ever been with any woman. I've been alone most of my life, Cindy. I am nearly thirty-six years old, and it had not occurred to me, until I saw you in that telegraph office, that I am lonely, but not lonely for just any woman. I suddenly realize I'm lonely because I have seen you, and talked to you, and been close to you. No, it never once occurred to me that I was lonely. And then, there you were, quite beautiful and fascinating, not words my lips are accustomed to uttering. You have mystery and fight in you, Cindy, and these are qualities needed in this new, Western, spreading-out country."

I brought the tin cup to my lips and hesitated. "You must have many women who bat their bright, Colorado eyes at you, Marshal Vance. You must know you're crazy handsome, and for lack of better words, totally masculine."

"I will not lie about what I have done, Miss Downing... Cindy. I am a man who has often sought the company of a woman, like any man."

I grinned at him. "I'm glad to hear it. I've never been attracted to saints."

"Then are you attracted to me, Cindy?"

My voice was a silky caress. "Yes... Yes, Marshal Bryce Vance, I am, and you know it."

He leaned back with a little sigh of relief. "Then I am pleased that my instincts were right."

"Only pleased?" I smiled flirtatiously.

He reached for his tin cup of coffee and took a generous drink, keeping his warm gaze on me. "I have a cabin. I built it myself. It is private, and it is warm, and it is not so far from here."

My excited gaze traveled over his face. "And I bet you want to show it to me?"

"Yes, Cindy, I do. I want to show it to you, and I want to share it with you."

I smiled, and he returned my smile.

"You do have a way with words, Marshal Vance, and I've always been excellent at reading between the lines. Don't you have to work?"

"If there's any real trouble, Deputy Clay Fallon knows where he can find me. But I don't think there will be trouble at this time of year. In the spring and summer during the cattle drives, yes, but not so much now."

"I'm so glad to hear it," I said, feeling my body heat up.

Marshal Vance kept his eyes on me, and I gave him a teasing smile.

"Can I trust you, Marshal, all the way out there in the wilderness, in a cabin? Just the two of us?"

His eyes shined with playfulness. "No, Miss Downing, I do not for a minute think you can trust me."

"Good... then as soon as we finish this delicious lunch, let's go."

CHAPTER 40

A half hour later, we were back in the buggy, trotting off on a side dirt road with a breathtaking view of towering, snowy mountains on one side and thick groves of glorious trees on the other.

We didn't say much as the sun lowered, the cold wind circled, and the howling sounds of wolves echoed across the land. The road angled left; we rounded a bend, and I saw a single-story log cabin loom in the distance, nestled in firs and birch. Next door was a log barn and a cord of wood, neatly stacked and sprinkled with snow.

"There it is," Bryce said.

"Wow, it really is a log cabin out in the middle of nowhere, isn't it?"

"I wouldn't say this is nowhere, Cindy. The cabin sits near a clear, sparkling stream, and it's tucked away in a forest of magnificent trees, with God's own view of those majestic mountains."

I looked at him, impressed. "You're a poet, Marshal Vance."

He grinned. "And I believe that you are having a jolly old jest at my expense, Cindy."

"Not at all. I think spending time out here would make anyone a poet. I love it."

Bryce tied up the horse, helped me down, and led the way up the four stairs and across the porch to the front door. To our right, firewood was neatly cross-stacked in rows using irregularly shaped logs; to the left, a simple rocking chair sat facing the distant mountains.

Inside the cold cabin was a knotty pine interior, handcrafted windows and doors, and an impressive stone fireplace enclosed by a fire shield. The furniture was solid wood, beautifully handcrafted, with pillows of dark green and rich burgundy. Beside the fire was another rocker, and on two side tables were oil lamps, with a large, mother-of-pearl wall lamp near the front door.

On the wall above the fireplace hung an unexpected sepia photograph in an oval frame, featuring a stern, square-jawed woman in her fifties, with a determined stare and braided hair arranged tightly on the top of her head.

"Who is that?" I asked.

Bryce wandered over, placed his hands into his back pockets, and gazed up at it. "That is my mother, and though she doesn't look to be so friendly in that likeness, she was as kind-hearted a woman as there ever was. My father was killed at the Battle of Cold Harbor in 1864, and she was never quite the same after that."

"Was?"

"My dear mother died of consumption only three

years after that image was composed."

I turned to him. "I'm sorry. You must have been so young when you fought in the war."

"I was, indeed. Just a kid who took too many chances and had more luck than was due him."

"And your father must have been relatively young."

"Yes, I was born when mother was but sixteen and he was seventeen. He insisted on getting into the fight, against my mother's wishes, and I think she never forgave him for it."

"Do you have any brothers or sisters?"

"I have a sister, Lydia, who is married and lives in Indiana with her good husband and four children."

Bryce returned his eyes to his mother's photo. "I think you would have liked her, Cindy. Mother had fight in her, too, as you can see in her eyes. She fought that dreadful disease with all her strength, but when the damned thing won, she just laid back, let go and said, 'It's time for me to see Adam again, and give him the devil's own, for running off to that war and leaving me.'"

I touched Bryce's arm. He looked at my hand and smiled. "I'm glad you came."

"Me, too."

I turned to my left and saw an iron-framed double bed in the back corner, covered by a heavy, patchwork quilt. Opposite the bed was a wood-burning stove, hanging pots and pans on hooks, a wooden kitchen table and chairs placed near a bare window.

"This place is awesome, Bryce. Totally awesome."

Bryce laughed a little. "Awesome? Well, why not awesome? The walls are five-inches thick," he said with pride. "I built it to be simple, comfortable and peaceful, but I didn't build the furniture. That was made by a craftsman in Denver, the best I've seen anywhere."

I sat in the rocker while Bryce made a roaring fire, and within a few minutes, the cabin was warm and cozy.

"So, what do you do here all by yourself?" I asked, gently rocking, while he stood near the fire warming himself.

"I come here to let my mind ease and stretch. I come here to get away from the rough and tumble of the town, and the people."

"So you're a loner?"

"When I can be."

"Have you ever brought anyone else here?"

He studied me while he rubbed his hands together near the fire. "No... I haven't."

I lifted an eyebrow. "Really?"

"Well, bears come wandering in now and then, snooping around, and a bobcat or two has stopped by to say hello, but no humans to speak of."

I looked at him meaningfully. "Then, I'm very... flattered. Why me?"

"I told you. We seemed to know each other at our first meeting."

I couldn't deny it.

"Are you still cold?" Bryce asked.

I faced away. "No. I'm just... I don't know."

"Why did you agree to come, Cindy?"

I ignored the question. "I don't know if I can stay here," I said. "I mean, in Denver."

He stared into the fire for a moment. "Cindy, a woman of class and deportment, as yourself, would do well opening a ladies' shop. I know you'd do well. Denver is growing very fast, and you could grow along with it."

"I'd prefer real estate," I said, staring into the crackling fire. "I like it, and I know I'd be good at it."

Bryce lowered his head. "That would prove difficult."

"Because I'm not a man?"

Bryce sighed. "Men steal land, Cindy, and they fight over land, and they kill for it. It is not a respectable occupation, nor a safe one for a lady, I fear."

I let out a sigh. "And I fear I'm not living at the right time."

"I don't get your meaning, Cindy."

When I looked at him, I really looked at him, as if he were an unsolved mystery, or a fantasy, or some watery vision from a lucid dream. Had I already fallen in love with this guy? There was an easy, electric magnetism between us, a full moon kind of primal attraction that was hot and a little scary. How could I leave this guy? He was everything I'd ever dreamed of, and not dreamed of, because I'd never thought that a guy like Marshal Bryce Vance existed.

A simple movement of his big hand, the tilt of his head as he removed his hat, and the cut of his jaw, all nudged me to be reckless. His wide chest, taut waist, and long, sturdy legs brought the impulse to reach for him, this dream of a man from 1880.

And then he left the cabin for the stable to water and feed the horse, returning about a half hour later.

I'd removed my coat and hat, and I was standing, facing the door, when Bryce entered, shuddering from the cold. My emotions churned, and I felt distant from myself, and I felt disoriented, and I felt fearless, as if time would never own me again. Time was a plastic thing, a malleable thing and, when it was all said and done, maybe it was a false thing.

That sharp thought drove me to step fully into this time—this wonderful moment—and embrace it with radical emotions. To my surprise, I bravely considered the possibility of marrying Bryce Vance.

Yes, I could marry him, find Tara, open a ladies' shop, and live happily ever after in Denver, Colorado, in 1880.

I looked directly into Bryce's eyes as I plotted my next move. And then there was the call of a bird nearby, and Bryce came to me, and our breath seemed loud in that private silence. When we touched, it was natural. We were new lovers, but old soulmates. With my eager fingers, I explored his face, his hot eyes searching my lips and neck, his hands finding my breasts.

His muscled arms wrapped and held me, his kisses brought heat, and his hands, tangling my hair, brought shivering spasms and an urgency to move to the bed.

As we made love, a kind of glory lit up the moments, lit up my emotions and my body. I reached and touched him, and his strong hands and firm control had me gasping, lost in a timeless pleasure. There was heat and rapture, and each intake of my startled breath was sweet, each kiss a brand new thrill.

Bryce Vance had the power and the stamina of a wild thing, but he also possessed a tender grace that ignited my passion, boosted my fantasies, and melted any resistance.

Darkness crept in slowly, and by the time I was aware of it, I awoke with Bryce asleep beside me, our legs tangled, my hair scattered, my body weary from sexy play.

I'd spent my life in the gray areas of love, in the cold shadows of love, and in the dark caves of love, asleep and wanting. I hadn't even been aware of it until Marshal Bryce Vance came along, awakening me from that deep, unhappy sleep into a vibrant world that offered unimaginable delight. A world I'd never experienced and never thought was possible.

But feeling blessed and liberated; feeling in love for the first time, I also felt fragile, and I'd never felt fragile before. Was it fear? Fear of what was to come and what I could lose?

Would I find Tara? Would John Gannon come for Bryce and me and destroy our love before it had a chance to grow?

I lifted on an elbow and, as night settled in, I wanted all the love I felt for Bryce to come bursting out and shower him, to seep into his skin and his heart and the marrow of his bones. When he was a silhouette, I watched him sleep, and I whispered into the darkness.

"Yes, Marshal Bryce Vance, I love you, and I'll marry you."

CHAPTER 41

Four days later, at 9:30 in the morning, the maid knocked on my hotel room door. "Miss Downing, Dr. Broadbent is in the lobby, and he wishes to speak with you."

A jolt of hope drove me to my feet. I'd been at the writing desk, examining Rosamond's jewels more closely, speculating as to how much each piece might bring.

Ten minutes later, I left my room and started downstairs, finding the doctor standing near the newsstand. When he saw me descending the stairs, he walked toward me, his expression grave.

"Good morning, Dr. Broadbent."

"Yes, Miss Downing, good morning," he said, obviously agitated.

He pointed to a golden sofa positioned to the right of the dining room doors, and we went over to it and sat, my eyes immediately coming to his.

"Miss Downing, I have found Tara O'Hanlon."

I sat up at attention. "Where? Is she all right?"

The doctor adjusted his spectacles and then ran a shaky hand over his beard. "She is working as a maid in a hotel in Bart's City."

"Where is that?"

"About twenty or so miles from here."

I heaved myself up. "Okay, I'll go get her."

Dr. Broadbent shook his head, lowering his voice. "Please sit down, Miss Downing. There is more I have to say."

I eased back down, my temples throbbing, my attention acute. "Tell me, is she all right?"

"It's a so-called hotel, owned and operated by Carson Kreet. Marshal Vance knows the man. He used to run a place not far from here until the marshal ran him off."

"Okay... So what is a so-called hotel?"

Dr. Broadbent lowered his eyes. "It is a house of ill fame."

A sickening dread pooled in my stomach, and then a rush of panic. "I've got to get her out of there! Now!"

Dr. Broadbent leaned closer to me, keeping his voice low. "I'm not saying Tara is being... well, abused in that way, but I also cannot say that she is not."

I shot up again. "Just tell me where she is."

"It is not that easy," the doctor said, soberly, his eyes blinking fast.

"Why? Tell me!"

"Please lower your voice and sit down, Miss Downing."

I hesitated, then did so, waiting for his explanation.

"Mr. Kreet is a low ruffian, and the hotel will certainly be guarded by such low men."

"I don't care! I'm going. I'll catch the next train or whatever, carriage, horse, I don't care."

"You must keep your head, Miss Downing."

Rage burned my face. "Did Mrs. Grieve send her there?"

Dr. Broadbent turned his sorrowful head toward the front door. "I'm afraid so."

"I'll kill that woman!"

"Miss Downing," the doctor said, shocked.

"What kind of sick woman is she?"

The doctor raised both hands, like stop signs. "Please, Miss Downing. Keep your wits about you. We must focus all our efforts on securing Tara's release and not waste our time and energy on Mrs. Grieve's despicable character."

I was so angry, I barely heard him. "Was Mr. Gannon in on this?"

"I do not know, and I say, once again, let us not waste our time on those people."

"Are you sure about this, Dr. Broadbent? Absolutely sure?"

"The information came from a dependable source, who is both frightened and wary."

I put a hand to my forehead and massaged it. "Okay, I don't care, I'm going. I've got some money and jewels, and I'll pay the man whatever he wants. I'll give him everything I've got."

Dr. Broadbent raised his narrowed eyes. "And what if he doesn't want money or jewels, Miss

Downing? He is a dark-hearted devil of a man. I treated him once for a gunshot wound."

"Okay, fine, then what the hell will he want?"

The doctor's hard stare said it all.

Of course, if I'd been in my suspicious, jaded mind, I would have realized it right away. I knew what Carson Kreet would want, and even if I gave it to him, it wouldn't be enough. Not with a man like that. I slumped back into the sofa, cursing.

The doctor cleared his throat. "Miss Downing, I will go with you, and I will endeavor to negotiate with the man. He knows who I am, and if I offer him money, Mr. Kreet might consent to let the girl go free without any fuss."

I sat up, anxious and relieved. "When can we go? Let's leave now. I can't stand the thought of her being in that place alone. I can't. It makes me sick, and I hate it! So help me God, I'm going to punch that woman for what she did to Tara!"

"You must calm yourself, Miss Downing. Your anger will not help us or Tara. Your emotion is the reaction of a child. Please!"

I shot him a vicious stare and almost lashed out, but I didn't. He was right. I was acting like a child. I fought to regain control of myself, heaving out a breath, and relaxing my fisted hands.

"All right... All right. Is there a train to Bart's City?"

"Yes, Bart's City is a water stop."

"How long does it take to get there?"

Dr. Broadbent rose. "Because of the rough terrain,

over two hours."

I stood up. "Do you know when the next train is?"

"Yes, I checked the schedule before coming here. The train arrives in Denver at 11:10 a.m. and will arrive at 1:20 p.m. in Bart's City."

I released a grateful sigh. "I can't thank you enough, Doctor, for finding Tara, and for going with me."

"There is something more to be considered," Dr. Broadbent said, as he straightened his silver and blue silk vest. "We should consult Marshal Vance on this matter."

"He's not in town," I said, having already thought about it. "He left early this morning for a ranch up north. A rancher and one of the ranch hands got into a fight and shot each other."

"Then perhaps we should wait?"

I gave an emphatic shake of my head. "No... I can't wait. I've got to catch the next train."

Dr. Broadbent removed a handkerchief from his breast pocket and blotted his damp forehead. "All right, Miss Downing, if that is your wish, then I will meet you on the train platform promptly at 10:45."

CHAPTER 42

I down-dressed for the trip and for Carson Kreet, wearing a frumpy day dress and a flat, dark hat with a wilted embroidered flower that looked like someone had sat on it.

Dr. Broadbent was mildly amused by my outfit and then very restrained as we purchased our tickets and boarded the train, taking our second-class seats.

The train was narrower, dimmer and smellier with cigar smoke than the train to Denver had been. Newspapers crinkled, women chatted, and an annoying kid of about five or six kept racing up and down the aisle, waving his arms. Normally, I wouldn't have cared, but I was a nervous wreck, trying not to anticipate what was about to unfold.

I prayed for Tara, and realized that, in my entire life, I'd prayed for only two other people: my mother and my sister Casey. I prayed that Carson Kreet would let Tara go without a fight. I prayed for his indifference. I imagined him saying something like, "Go ahead, take the girl. She's nothing to me." Or maybe he'd be drawn to the rose gold earrings, or the rose gold diamond ring, or the silver bracelet. And I prayed that Kreet wasn't the evil man the doctor had said he was.

Dr. Broadbent looked at me. "Miss Downing, as I have considered the situation, I have come to the conclusion that it would be best if I see Mr. Kreet alone. I will simply state that I wish Tara to join my servant's staff. It will be a business transaction, a direct and practical transaction between two practical men. You should remain safe in the train station restaurant and wait for me."

It made perfect sense, of course, but I was too emotional and too anxious to stay behind. "But what about the jewels and the money, Doctor?"

"I have money, Miss Downing. I want this transaction to seem entirely commercial between two gentlemen, although one of those gentlemen is of the lowest character. No, it is better this way. I am sure of it."

"Why are you doing this, Dr. Broadbent? Why are you going to use your own money for Tara, a girl you hardly know?"

"Because where I see a wrong, I try to right it. To put a young girl into the clutches of that man is an abomination, and I could not live with myself if I stood by and did nothing. I am a doctor, a healer, and sometimes, perhaps, a crusader for the wretched, the poor, and the infirmed."

I was humbled by his words, by his sacrifice, by his good character and by his courage.

He narrowed his eyes on me. "Why do you want to help Tara, Miss Downing? Why haven't you boarded a train and returned to New York?"

The strangeness of time travel struck me again. I was on an old train, thumping along the tracks out in the Old West, with kerosene lamps hanging at the ends of the car, in a coach where the people I was traveling with were long dead in 2022.

I thought about angels and devils, and I was all too aware that they lived inside me. I was not religious and had never thought much about religion, but I did know about angels and devils because I had experienced them, mostly the devils.

My mother and my sister were angels. I had no doubt about that. My father had been a devil, and maybe I got some angel from my mother and some devil from my father. I had been abused by devils, and I had been a devil when I stole, and schemed, and used sex and my good looks to get money.

I thought about Tara, and I felt love for her, a warm, spreading love that actually hurt. Inside my heart and in the core of my soul, I felt an animal's need to protect and nurture her, to save her, even if it killed me.

I thought about Bryce, and my spirit rose, flying. I felt free, liberated from my cynical, dark past... or more correctly, free from my future self, the murderer who had killed Cliff Prince, even if it *was* in self-defense.

I stared into Dr. Broadbent's expectant face as he waited for my answer, and I realized I had changed. I was not the same woman I had been when I'd vanished in 2022, only a few short weeks ago.

I had my answer. "Tara took care of me when I was sick, and she didn't have to. She sat with me for hours, and she said I was her friend. So, I love her, and she's like a sister to me, and I lost a sister, a younger sister. And it's because of me and my big mouth that Tara's in this mess. So, it's simple. I've got to get her out of there."

Dr. Broadbent turned away, giving a little nod of his head. "I see... Then, by the grace and compassion of the Almighty, we shall free her."

When the train slowed down, and the pounding wheels lessened, and the whistle blasted our approach, I struggled to settle my nerves and relax. I failed. I was sweating.

The conductor poked his head into the door. "Bart's City, next stop! Bart's City!"

I glanced out the window and saw shacks and old sheds and the spout of a water tank, appearing like the upraised trunk of a giant elephant.

The train pulled into the Bart's City station, a wooden depot, with deeply set eves and windows, that were shaded by a blue canvas awning.

We left the train, stepping down onto the wooden platform, and the December wind punched at us and whipped up the red in the doctor's cheeks.

"Let us go into the train station for warmth, Miss Downing. This wind is like liquid ice."

We entered the station restaurant, sat and ordered two coffees, some cheese and a piece of cake.

"I don't think I can eat a thing," I said.

"You must keep up your strength, Miss Downing.

We do not know what we are about to meet, so we must have God's own courage and some food in our stomachs."

I noticed the smoke-grimed hands and faces of the trainmen hunched at the counter on bare, hard stools. The weary-looking waitress slouched across the black and white tiled floor, carrying two blue plates of food, ignoring a lewd comment from one of the men at the counter. Some things were the same at any time, past or future.

I glanced about and saw a lopsided, dusty-looking calendar on the wall, and it startled me for a few seconds. When I was caught off-guard, it was still hard to believe. The calendar said it was December 8, 1880.

The food came quickly, and Dr. Broadbent ate a little cheese and half of the stale chocolate cake.

"What's the name of the hotel?" I asked.

"It's called the Bramble House."

The doctor checked his pocket watch and nodded. "It is time."

He stood up, shouldered back into his overcoat, put on his bowler, and told me he shouldn't be more than an hour.

"The hotel is only three blocks from here, on Pike Street. Let us hope the man is reasonable and not so ornery as I remember him."

Ten minutes later, I finished the coffee, the cheese and the cake, but the food didn't calm my jittery nerves.

I gently snaked a hand into my purse and felt for

it. The 5-shot revolver that Bryce had given to me for protection only the day before. He'd heard rumors that John Gannon might be coming to town looking for me.

"I don't think he will, but just in case, you take this. Do you know how to shoot, Cindy?"

I took the revolver, feeling the cool weight of it in my hand. "Yeah… I learned from a kid who lived in a trailer next door. We used to go shooting in the Florida swamps, and there are a lot of things to shoot at in those swamps."

"More of your mystery, Cindy," Bryce had said. "Florida and a trailer? Someday, you must tell me all your secrets. For now, I'll be back in town as soon as I can."

The minutes ticked by, and I had the sinking feeling that things weren't going so well with the doctor and Carson Kreet.

CHAPTER 43

I waited an hour and a half, and when Dr. Broadbent and Tara didn't appear, I knew it was time to leave for the Bramble House. I breathed in and exhaled a trembling breath, hoping to soothe the hot storm brewing in my chest. If Dr. Broadbent hadn't returned with Tara, then something bad must have happened, and I didn't even want to think about what that might be.

Dr. Broadbent had paid the check, and the place was filling up as new trainmen entered, searching for a table. Standing, I slipped into my coat, donned my pitiful looking hat and reached for my purse. As I left the restaurant out the front door, I patted the pocket of my dress, feeling the wad of jewels. I had no doubt I'd need them.

Bart's City was an unfortunate-looking town, a sprawling town, a temporary-looking town, cut by rutted streets. It appeared as though they'd built it recently, with no intention of anyone hanging around for very long.

On Main Street, I saw the square, high fronts of stores, the raised, planked sidewalks, and the lopsided, wooden hitching rails. I smelled sawdust and new paint, and passed scruffy-looking men in scraggly beards and mustaches. They wore tattered clothes and floppy hats, and even in the cold, moving wind, their body odor was nauseating.

I stopped short when I saw the Bramble House. It was a frame building with a false front, and something that passed for curtains, but appeared more like hanging burlap sacks. My heart sank when I thought about Tara being trapped in that dirty, foreboding place.

I didn't have a plan. I once dated a New York City cop who told me, whenever he had to confront the unknown, he always tried to have a plan. If he didn't have a plan, he went in "all confident and aggressive," expecting the unexpected.

Okay, so I reached into my purse and felt the security of the cold revolver. I had never fired a gun at anyone, only tree stumps, tin cans, soda bottles and snakes; maybe an alligator or two, when they broke from the water and rushed us. Jimmy Deck, my fifteen-year-old boyfriend at the time, had said I was a better shot than he.

But who was I kidding? This was 1880, and the men inside that hotel were no doubt professionals who'd been using pistols and rifles since they were kids. I wouldn't stand a chance. I glanced around, wishing Bryce was with me.

I slowed my pace, having second thoughts, my heart hammering. I thought *Maybe I should catch the next train back to Denver and return when Bryce can come with me.* I should have listened to the doctor. But what had happened to Dr. Broadbent? Was he in there? Maybe everything was fine, and he and Carson Kreet were having friendly negotiations.

I squared my shoulders, kinked my neck, and marched forward. There was no way I wasn't going in there. There was no way I was going to let Tara stay in that place one more day.

I lifted my skirts and crossed the hard dirt street, dodging horse crap, and then I climbed to the wooden sidewalk. As I stood directly in front of the "so called" hotel, I made up my mind. I marched across the front walkway, mounted the four stairs to the narrow porch, reached for the doorknob, and opened the door.

The door creaked open, like the sound effects from a horror movie. I entered the small hallway and saw a staircase on my left, leading up to the second floor. To the right was a parlor with a threadbare gray and red carpet, a potbelly stove in the room's rear, a sagging sofa, two tattered armchairs, and a fireplace, the fire crackling.

I tried to swallow down the fear, but I couldn't. Two men faced me. A heavy one, wearing a bowler hat, was sitting in one of those lumpy armchairs. The other man, to his right, stood near the fireplace, with a holster and revolver on his hip.

The man in the armchair regarded me with shrewd eyes. The standing man was stringy, looked mean, and had a cruel, frosty gaze. His black hair was parted in the middle and pomaded flat over his forehead. He rubbed his stubby cheek as he looked me up and down.

The man in the chair bent his lips into a half-humorous smirk. "Well now, Buck, lookee who we have here. A girlie the miners would pay silver and gold for."

I hoped my raw fear didn't show. I had no plan. I'd have to bluff and improvise. "Be confident and aggressive," the New York cop had said.

I cleared my throat and lowered my voice. "I'm looking for Dr. Harlan Broadbent. Is he here?"

The heavy one kept his smirk and his reptilian eyes on me. "And who wants to know?"

"I suppose that would be me, since I'm the one who just asked," I said, much too smart-alecky. Why did I get all sassy with anyone in authority? This was not the time to be a smart ass.

The stringy, homely man looked at me with dark, mean eyes. He cracked his knuckles, flexed his fingers, and said, "A girlie with a smart mouth. Maybe she needs to feel the back of my hand."

I ignored him. My purse was within easy reach, the revolver waiting, but my hands were shaky and clammy. I tried to keep my voice steady. "Is Mr. Carson Kreet around?"

The heavy man looked me fully in the face. "Who are you?"

"I asked first," I shot back, again wishing I could keep my big mouth under control.

He pointed a warning finger at me. "You've got a smart mouth on you, all right, and I don't like smart mouths on girlies, you hear?"

I waited, staring him down, part of me, the rebellious part, surprised I was staring him down. Suddenly, he was my drunken father, and he was a nasty Florida cop who'd just cuffed me, and he was Cliff Prince, ready to whack me across the face with his big hand.

I raised my voice. "Then tell me who you are and where Dr. Broadbent is, and I promise to shut up."

The heavy man sat up, a little insulted but curious. Then he laughed. "A pretty girlie with a spicy mouth, and a back like an ironwood. Ha! You came with the doctor, didn't you?"

I said, "And you must be Carson Kreet."

His fat chin came up a little, as if my knowing and speaking his name was a reason for pride. "And if I am?"

"Then, I'm going to be nice and ask you politely, once again, please, do you know where Mr. Broadbent is? He told me he was coming to see you."

Kreet's eyes darkened. "Yeah, girlie, I am Carson Kreet. The one and the only Carson Kreet," he said, with self-importance.

Carson Kreet was about forty years old, with thick liver lips, an ugly mustache, and a pudgy, ugly face. His thrusting jaw suggested force, his pot belly and florid face suggested overindulgence. His dusty suit was tight, his vest strained the buttons, and the trousers had long lost their crease, if they'd ever had one. There was a violent, greedy restlessness in his eyes that was terrifying, so I avoided those eyes and looked above him.

I'd seen faces similar to Carson Kreet's in some ex-cons and professional gamblers, and I'd seen the same sneering face when I was a teenager, hitting dive bars in the Florida swamps.

"If you are Mr. Kreet, then I have come for two reasons," I said, frankly.

His broad grin was menacing, and it revealed tobacco-stained, gapped teeth. "And what would those reasons be, girlie of mine?"

I didn't let his insult provoke me. "First, I'd like to see Dr. Broadbent. Second, I understand Tara O'Hanlon works here. I want to take her with me and return to Denver. I will pay you, of course, for your trouble. I can pay any reasonable amount."

His dark, hoarse laughter started low and then rose to a crazy cackle. The other guy laughed too, but there was no joy in it. It sounded like some kind of war cry.

Carson Kreet made a gesture to him. "Go get the doctor, Buck, and bring him out here. Let the girlie see the good doctor."

Buck pushed away from the mantel, swaggered across the room, and left through a rear door. I felt Kreet's eyes on me, but I ignored him, staring into the fire. My heart was beating so hard it hurt.

It seemed an eternity before the door opened and Dr. Broadbent appeared, his face red and swollen, his eyes dazed and filled with pain. He shambled forward a few feet into the room. From behind, Buck gave him a violent shove, and the doctor staggered forward, stumbled over his own feet and fell to the floor in a cry of pain.

A gut-wrenching twist of anguish engulfed me. Rage pumped adrenaline through my veins.

"There he is, girlie girl," Kreet said, giving me a sardonic look. "There's your old fool of a doctor, who came in here talking his high and mighty words at me. He wasn't no good as a sawbones when he treated me all those months ago, and I'll bet you my best Saturday night whore that he ain't a fit sawbones now. So, take him, and you get out, before I rip that dress from off you and take my bullwhip to your bare arse."

Something happened to me that had never happened before. The boiling rage in my gut and in my brain exploded, but not the way it always had before—shooting out in a chaos of curses and in a clumsy attack.

This time, I grew quiet. My eyesight sharpened, my muscles pulsed with expanding strength, and my reflexes were coiled springs. My voice was soft, but with a biting purpose. "I want Tara O'Hanlon."

"Did you hear me, you stupid woman?" Kreet said, his face pinched with anger. "Get out of here, now, before Buck here shoots this no-good bastard of a doctor, and I come for you with my hands and my whip."

I repeated my request, my voice controlled, my words crisp. "I want Tara O'Hanlon and I won't leave without her. Get her! Now!"

There was a long, hanging moment of threatening silence.

CHAPTER 44

C arson Kreet narrowed his flat, cold eyes on me. "All right, girlie girl, your time is up. Get her, Buck!"

Buck lowered his head, ready for wicked business. He fixed his mouth into a grim determination and started toward me.

My reflexes were cat-quick. The 5-shot revolver was in my hand in a second and it was pointed at Kreet. His eyes opened fully, stunned. Buck froze.

"She ain't gonna shoot nobody! Get her, Buck!" Kreet barked.

Buck reached for his gun, and just as it left his holster, I swung my revolver at him and squeezed the trigger. There was a loud pop and the smell of gunpowder. The bullet struck Buck just above the right knee. He screamed in pain and staggered. I was ready to shoot him again, but he dropped his revolver and crumbled onto the floor, rolling about in pain, both hands gripping his injured leg.

Kreet froze. A deer in headlights.

Movement, up and to my left, drew my eyes. A man scrambled down the stairs, rifle at the ready.

As he leveled it on me, I turned and, with the calm aim and sure confidence of a gunslinger, I fired two shots. One missed, digging into the wall, the other slammed into his chest just as he fired the rifle. His bullet was high. My second shot got him. He jerked backwards, slammed back against the wall, dropped the rifle and went tumbling down the stairs, landing hard and still.

Kreet's hand went for his inside coat pocket. I was there, the revolver swinging toward him, pointed at his head. My eyes were burning with fury, and strangely, I was as calm as a yoga teacher. I felt no fear.

"Draw your gun and you're dead!" I threatened.

Kreet stiffened and swallowed, his Adam's apple moving, his bug-eyes spooked.

I crossed to him. "Now get Tara. Right now!"

He stammered. "I... I..."

I took two steps forward and rammed the barrel of the revolver into his forehead, forcing his head back. "Get her, or so help me, I'll shoot you, and love every minute of watching you die!"

At the top of the stairs, I heard a faint, small voice. "Miss Adams?"

Keeping the revolver at Kreet's head, I glanced up and saw Tara. A tidal wave of relief washed through me.

"Tara... Tara. Come down. Come down, now. We're going. Hurry!"

But Tara didn't move. She seemed lost in a panic-dream.

"Tara! Come down. Now! I'm getting you out of here!"

Tara descended two stairs, then stopped, glancing about, frightened as a wild animal.

"Tara! Come on! We're going!"

"Miss Adams?" Tara said in a strangled voice, still uncertain, staring at me with round scared eyes. She saw Buck on the floor. She saw the dead man at the bottom of the stairs. She saw Dr. Broadbent sprawled and breathing heavily.

Her wide eyes returned to me, and at the gun pointed at Kreet's head.

"Yes, Tara. Yes. It's me. We're getting the hell out of here."

Tara's lips quivered. She crossed her arms tightly against her chest and I saw the tears start. Her face broke up, her eyes pinched shut, and she sobbed, her thin hands flying up to cover her face.

I felt compassion, anxiety, and then, inevitably, the slow spread of fear, as I realized what I'd done. "Tara, honey. Please... we've got to go."

Still fighting emotion, Tara slowly descended the stairs, edged away from the dead man and his rifle, and stopped a few feet from me.

I tried a smile of confidence. "It's okay, Tara. I'm taking you away from here."

Dr. Broadbent struggled to his feet, leaning back against the wall near the staircase, his hands trembling.

"Can you walk, Doctor?" I asked.

He nodded, pretending strength. "I am quite all

right. Yes. I can walk."

Tara wiped her wet, disbelieving eyes.

I looked at Kreet, the anger rising again. "We're leaving now. If you follow me, I'll shoot you. Do you understand?"

Kreet's frightened, questioning eyes looked first at Tara and then at me. "You did all this for that girl? For that ragtag, nothing of a girl?"

I wanted to pull the trigger, and it took all my strength not to. "You are a sorry, worthless piece of sh…"

A voice stopped me. And then I saw him. John Gannon entered the room from the back door, with a revolver pointed directly at me!

"Hello Cynthia…" he said smoothly, his eyes veiled and unreadable. "My, but don't you have a dangerous surplus of fantasy? Do you really think you're going to leave here alive?"

I kept my revolver pointed at Kreet's head. Buck was still on the floor, a grimace of pain on his snow-white face, his eyes glazed, blood oozing from his leg.

"Help…" he called, faintly.

No one moved to help him.

"Drop the gun, Miss Downing," Gannon said.

Tara stared at me, confused by a name she'd never heard.

"That's not going to happen," I said, my pulse drumming in my ears.

"I won't miss, Miss Downing, and I will kill you."

"Not before I shoot this son-of-a-bitch, who I

assume is your friend?"

"Business partner. Nothing more."

"Nice company you keep, Mr. Gannon."

"I heard you were coming for the girl. I have friends everywhere, you know, even in the Hotel Denver. Why you came for her, I don't know, but I wanted to see you again. Well... I had to see you again, didn't I, after you ran off like that."

Most of the calm had left me. I was scared, but I tried not to show it. "Now you see me."

"Just let her go, Gannon!" Kreet pleaded. "I tell you, she's not right in her head. She shot Buck and Stubby."

"What a fool you are, Kreet. Haven't you heard that Miss Downing is all spit and fire, with the hot blood of a gypsy? But she will not be shooting anyone else today. Now, Miss Downing, I said to drop the pistol."

I looked at him, mustering all the courage I had left. "You'd better not miss me, Gannon, because I'm a helluva good shot and I won't miss this bastard, and I won't miss you."

For only a second, I saw the flash of fear in his eyes, and I reveled in it.

Then he said, "You should have stayed with me instead of running off with Marshal Vance, Cynthia. I would have given you anything you ever wanted."

"I didn't want anything you had to give. Now, drop your gun and let us go. You'll never see me again. I promise."

He shook his head. "No, Miss Downing. You

betrayed me. No one who betrays me stays alive."

"Are you crazy?! I didn't betray you. You betrayed yourself when you killed your wife."

He tensed. Carson Kreet tensed. Tara tensed, and Buck's body went slack as he lost consciousness from shock and the loss of blood.

I had to buy some time and figure out what I was going to do. I saw Buck's big revolver on the floor. He'd accidentally kicked it when he fell, and it lay only a few feet from Dr. Broadbent.

I glanced at the doctor and saw that he was thinking what I was thinking.

"All right, Miss Downing," Gannon said. "I'm finished here. Drop your revolver now, or I will shoot you."

At that moment, the front door burst open. To my utter shock, Marshal Bryce Vance entered, his revolver drawn and aimed at Gannon.

The room gathered into a stunned silence, as everyone calculated position and possible attack.

"You have a choice, Mr. Gannon," Bryce said, in his low, measured voice. "You can walk out now, no questions asked, free and clear. Or you can stay and die. Simple choice."

"Simple!?" Gannon snapped. "You know your days are numbered, Marshal. The town has turned on you, haven't they? Turned on you because of this low harlot you picked up at my house."

"As with most things, Mr. Gannon, some people have turned. Some haven't. It's the way of things."

Gannon's voice growled with anger. "I'll make

sure you're ridden out of town on a rail—tarred and feathered!"

"Not before they're told the truth about you killing your wife."

"That's what you say and nobody else!"

"There was a witness, Mr. Gannon! All your hired hands didn't ride away. One of them hid out and watched everything you did."

I glanced at Bryce. I knew he was bluffing. Thomas was dead.

Gannon's face fell a little. "What witness?" Gannon bellowed. "There was no witness!"

"You strangled your wife, Mr. Gannon. Do you think I'm a fool? You broke her neck with your own hands when you caught her with the groom, Jubal Banks, in the carriage house. Then you took her and her horse out to the pasture and left her there. Like I said, there was an eye witness to the whole event."

John Gannon's hand trembled. "You're finished, Marshal. Do you hear me? I'll see to that. I'm the one with the money and the power, and you're finished!"

"Drop the gun, Mr. Gannon. It's my last warning to you."

And then everything happened so fast it was a blur.

Gannon fired, and the bullet glanced off my right side. Tara screamed. The force drove me left, and I toppled to the floor, dropping the 5-shot. Gannon aimed his revolver at Bryce and fired. It missed. Barely!

Standing tall, Bryce used both hands to steady

his Colt Six-gun, then he fired two shots at Gannon. From the corner of my eye, I saw Gannon jerk erect, drop his revolver, grab his chest, stagger a few steps to his right, then drop to the floor.

Kreet held up his hands, shouting. "Don't shoot me! Don't shoot me!"

Bryce moved forward, his revolver aimed at Kreet's head. In a calm voice, Bryce glanced at Dr. Broadbent. "Doctor, attend Miss Downing."

Dr. Broadbent hurried over and knelt down beside me, searching for the wound.

Bryce stood over Carson Kreet, his Colt aimed at Kreet's head, his hot eyes glaring at him with a threat. "Keep your hands up!"

Kreet's hands reached toward the ceiling as Bryce reached into Kreet's coat, and pulled a revolver from the shoulder holster. "If Miss Downing dies, Mr. Kreet, you're a dead man."

Kreet's face went blank with shock.

Tara rushed to my side, dropping down, weeping. "Miss Adams... Miss Adams, please don't die. Please..."

CHAPTER 45

We sat at a table in the Bart's City train station restaurant, without Bryce, who had stayed behind until the local mortician arrived. He'd also called for a doctor to come and treat Buck's leg, and sent a local man to a ranch two miles away, where the town sheriff, such as he was, was out prospecting.

Before we'd left the Bramble House, Bryce had said, "I don't know how long this is going to take. I know the sheriff, and he ain't going to like any of this, especially me shooting John Gannon dead in his town. So, you all catch the next train back to Denver, and I'll return as soon as I can."

I was experienced in police matters, so I asked, "But won't the sheriff want our statements?"

Marshal Vance nodded. "Back in Denver, all of you will write down your statements, and I'll have them forwarded. That will be all right. Now, you take Tara and the doctor, return to the train station, and get back to Denver."

In the busy restaurant, we all sipped coffee and nibbled on oatmeal cookies that were soft and tasty.

It was late afternoon, and the next train to Denver wasn't scheduled to arrive for about an hour. I kept glancing back at the front door, hoping Bryce would finish his business and travel back to Denver with us.

Tara rested her head on my shoulder, her packed canvas bag near my feet. Dr. Broadbent sat across from us, holding an ice cloth over his swollen left eye.

"Are you feeling better?" I asked.

"Not so bad. I fear my wife, Tilly, will find me less than desirable to look at, but I'll play up the story so that I am the hero. I'll tell her I got some good punches in. That should impress her. And she'll want to hover over me, and fuss over me, but that will be all right. And you, Miss Downing, are you recovered from all that terrible violence?"

"I'm still shaking inside," I said, as I stroked Tara's head. "And thanks to Rosamond's jewels that helped to cushion Gannon's bullet, I'm still alive."

"Yes, but you have a wound on your left hip where the bullet grazed you, and you must keep it clean and dressed, Miss Downing. You do not want infection to set in."

Tara nestled in closer. "I was so frightened, Miss Adams, and I am so grateful that you're alive and that I am released from that terrible place."

I hadn't had the time to tell Tara who I truly was, so she continued to call me Miss Adams. I'd explain it all later.

"You are a brave woman," Dr. Broadbent said. "I

must say that I have never seen the like of it before. I was sure you would be killed."

I screwed up my lips. "Yeah, well, you're not the only one. Let's face it, I was lucky."

"But you are a dead shot with a pistol. I dare say, there are not many men, myself included, who could shoot as sure and true. It was most remarkable. Yes, most remarkable."

I was aware that other diners were staring at us. It was obvious that they'd heard what had happened and most didn't look pleased to have us there.

"It all happened so fast," I said. "I didn't have time to think about it."

The doctor lowered the ice cloth and reached for his cup of coffee. He took a sip and replaced the cup in the saucer. "What will you do now, Miss Downing?" the doctor asked. "Will you stay in Denver?"

Tara spoke up. "Why are you being addressed as Miss Downing? I don't understand."

"I'll tell you later, Tara. For now, let's just relax."

I wrapped an arm around Tara's shoulder and held her close. "As to your question, Doctor, Tara and I are going home, aren't we, Tara?"

She looked up at me. "Home to New York?"

"Yes, back to New York, where we belong. We'll start a new life there."

The doctor cleared his throat. "Miss Downing, pardon me for saying so, but it is known throughout the town that you and Marshal Vance are, shall I say, fond of each other's company."

"He'll come with us," I said confidently. "I don't think the town will want him in Denver after he shot and killed John Gannon, do you? And I'm not going to win any popularity contests. Most people already want me to get out of town, don't you think?"

The doctor lowered his head. "Perhaps you are right. The ugly truth of John Gannon's dastardly murder of his wife and that poor young man will never be believed, and anyway, I doubt whether Marshal Vance will ever tell it. So, unfortunately, I believe you are correct in your supposition, Miss Downing. The town might turn against him, and he could be dismissed by the territorial governor, who knew John Gannon well. But I, for one, will lobby for him to stay. The town will never find a better lawman than Marshal Bryce Vance."

Bryce didn't meet us at the restaurant as I had hoped, so the three of us took the train back to Denver, arriving late, all of us drained of energy and longing to sleep away the awful images of the day.

In my hotel room, I ordered a hot bath for Tara. While she bathed, I helped wash her hair and scrub her dirty fingernails.

Later, yawning, she buttoned on one of my nightgowns and slipped under the warm quilt, and I tugged it up to her chin.

And then, unexpectedly, she began talking about Irish fairies.

"What are these fairies, and where do they live?"

I asked, easing down next to her on the edge of the bed.

Tara lifted up on elbows and her eyes lit up. "They live underground beneath grassy mounds, and in trees, and some live in an invisible world that hovers close to this one."

"Have you ever seen a fairy?"

"Oh, no, Miss Adams, you must have the gift to see them. My mother said she could see them, and she said they existed in a timeless world."

And then Tara's eyes fluttered. She dropped back down, her head deep into the pillow and she was asleep. I watched her sleep for a time in the dim light of an oil lamp, and I stroked her hair, and I swelled with love for the girl, a love I hadn't experienced since before the death of my sister. It was a healing love, a tenderness that seemed to fill the room, and there was a sweetness in those peaceful moments that I can't describe.

As the night lengthened, I rose from the bed and moved to the window, pulling back the curtain, and staring out into the quiet night. Would Bryce come with us to New York? I silently prayed that he would. He would be the perfect father for Tara and the perfect man for me. Bryce Vance and I knew each other. Deep down in our souls, we knew we were meant for each other, that we loved each other, and that we always would. There was no doubt about it.

Whatever we encountered in the New York of 1880, I knew Bryce could handle it. And I knew he'd thrive there, as a policeman, or at whatever he put his mind to.

I knew I'd love him no matter what profession he chose. I'd love him if he dug ditches or hauled coal or drove a horse wagon, although I was certain he'd rise to the top of any trade he chose.

Love had come into my life, and it absolutely astounded me. I loved Bryce with all my heart, and I loved Tara with a heart so full I could hardly contain it. So, is that why I had time traveled? Had the universe singled me out, saying, "Hey, you Lost Cause, we're going to give you one more chance—an opportunity to make something of yourself instead of throwing your life away. We're going to give you two people to love. Now, girl, what are you going to do with it?

A clopping horse rode by, a silhouetted rider in the saddle.

I thought about time travel, and the strangest thoughts about it went streaming through my head, concepts I'd never thought I was capable of having.

I imagine myself on a train that's moving through a large pass between mountains. Standing in the caboose, I look backwards, and there it is, the past I've just lived, and it's still there. Then I see myself up front, looking forward, and I can see the future, that is, where I'm going.

And then I'm walking back and forth on the train, which is moving in a single direction. If each time I change direction, am I moving for a time in the past, and then, for a time, in the future? Am I moving back and forth in time, a kind of forever time passenger?

I nodded off and finally slipped into the bed next to Tara. For the first time in a long time, I prayed I wouldn't wake up and find myself living in 2022, finding that my entire experience in 1880 was only an elaborate dream.

CHAPTER 46

T he next morning, I let Tara sleep in, and I left the hotel, arriving at the Denver jail just after nine o'clock in the morning. To my delight, Bryce was behind his desk, signing some papers, and Deputy Clay Fallon was standing by one of three jails, talking to an inmate while eating his breakfast.

Hanging on the wall, near some wanted posters, was a sign that read:

No person shall fire or discharge any cannon or gun, fowling piece, pistol, or firearm of any description, or fire, or explode any squib, cracker or other thing containing powder, or other combustible or explosive material... without permission of Marshal Bryce Vance.

When he saw me, Bryce rose and smiled a greeting. "Good morning, Miss Downing. I was going to pay you a visit around ten o'clock. I supposed you were catching up on your sleep."

I acknowledged Deputy Fallon with a smile and a "good morning," and approached Bryce's desk.

"Well, Marshal, I can see from your red-rimmed

eyes that you didn't get much sleep."

"No, I arrived only an hour ago, but I slept some on the train."

I lowered my voice. "I'd like to talk to you. Can you join me for breakfast at the hotel?"

"Yes, I can use some ham and eggs and fresh coffee."

He turned to his deputy. "Clay, I'll be back within the hour."

We sat at the same table as before, ordering mostly the same breakfast items we'd ordered all those days ago. It seemed weeks ago. The diners around us stole curious glances, but Bryce didn't seem to care and Dan, the waiter, was his usual, pleasant self.

When the coffee was poured and Dan withdrew, Bryce mixed in some cream and stirred. After he'd taken a generous drink, I leaned toward him, speaking in a near whisper.

"Is everything okay?"

He shrugged a shoulder and gave me his fetching, slanted grin. "Well, let me see now, Cindy. The newspapers say I'm a killer. The mayor wants to see me at one o'clock. He says the territorial governor wants answers about how John Gannon was killed. I've received several threatening anonymous letters, and many of the more respectable residents of Denver want me tossed out on my... shall I say, ear?"

I frowned. "I'm so sorry I got you into all this."

He made an empty gesture with his hand. "Not your fault, Cindy. It's just the way of things, and how events take form and play out. After being in those Civil War battles, where so many lives were lost and so much was at stake, these little fights don't get to me much. Maybe they should, but they don't."

"And what is being said about me?" I asked.

"You haven't read any of the morning papers?"

I lowered my gaze and reached for my coffee cup. "No. Not before breakfast."

"Suffice it to say that the opinion of the paper is that you are a loose female who has brought nothing but the foulest trouble to our fair city. To be bare-back honest, they are blaming you for John Gannon's death, and blaming me for falling head-first into your, and I quote, 'love-web trap.'"

"'Love-web trap?'" I almost burst out laughing. "Wow… that bad, huh?"

"Yup."

I looked directly at him and just let the words fly. "Come with me, Bryce. Come with me and Tara on the next train out of here to New York."

A little breath of laughter left his lips. He studied me. "Do you mean run away from all this, like a whipped dog?"

"No, not run. Leave."

"Same thing."

I leaned toward him. "No, it isn't. You choose to leave. You choose something better, and that something better is us, and it's Tara, and a life together."

He ran a finger around the rim of his coffee cup. When he raised his eyes to me, I saw a weary fatigue, and I saw questions. "Who are you, Cindy Downing? You have never answered that one simple question, and I cannot find an answer."

For a few seconds, I considered telling him everything: how I killed Cliff Prince and about time travel. He waited, and I struggled to answer his question once and for all. But again, how could I? I would lose him for sure.

I sat back in my chair, releasing a little sigh. "I'm a girl who loves you, and who wants you; a girl who will explain everything to you once we're on that train heading to New York. Promise."

Our breakfast arrived, and we ate in silence for a while. After Bryce had eaten most of the eggs and ham, he slid his plate aside, blotted his mouth with his napkin, and folded his hands on the table.

"Cindy... I will travel to New York."

I wanted to jump up like a cheerleader and scream "YES!"

Then what he said next brought me back down to earth.

"But not now. I will not run from this fight, Cindy. I cannot. If I did, I couldn't live with myself."

My body slumped in defeat. "I think what you're really saying is that you'll never come."

"No, it does not mean that. It means I will travel to New York and meet you and Tara when all this business is cleared up. That is a promise."

"And what if they toss you out on your ass? Excuse my modern mouth."

"Then I will get on that train and meet you in New

York all the sooner. I will ask you to marry me and, I suppose, as the stories often say, we'll live devotedly, and in love, and happily ever after."

I saw the truth of it in his eyes. "And what if they don't toss you out on your... very nice ass?"

Bryce's lips were curved into a smile as he spoke. "Oh, my, Cindy, but aren't you always a surprise, and a touch wicked, I believe."

I reached and placed my hand on his, batting my eyes flirtatiously. "I'm trying to be better."

"Don't be better. Don't change. You bring a morning gladness to this lawman, and it stays with him the day long, and it warms up his night, especially if you're with him."

I gazed adoringly at him, melting into his gorgeous eyes, taking in his ruggedly handsome face.

When Dan appeared to remove our empty plates, I removed my hand from Bryce's hand, and he averted his gaze. When Dan was gone, Bryce looked at me earnestly.

"I will not run off like a scared rabbit. I will stay and fight. But as soon as it's over, one way or the other, I'll catch the next train to New York."

I nodded decisively. "Okay. Fine. Then, I'll stay, too."

"No... You should go. Things will get ugly, and I don't want you or Tara here when it does."

"But how can I leave without you? What if something happens to you? How will I know?"

"Nothing will happen except a 'Yes' or a 'No' vote.

Whichever it is, then I will leave, and I'll be in New York as soon as I can."

The next train for Chicago, and then to New York, left at 4:10 p.m. that afternoon. Bryce said he wanted me and Tara on it.

I didn't want to add to his problems, and I was certain most of the town would turn on him even more if I stayed, so I agreed to leave. But it didn't feel right, and it didn't feel good, and for the first time in my life, I knew what an aching heart felt like. I was leaving the man I loved, and I had no idea when, or even if, I'd ever see him again.

Bryce had paid our hotel bill, and he was waiting for Tara and me outside the hotel on a buckboard at three o'clock. Because I knew there would be a curious crowd gathered to watch me leave town, I'd dug deep into Rosamond's trunk and put on a stunning, purple silk and crushed velvet bustle dress, and a lavish matching hat with feathers. Tara wore a lovely blue and tan dress, with a stylish felt hat that I'd bought for her at the only basic ladies' shop in town. She'd stared at herself in the mirror for a good five minutes, turning this way and that.

"I don't look like myself, Cynthia." She insisted on calling me that, saying she liked the sound of it better than Cindy.

"You look beautiful," I'd said. "And you *are* beautiful."

I wanted to make a lasting impression on these people, one they'd never forget. As I exited the hotel in that fine dress, I took Tara's hand and lifted my proud head. From Bryce's wide eyes and the crowd's gossipy whispers, I knew I'd achieved my goal, and I was delighted.

The teenage hotel steward loaded my trunk and Tara's canvas case into the rear flatbed, wished us "Godspeed," and then he winked and smiled at Tara. Bryce climbed down and helped me and Tara aboard, while the crowds thickened, and someone shouted an insult. The marshal ignored it as he climbed up next to me. He shook the reins, and we lurched ahead.

As we trotted along the streets, a few cowboys waved at Bryce, but many other townsfolk ignored him, including the ladies, who didn't glance my way.

Bryce's eyes shifted left and right, watchful and wary. I thought, how easy it would be for someone to take a shot at us from one of those shop windows, from a roof, or from inside an alley. If I was thinking about it, then Bryce was thinking about it, too.

CHAPTER 47

At the train station, we waited under the protection of the platform roof, as snow flurries fell, and a snappy wind gathered, then died away. I reached into my coat pocket, removed the statements Tara and I had written down two hours before, and handed them to Bryce.

"I hope these help."

He took them, slipping them into his inside coat pocket. "Thank you. The sheriff was asking for them. They may not help, but they certainly won't hurt."

"Something that I keep wondering about is, how did you find me at Bart's City?" I asked.

"The rancher I was with told me John Gannon was on his way to Bart's City. I flagged down the west-bound train at a whistle stop, two miles from Denver, and ordered it to take me to Bart's City. That's one advantage of being a federal marshal and not just a sheriff."

Bryce, dressed in his black woolen frock coat and cowboy hat, checked his pocket watch, then glanced toward the tracks. "If it's on time, we have about four minutes."

I gave him a tender, longing look. "By the way, thanks for giving me your revolver. It saved my life."

He smiled. "With your shooting skill, I could hire you as a deputy, if you stayed."

I turned my eyes away. "It doesn't feel so good killing a man with a gun, does it, even when they want to kill you?"

"No, killing anything never feels good, but if you hadn't shot the man, you and Tara wouldn't be here. You saved your own life and Tara's. Now, that's something to think about whenever bad memories come in the night."

Tara stepped over, wrapped in her long woolen coat. "Marshal Vance, what will happen to the servants who work at the Gannon Mansion?"

"John Gannon's younger brother is coming from Kansas City. He will inherit the estate and, from what I have heard, he is a kindlier man than his older brother was, and from all accounts, he is married to a fine woman, and they have two children."

Tara was thoughtful. "I hope he keeps the house, for the servants' sakes. They need their jobs."

Tara moved away toward the tracks, leaning out to see if the train was approaching.

Bryce looked at me, and his eyes said something hopeful and warm. "You take care of yourself and Tara, and don't worry about me. I'll be all right. Once you get settled, send me a telegram with your address, and I'll send some money. And, of course, I'll wire you just as soon as this bad business has been concluded, one way or the other."

I didn't care if people were watching. I faced him, reached a gloved hand, and touched his face and his lips. "I love you, Bryce Vance. I know it was fast and I know it's crazy, but that's just the way it is. I love you. Come to me as soon as you can."

The haunting blast of the train whistle startled me, and Tara spun around. "It's coming! It's coming, Cynthia."

Earlier that morning, I had ordered a room-service breakfast for us, and while we ate, I told her the entire story about Rosamond, Thomas, and me. I didn't tell her about time traveling, because I didn't want to freak her out.

She took it well, standing, wrapping her arms about my waist, hugging me tightly. "I'm so glad you're with me. I prayed so hard that you would find me, and you did. You came for me."

The train had almost reached the station when Bryce said, "We'll be together again before you know it."

We embraced and kissed, something that was scandalous in 1880, but since we were already considered outcasts, it didn't matter, did it?

Tara turned away from us, embarrassed, as Bryce kissed me one last time, long and warm. And there it was again, the glory and the magic of love.

The train rumbled into the station, hissing steam, brakes squealing. A porter toted my trunk and Tara's bag up the stairs and into the coach, and Tara climbed aboard and found our seats, giving me another minute alone with Bryce.

He touched my nose with a finger and said, "She was a phantom of delight, when first she gleam'd upon my sight. Her eyes as stars of twilight fair; like twilight's, too, her dusky hair."

I drew back in surprise. "A poem? From you? Big and tough Marshal Bryce Vance reciting a poem? I don't believe it."

He slanted an apologetic grin. "My old schoolmarm, Miss Jenkins, made us memorize that William Wordsworth poem all those years ago. I thought I'd forgotten it."

I kissed him again, broke away, lifted my skirts, and darted up the stairs. Not looking back, I entered the coach and sat down next to Tara.

The clanking bell seemed loud as we lurched ahead, and clouds of steam obscured my view of Bryce for a few seconds. He waved, and he smiled, and as he faded from view, he already seemed light years away.

The train rattled along the tracks, and Tara was soon asleep, her head resting against my shoulder. I ached for Bryce, and I felt an unspeakable love and gratitude for Tara. The depth and the range of my emotions were new to me, and they hurt, and they were mysterious.

It was after we'd changed trains in Chicago and were thundering across the tracks somewhere in Pennsylvania when it happened.

We shot through a tunnel. I heard and felt the whoosh of wind and I sat up, fully alert.

"What's the matter?" Tara asked, glancing about nervously. "What's going on?"

But I couldn't speak. I seized Tara's hand and pulled her close.

Just as before, a smoky, yellow fog rolled into the coach, and I coughed, frantically struggling to wave it away. It thickened, and the surrounding passengers were ghostlike, and then they vanished. Tara cried out, panicked.

All around us, glittering light sizzled and flashed; bright blue tentacles were frenzied, crawling along the seats, the windows and the ceiling, a hot electric current stinging my skin.

Tara screamed as the train bucked and groaned like something wounded, and I wrapped her tightly in my arms, clutching her, expecting the train to jump the tracks and go barreling off into oblivion.

A sharp blast of frigid wind battered us, and I held fast to Tara with all my strength, as the train went hurtling off into a stormy cloud of flashing blue lights.

CHAPTER 48

T he impact of the return was jarring, like being yanked from a deep-sleep dream and flung into a pool of icy water. I was gasping for air, shivering and fighting panic.

The conductor seemed to tower over me, like an alien giant in a sci-fi movie. He spoke in a deep, slow-motion voice. "Miss... Are... you... all right...? Can... you... speak?"

I couldn't speak, and my brain was a scrambled mess of tangled words, thoughts, and faces. My heart slammed in my chest and my head was pounding.

A doctor was called. There was one in the next car.

He asked me questions, but I don't remember anything. He lifted my wrist and checked my pulse. It was racing, of course. And then everything went black.

The next thing I remember, I was strapped in a gurney inside a speeding ambulance, the siren screaming. I passed out again.

My eyes popped open, and a doctor wearing blue scrubs, complete with a cap, a blue face mask, and a stethoscope, was hovering over me, shining a pin light into my left eye.

I squinted and swallowed. "What?"

He switched off the light. "How are you feeling?"

I swallowed again. "I don't know."

"Any pain?"

"I... I don't think so," I said, blurring the words.

"Are you sure? No pain, anywhere?"

"My head hurts. Headache."

"Have you taken any medication?"

"No. Where? Where is this?" I asked. My lips felt made of rubber.

"Can you tell me your name?"

I thought about it. "Cynthia..."

"Last name?"

"Downing. Where am I?"

"This is the ER at New York Presbyterian Hospital."

"In New York?"

"Yes."

"Who are you?"

"I'm Dr. Philbin. Miss Downing, did you fall recently?"

"No..."

"Have you taken any drugs or consumed alcohol?"

"No..."

"Do you have a history of seizures or fainting?"

"No."

"Were you in some kind of play, or maybe you were an extra in a movie?"

"What?"

"The clothes you were wearing were... well, they were quite retro, like something from the nineteenth century. You also have a wound on your left side, which we have cleaned and dressed."

My thoughts and memories were swirling whirlpools, and my head was still pounding. A minute later, as the doctor was keying info into his digital tablet, I saw, in my inner mind, Bryce's face. Then Cliff's face flashed in. I inhaled a breath and made a startled sound of panic. "Why am I here?"

The doctor didn't look up from the tablet. "You fainted on the train."

The word "train" rang a bell. "Train? What train?"

The doctor raised his eyes from the screen and explained that I was found passed out on an Amtrak train traveling to New York from Chicago.

I sat up, my eyes searching the walls, the doctor's face, and the beeping machines with their blinking, red, digital numbers. "Oh. My. God!"

The doctor laid his computer tablet aside. "What is it?"

I shot him a look. "What's the date?"

"The date?"

"Yes! What's the date!? Tell me the date!"

"It's Wednesday, November 2, 2022. Miss Downing, we will need to run some tests, and when you're feeling better, we'll need your insurance information."

Before he finished the sentence, I'd whipped back the cover sheet and swung my legs to the floor. "I've got to get out of here!"

The doctor took a step back. "I don't recommend..."

Tara's face came crashing into my head. "... Tara! Where's Tara?!"

I shot to my feet, and white dots swam across my eyes. Staggering, I dropped back down onto the edge of the bed, placing my head in my hands.

"Please, get back into bed, Miss Downing. Let me help you. Nurse!"

I obeyed, lying back, closing my eyes.

"Did they find me alone?"

"Alone?" the doctor asked.

"Yes. Yes! On the train, was I alone or was there a young girl with me?"

A nurse entered and walked to Dr. Philbin. They whispered, and that irritated me.

"What are you saying?" I demanded. "Tell me what you're saying!"

The doctor turned to me. "Miss Downing, a young girl was found hysterical in the next seat over from yours. The police were called. She's here at the hospital. She's been sedated, and she's sleeping. Perhaps this is the young girl you're speaking of?"

I lifted my head. "Yes! I've got to see her! She must be out of her mind, scared to death! Where is she?"

Again I got out of bed and on to my feet, noticing I was wearing a blue hospital gown.

"Take me to her. I've got to see her. Now!"

The doctor looked at me with a warning. "We'll take you, but only if you're sitting in a wheelchair."

Minutes later, a beefy, bald orderly rolled me

down the gray, polished hospital corridor to the elevators. On the fifth floor, we exited and traveled down another long corridor until we came to a quiet lounge and a nurse's station. The orderly spoke to the nurse, and she led the way to room 518.

Inside, the lights were dim, and I saw two beds. The orderly rolled me to the bed on the left and stopped.

I opened my eyes fully on Tara. She was asleep, covered by a blanket. With effort, I used my hands to pushed to my feet, my legs weak and rubbery. Tears of relief rolled down my cheeks as I gazed down at her.

"It's okay, Tara. I'm here. You'll be just fine."

The nurse drifted over. "Do you know her?" the nurse said, speaking in a Jamaican accent. "She had no identification, just a canvas bag with old clothes inside."

"Yes, I know her. Her name is Tara O'Hanlon."

"Is she a relative?"

"Yes, she is. She's my sister."

The nurse smiled. "Well, I'm sure she'll be fine now once she sees you."

I let out a long, weary sigh. "I hope so."

I lowered my head and clasped my hands, whispering, fighting tears. "But Bryce is gone forever... Gone, just like a fading dream."

With kind eyes and a soothing voice, the nurse said, "I'm sorry, what did you say?"

I shook my head. "Nothing... It's nothing. This is November the second, isn't it?"

"Yes…"

"And it's definitely 2022?"

"Yes, it is."

I sat with Tara until her eyes fluttered and opened. I spoke gently to her, and she turned her head and saw me. Tears flooded her eyes, and I stood and kissed her forehead. I told her she was safe, and that I was going to take her home.

We both cried for a time, from fear and relief, and I promised I'd explain everything once we were home, and she was rested.

I called my friend and real estate co-worker, Alina, who had an extra set of keys to my condo. I asked her to come to the hospital and bring my insurance card and any credit cards, cash or identification she could find in my desk drawer, along with clothes for me and Tara. I told her I'd explain everything later.

The doctor suggested they keep Tara in the hospital for observation, but I declined. Tara and I agreed she'd be better off with me, safe and at home, than in any hospital. I was going to have to explain my entire time travel journey to her, and I wasn't sure if I could fully explain it even to myself.

And although my heart was broken, knowing I'd never see Bryce Vance again, I had Tara, and I vowed she'd be safe, and never alone again.

And then there was Cliff Prince. I had one week before the horrific event of November 9 would occur. Cliff and I had had a violent argument on November 9. I had struck him with that clock and killed him. I had run away, and time traveled to

1880.

Would that event be repeated? Would history be repeated, or had I been given a second chance?

My next thought seemed silly, yet poignant. Only *time* would tell.

EPILOGUE

On the full moon night of November 9, 2022, Tara and I strolled arm in arm in a chilly autumn breeze. New York City was flooded with moonlight and Tara said it looked like "a magical, romantic wonderland."

"I still cannot believe I am living in a city of soaring towers and glittering lights and flying machines," she said. "And I cannot believe that I am here with you, Cynthia, in this most marvelous of futures."

During the past week, I had carefully explained my time travel experiences to Tara, while helping her cope with her own time travel experience. Her response had been understandable. She was frightened, tense, and confused, and for the first day, she wouldn't leave her room. On the second day, for long periods of time, she stood before my condo windows, staring out onto the street below, watching the cars, the scooters and the people pass, not willing or able to leave the safety of my place.

I cooked for her, ordered pizza and gourmet dinners, and I stepped lightly, not forcing anything, letting her adjust to all the modern conveniences.

By the third day, she joined me on the sofa and watched part of a movie on my wide screen TV. She sat as still as a statue, her eyes round and wide, her hands trembling, but she didn't run back to her room.

I bought her clothes online. I gave her a cellphone and taught her how to use it. To my surprise, she took to it eagerly, and within days, she was watching *YouTube* and *TikTok* and texting Alina and me.

Tara was a stronger girl than I'd first thought. Perhaps it was her youth—the ability to adjust to new situations—but after only six days, she was blossoming, anxious to explore the modern New York City.

Nonetheless, she had been through a lot of emotional upheaval in a short amount of time, and I knew it would take both of us a while to work through the trauma of that day at the Bramble House, when I'd killed a man and she'd seen Mr. Gannon shot and killed.

I'd thought of finding a therapist for Tara, but I was uncertain. What about the time travel problem? I didn't want anyone—especially a therapist—to think Tara was delusional or schizophrenic, which would make things even worse. I assured her that time travel was not a common occurrence in 2022 and that even I didn't understand how it had happened.

The first thing we had to do was come up with a story of how Tara had come to New York in the first place. After some thought, we created what we hoped was a plausible story: Her family had all died in a house fire in Denver when she was three years old. She'd been moved from one foster home to another, and she was living in a small town in Colorado when I went there to visit a friend, who happened to live next door. We'd spent time together and become friends, both of us feeling there was a special kind of bond between us. She reminded me of my deceased sister, and I reminded her of a young foster mother she'd particularly liked, but who hadn't been able to adopt her.

My second challenge was getting Tara a birth certificate, a social security number, and a traceable past, but I had no idea how to go about it. I'd already hired a private tutor to come to the condo right after Thanksgiving. Tara was behind in her education, having only attended school as far as the fourth grade.

I was also concerned that she needed to meet girls and boys her own age, so that she could blend in. But kids will be kids. Tara's formal, nineteenth-century speech and manners would be a reason for ridicule, so I planned to have her watch TV shows and movies so she could pick up words, slang and speech patterns, while hopefully ignoring the profanity. She'd already been shocked by the language she'd heard on TV, as well as by the advertising, the cars and the fashion, especially the tight pants, halter tops and ripped jeans.

My love for her deepened every day, and it was

an indescribable delight to see her flower and shine, and hear her say, with a beaming smile, "I love you, Cynthia."

The old Cindy would have said Tara's sentiment was sickening sweet. The new Cynthia didn't care. I loved it and I loved Tara.

And, yes, I did search for Marshal Bryce Vance on the internet. I *Googled* his name but found nothing. I guided my laptop cursor and clicked links to old Western historical sites, including Denver and Leadville, but I found nothing.

On the third day, I found it. Buried within a link was an old Denver newspaper article from 1881. When I saw the name Marshal Bryce Vance, I stiffened, my pulse racing. I expanded the page and nosed in toward the screen. There it was!

Yesterday morning, Marshal Bryce Vance left our fair city, boarding an east-bound train, en route to New York City, where he is to begin a new life.

Let it be known that he departed without any fanfare or venerated sendoff, the like of which the late John Gannon had received. There were no speeches, nor marching bands, nor hanging banners to hail him and send him triumphantly on his way.

It is the opinion of this newspaper that Marshal Vance was not afforded the gratitude and respect that he so justly deserved from the peoples of Denver, for his courageous and skillful execution of his duties in the years he was marshal.

*Therefore, we at the **Denver Gazette** would like to*

extend our sincere thanks to Marshal Vance for a job well done. We want it to be noted on these pages that we will not see another man like him for many years to come—a man of steadfast determination and strong moral fiber, possessing a true, independent, Western spirit.

Godspeed, Marshal Bryce Vance!

I called Tara over, and she sat down beside me and read it. When she'd finished the article, she turned her sorrowful eyes to me. "He left for New York like he said he would. I'm sure he tried to find us."

I read the article again and again. "Yeah… he did. Of course he did. He searched for us, but he never found us. How sad, Tara. How depressingly sad is that."

The softness of fond memories, of his lopsided smile, of his kisses, brought tears, and I couldn't stop them. Tara and I hugged, and we were silent, and we let the tears flow.

Tara and I were walking under that magnificent full moon on November 9, 2022, having just had dinner at a local restaurant. I glanced at my cellphone—it was 8:43 p.m., the exact time that, in another life and another time, Cliff Prince and I had argued, and I'd accidentally killed him.

And then my phone rang, and Cliff's name popped up on my screen. Should I answer it?

As Tara and I passed a Starbucks, I hesitated and then asked her to step inside and buy us some scones for the morning. She entered, then turned back to look at me, concerned, as I answered the call.

Since I'd returned, I had not called or talked to Cliff. I had been too scared, and I'd not answered his emails or texts. Hearing his voice brought a sour stomach.

"So, Cindy, what's up with you?" Cliff said, in his usual strong, husky voice. "I mean wassup, girlfriend? I keep calling, texting, emailing and nothing. Then I get one email that says, 'It's over, Cliff. It's time for us both to move on.' What's that all about? Is that all you have to say to me?"

"Yeah... that's about it," I said.

"What the hell's the matter with you? What do you mean, it's over? What's over?"

"We're over," I said quietly.

"Look, I know I've been crazy busy and out of town a lot, but come on, Cindy, give me a break here. Don't go off the deep end on me. Come over. Let's have a night together. I'll open some champagne and order dinner from Lennie's. You love his steaks. You love his cheesecake. I'll order the whole cake, with extra strawberries for the champagne. Come on, come over. I want to celebrate. This morning, I closed a big deal."

I turned my back against the wind and gazed up at the buttery, full moon. And then I looked into the window and saw Tara pointing at the glass dessert case, and I knew she was also ordering each of us a hot chocolate.

"Cliff... I'm not coming. It's over. We're over."

"Who is he!?" Cliff snapped.

"No one. Nobody. I'm not seeing anybody."

"I hear you have some teenage girl staying with you. What's that about? What the hell has happened to you?"

"It's about love, Cliff. It's about me having a new life. It's not about us anymore. Please don't call me or text, Cliff. Move on with your life, because I've moved on with mine."

I disconnected the call and blew a grateful sigh into the wind. I was free! I had been given a second chance, and I was going to take it!

As I turned to enter Starbucks, something to my left caught my eye. A black sedan had pulled to the curb, and a man climbed out. I stilled and watched the man approach, pass me, and enter Starbucks.

Once inside, he stopped, turned, and looked at me. I was outside staring into Starbucks, and he was inside, staring back. Our eyes met. The power of his gaze startled me. I knew this guy. I mean, there was no doubt about it. I did know this guy! He wore a dark suit and blue tie that set off his eyes, and I had the ridiculous impulse to burst through the glass door and run into his arms.

I opened the door with care, keeping my eyes on him, feeling his eyes on me. I moved toward him and stopped about four feet away, and I had no awareness of anyone else being in the room, not even Tara.

There was no logical reason that we stood there holding each other's eyes, and I couldn't have explained that strange and magical moment to anyone, because there was no language for it. The silent communication between that gorgeous looking man and me could not be translated into words.

"Do I know you?" he asked.

I took him in fully. "No, we've never met."

"Yeah, I thought so. Still..."

"What's your name?" I asked boldly.

"You'll laugh. It sounds like the name of a TV cop."

"I won't."

"Brett Vaughan. And yours?"

"Cindy Downing."

He held out his hand. I took it and we shook. "Well, Cindy Downing, it's nice to meet you. Can I buy you a coffee?"

"Where are you from, Brett?"

"Originally? Denver."

"Really? Denver?"

"Yeah. Is that okay?"

"Yeah, sure. Okay... What do you do?"

He made a face. "You won't like it."

"Try me."

"I'm a detective."

Words escaped me.

"See, I said you wouldn't like it," Brett said.

"No... No, I totally like it. Actually, I love it."

He cocked his head, trying to read me. "Love it?"

"Yeah, why not? A detective from Denver. Yeah..."

"Okay, and what do you do?"

"Real estate."

"Here in the city?"

"Yeah..."

"Funny thing. I'm looking for an apartment."

I smiled broadly. "I'll find you the perfect one."

"I have a dog."

"I love dogs. New York City loves dogs."

He smiled, raising his eyebrows and turning his head ever so slightly, curiously.

"No wife?" I asked, without thinking.

He shook his head. "Almost. But no. You? Husband? Maybe a boyfriend or three?"

"I just left one in Denver," I said, with a shrug.

"Denver? Hmm. Maybe I know him."

I shifted my eyes. "Maybe."

He scratched his head, keeping his eyes on me. "You know, I'd swear I've seen you someplace before, and that's not a line or anything."

I let my eyes linger on him, feeling the surge of an impossible thrill. Brett Vaughan was Bryce Vance's double: the same eyes, the same great body, the same handsome face and hair. And, amazingly, he had the same slant of a smile as Bryce had.

I smiled flirtatiously. "Yeah... so maybe we have met before someplace. Maybe I saw you in Denver."

He shrugged. "I was there in October, for my sister's birthday."

I secretly smiled. Brett, the detective, would know how to obtain identification for Tara, wouldn't he?

Tara drew up, carrying a paper bag. "I got two hot chocolates and two scones."

And then Tara glanced at Brett, and she gasped, taking a step back. "Oh, but... It can't be."

"What?" Brett asked, spreading his hands innocently. "I didn't do it. I promise, and I have witnesses. I'm not the guy," he joked.

I thought, *Yeah, Brett, you are the guy. You are definitely the guy.*

Tara and I exchanged a disbelieving glance. "Tara, meet Brett Vaughan, a New York City detective, who moved here from Denver. Brett, meet Tara, my sister."

Brett extended his hand and Tara took it, not pulling her wide, disbelieving eyes from him.

"Hello," Tara said numbly.

"Hello, Tara. Nice to meet you."

Brett turned to me. "Look, I was going to grab a coffee. Would you mind waiting for me? Maybe we could all go for a walk. It's a beautiful night. Not too cold."

I motioned toward the black sedan. "What about that someone in there waiting for you?"

"Don't worry about him. He has three kids. He'll catch up on his sleep. Anyway, just a short walk? A walk and a talk? The three of us should get to know each other a little bit, don't you think?"

I nodded. "Yeah, why not?"

Minutes later, we were strolling along West Broadway, under the lovely glow of a golden, New York City moon. And the world was magical, and the world was filled with wonder, and my world was filled with love.

THANK YOU!

T hank you for taking the time to read *Time Passage – A Time Travel Novel.* If you enjoyed it, please consider telling your friends or posting a short review. Word of mouth is an author's best friend, and it is much appreciated.

Thank you,
Elyse Douglas

Other novels by Elyse Douglas that you might enjoy:

The Christmas Diary (Book 1)
The Christmas Diary – Lost and Found (Book 2)
The Summer Diary
The Other Side of Summer
The Summer Letters
The Christmas Women
Time with Norma Jeane (A Time Travel Novel)

The Christmas Eve Letter (A Time Travel Novel) Book 1
The Christmas Eve Daughter (A Time Travel Novel) Book 2
The Christmas Eve Secret (A Time Travel Novel) Book 3
The Christmas Eve Promise (A Time Travel Novel) Book 4
The Christmas Eve Journey (A Time Travel Novel) Book 5

The Lost Mata Hari Ring (A Time Travel Novel)
Time Past (A Time Travel Novel)
Time Zone (A Time Travel Novel)
The Christmas Town (A Time Travel Novel)
Time Change (A Time Travel Novel)
Time Visitor (A Time Travel Novel)

Daring Summer - Romantic Suspense
The Date Before Christmas
Christmas Ever After
Christmas for Juliet
The Christmas Bridge
Wanting Rita

www.elysedouglas.com

Editorial Reviews

THE LOST MATA HARI RING – A Time Travel Novel
by Elyse Douglas
"This book is hard to put down! It is pitch-perfect and hits all the right notes. It is the best book I have read in a while!
5 Stars!"
--Bound4Escape Blog and Reviews

"The characters are well defined, and the scenes easily visualized. It is a poignant, bitter-sweet emotionally charged read."
5-Stars!
--Rockin' Book Reviews

"This book captivated me to the end!"
--StoryBook Reviews

"A captivating adventure..."
--Community Bookstop

"...Putting *The Lost Mata Hari Ring* down for any length of time proved to be impossible."
--Lisa's Writopia

"I found myself drawn into the story and holding my breath to see what would happen next..."
--Blog: A Room Without Books is Empty

Editorial Reviews

THE CHRISTMAS TOWN – A Time Travel Novel
by Elyse Douglas

"*The Christmas Town* is a beautifully written story. It draws you in from the first page, and fully engages you up until the very last. The story is funny, happy, and magical. The characters are all likable and very well-rounded. This is a great book to read during the holiday season, and a delightful read during any time of the year."

--Bauman Book Reviews

"I would love to see this book become another one of those beloved Christmas film traditions, to be treasured over the years! The characters are loveable; the settings vivid. Period details are believable. A delightful read at any time of year! Don't miss this novel!"

--A Night's Dream of Books

Editorial Reviews

THE SUMMER LETTERS – A Novel
by Elyse Douglas
"A perfect summer read!"
--Fiction Addiction

"In Elyse Douglas' novel *The Summer Letters*, the characters' emotions, their drives, passions and memories are all so expertly woven; we get a taste of what life was like for veterans, women, small town folk, and all those people we think have lived too long to remember (but they never really forget, do they?).
I couldn't stop reading, not for a moment. Such an amazing read. Flawless."
5 Stars!
--Anteria Writes Blog - To Dream, To Write, To Live

"A wonderful, beautiful love story that I absolutely enjoyed reading."
5 Stars!

--Books, Dreams, Life - Blog

"The Summer Letters is a fabulous choice for the beach or cottage this year, so you can live and breathe the same feelings and smells as the characters in this wonderful story."

ABOUT THE AUTHOR

Elyse Douglas

Elyse Douglas is the pen name for the married writing team Elyse Parmentier and Douglas Pennington.

They have completed numerous novels including, "The Other Side of Summer," "The Summer Letters," "The Summer Diary," and, "The Christmas Diary."

They live in New York City.

PRAISE FOR AUTHOR

"The Christmas Eve Letter" is a wonderful time travel book and one of my favorite books of the year!

- THE BOOK RETURN BLOG

"Time Zone" is unstoppable reading from start to finish!

- RED MOON BOOK REVIEWS

"Speakeasy" is a frolicky, jazzy blast that will keep you eagerly turning pages into the wee hours of the night!"

- BOOKSHELF REVIEWS

I love this book, "Time Stranger." A work of art!

- THE BOOK MARKSMAN

BOOKS BY THIS AUTHOR

Time Zone - A Time Travel Novel

In 2015, Pilot Mary McLane Carson struggles with a left engine fire. Her airplane plunges through a strange flash of light, crash-landing into a Kansas field. She wakes up, alone, in December 1942, being cared for by the handsome Dr. Thomas Fleming.

Time Past - A Time Travel Novel

You Never Forget Your First Love

In 2022, 74-year-old Kate Clarke returns to her Ohio college town seeking redemption from a tragic past. She bursts from a secret cave to discover it's 1968 and she's twenty years old again.

Time Visitor - A Time Travel Novel

In 1944 a Squadron of Navy Planes Disappears off the Florida Coast. One Lands in 2005... In Ohio.

The Christmas Eve Letter - A Time Travel Romance Novel (5-Book Series)

In an antique shop, Eve finds an old lantern with a dusty letter hidden inside. It's dated 1885, and her name is written on it.

Speakeasy - A Time Travel Novel (2-Book Series)

One minute, Singer Roxie Raines is in a 2019 West Village nightclub and the next, she's traveled back in time to New York's raucous Roaring Twenties!

Time Stranger - A Time Travel Novel

Anne Billings is tossed out of war-torn Britain in 1944 and flung into New York's Central Park in 2008.

Printed in Great Britain
by Amazon